SARAH MOSS is the author of seven novels, ~~Cold Earth~~, *Night Waking*, *Bodies of Light*, *Signs for Lost Children*, *The Tidal Zone*, *Ghost Wall* and *Summerwater*, as well as a memoir of her year living in Iceland, *Names for the Sea*. Her work has been shortlisted for the Women's Prize for Fiction, the RSL Ondaatje Prize, and the Wellcome Book Prize. Born in Glasgow, she lives in Dublin where she teaches at University College Dublin.

'An adventurous and original novelist'

Guardian, 'Best Books of the Year'

'Clever, well-constructed, moving, funny and very well-written ... It is rooted in domestic reality but able to take on the big themes of mortality and the fragility and preciousness of life. Excellent'

Daily Mail

'Moving [and] devastating'

Mail on Sunday

'An astute storyteller [...] Moss taps into a range of experiences that you do not need to be a parent to feel and tackles this extremely uncomfortable subject with tact, plausibility and flowing prose'

Scotsman

'Sarah Moss's great gift is as a first-rate depicter of human emotions. Her characters live and breathe in the way that readers need characters to do: as compassionate, sympathetic and recognisable individuals we can connect with utterly, as people struggling to cope with the realities of life ... This is grown-up writing for grown-up readers, the kind of story that makes you think about your own life choices and close relationships. Few novels do that with such depth and clarity as Moss's has done so here' *Sunday Herald*

'[A] sophisticated, state-of-the-nation novel ... Animated by wry intelligence, Moss's fifth novel reprises her exploration of mortal and moral paradoxes ... Bristling with contemporary teenage attitude, this coming-of-age story is about grown-ups, for grown-ups'

Country Life

The Tidal Zone

Sarah Moss

GRANTA

Granta Publications, 12 Addison Avenue, London W11 4QR
First published in Great Britain by Granta Books 2016
Paperback edition published by Granta Books 2017
This paperback edition published by Granta Books 2021

A CIP catalogue record for this book
is available from the British Library.

1 3 5 7 9 10 8 6 4 2

ISBN 978 1 78378 786 9
eISBN 978 1 78378 309 0

Typeset by M Rules

Printed and bound by CPI Group (UK) Ltd, Croydon, CR0 4YY

MIX
Paper from
responsible sources
FSC
www.fsc.org   FSC® C020471

then the daffodils pushed through the earth and began to open apple-white and yolk-yellow, the creature found itself cramped. The walls of the womb seemed to close on its arms and legs, to wrap even its ribs and behind, and soon the being was pushed down, its head held in the woman's bones and its hands and feet gathered in. The woman no longer swam. She walked less than she had, and she and the little stranger began to be sore and cross. At last, one bright April morning when white clouds drifted high in a blue sky and leaf-buds beaded the tired grey trees, it was time for the woman and the new thing to part, a painful work that took many hours, into the cold night and through the next morning, which the woman and her husband did not see because they were in a room with no windows, awaiting the child's birth. The heart had been working for months now and it kept going, sometimes fast and sometimes slow, but always beating the same rhythm. Our birth is but a sleep and a forgetting. When the child was born there came the ordinary miracle of breathing, that terrible moment when we are cast off from our mother and from her oxygenated blood, when we have never taken a breath and may not know how to do so, the caesura in the delivery room. She breathed. The music of heart and lungs began, and continued, and no-one listened any more.

The child was a girl, but the most important thing about her was that she was herself. She was someone new, someone who had not been before and so, like all babies, she was a revelation. She throve in her mother's arms all through that summer, watching the shadows of leaves on the parasol that shaded her new skin from the sun, watching her own hands drift and dance. She learnt to smile, to look her father in the eye and smile. By concentrating hard, she learnt to close her starfish fingers around the things she wanted to explore: stones, buttercups, the silk edge of her blanket. Suddenly, one

2

pale night, she learnt to roll over in her cot, and although it took her a while to learn to roll back, she began to work on lifting her heavy head. And all the time her heart beat, carrying the blood she needed to grow and learn around her changing body. All the impossible intricacies of her biology worked, and only in rare moments did anyone think to wonder at the astonishing processes of lungs and gut, of kidneys and brain.

By the time the next spring flowers came, the child was learning to walk. Her father took her to the park, where she held onto a bench surrounded by purple crocuses and then confided herself to the earth and the air, launched herself across the grass in four staggering steps to his waiting arms. She was finding her words by then: Dadda, bird, more, no. She learnt to hold a crayon and make her mark, to bat away anyone trying to feed her because she wanted to do it herself. She did not need to learn to dance, because she could already do that.

We know now that the first time the music stumbled, the child was five. She had started school that autumn and by spring was reading fluently, beginning to take over her own bedtime stories, although still uncertain about numbers and frankly not interested in learning to write. She was playing tag with her friends in the square of concrete that passed for a playground, running and shouting under a watery sky, her skin warm and her cheeks pink while the supervisors pushed their hands deeper into their coat pockets. Her feet slowed. Her muscles tired. Not enough oxygen, not enough sugar. Not enough light. Fear. Her lungs sucked hard and could not make a vacuum, could not pull in the air her blood needed. And yet by the time her mother arrived, by the time they had the child lying down in the room behind the reception-ist's desk, she was fine, was pink and cheerful and distinctly annoyed. They'd given her the inhaler they kept for forgetful

3

asthmatics, they said, they were sorry, they hoped it had been the right thing, only it had looked just like an asthma attack and look, it had worked. The child's mother knelt at her side, having been called from work took out her stethoscope and listened to her daughter's chest, to the free flow of air, to the percussion of her heart. There was nothing wrong. Asthma, she said, is over-diagnosed in children. Perhaps some virus, some passing disturbance, one of those things. And perhaps she was right. Perhaps it was not a warning that nobody saw.

After that, the child wheezed, sometimes, with a cold. It was nothing much, not often. Not, her mother said, asthma, not really, although yes, worth keeping an inhaler around, no harm to use it when the girl was uncomfortable at night.

The second call was louder. You knew that, of course; there are three warnings, three chances to stop the bad thing happening, although if we succeeded in doing so there would not be three, there would not be a story at all, only another in our unthinkable collection of things that didn't happen. The child had been swimming in the sea off the island of Kalymnos. The water was cold. At first she had been reluctant, chilly, afraid of the waves, not wanting the salt water over her fair head and in her ears and her nose, but gradually, hand-in-hand with her father, she had edged herself deeper into the Mediterranean, squeaking as the water gripped her knees and thighs and stomach but then learning to jump and mock the breakers on the sand and to let the smoother waves lift her body and set her back on her feet. There we go, up and down, swooping and landing. Her hand was blue with cold and slippery with sunscreen and sea but her father held on until the four of them were bobbing adrift, awash, afloat where the sirens sang, until the child's mother lost her nerve, wanted the air in her children's hands again and the ground beneath their feet, and she was right because the child was still

4

knee deep in the wine-dark sea when her breathing began to sound in her chest, to make a strange call. Mummy, she said, Mummy, and her mother took her hand and hurried her up the beach to where the inhaler, unused for months, lay at the bottom of a handbag. Here, she said, sit down, lean forward, you remember how to do this, and in half an hour they were all going for ice-cream. It is a strange moment for any body, for any arrangement of blood and skin and bone, leaving the water, cold water for hot air. Anyone's heart might miss a beat, might not know if it is on land or sea. Anyone's lungs might be surprised. Perhaps she did have asthma, after all. Lots of people do.

The third time, the girl was growing up, living between longing for and dismay at her own adulthood. She was as tall as her mother and heavier, more rounded, a less provisional presence in a room. She was clever and brave and stubborn and she didn't dance any more but she read and she wrote. She had joined Amnesty International and Greenpeace and the Green Party. She said patriarchy and hegemony and neo-liberalism, several times a day. She put streaks of blue in her hair and enjoyed baiting her teachers by wearing mascara: but Miss, you're wearing makeup. But Sir, aren't you just inducting us into a world more interested in policing women's sexuality than giving us knowledge?

They found her on the sports field. The PE teacher found her on the sports field, had looked out and noticed a huddle of clothes under a tree when everyone was supposed to be in lessons, and wondered what was going on. She was unconscious but making, he said, odd noises, her breathing like someone trying to saw through cardboard with a blunt knife, and before he'd had time to call the emergency services the noises stopped. The breathing stopped.

He did the right things in the right order. Pulled out his phone, pressed the 9 three times, pressed 'speaker' and laid the phone beside the girl among the dandelions while he rolled her onto her back, checked her mouth for obstructions, tipped her head back, the seconds dripping now like honey, held her nose and blew into her mouth, watched to see the chest rise and it didn't, not much, but since he knew how to do this and not how to do anything else he kept going. As he'd been taught, he sang in his head for the rhythm as he braced his arms and found the opening of her ribcage, felt her bra under the heel of his hand as he forced her bones down into the earth. Nellie the elephant packed her trunk and said goodbye to the circus. There was not much space between the girl's breastbone and the cold grass: easy, at first, to press a third of its depth. Ambulance, he said. School. Unconscious, not breathing. Doing CPR. Off she went with a trumpety-trump. More breaths.

Inside the girl's body, the teacher knew, inside her brain, cells were dying. Oxygen levels are reduced in exhaled air. Pressing on the chest, even hard, even this hard, does not move much blood. Her face and lips were turning blue. Keep on singing, keep on pushing down. Nellie the elephant. His arms tired. Harder. He heard sirens now on the road, blue lights coming across the field, a car bouncing over the grass. Said goodbye to the circus, off she went. Car door left open, engine still going, a woman in a green boiler suit. Blue plastic gloves on her hands. Running figures, an ambulance. We'll take over now, well done, and he stood to make room, stumbled. They knelt at the girl's side, four of them: Matthew, Mark, Luke and John, bless the bed that I lie on. A helicopter now hammering the sky, bending the trees.

*

6

Suddenly, your heart began; suddenly in the darkness of your mother's womb there was a crackle and a flash and out of nothing, the current began to run. Suddenly you began to breathe. Suddenly, you will stop, you and me and all of us. Your lungs will rest at last and the electric pulse in your pulse will vanish into the darkness from which it came.

Put your fingers in your ears, lay your head on the pillow, listen to the footsteps of your blood.

You are alive.

you can imagine it

There are no premonitions. The fact that you are eating a barely acceptable sandwich or devoting unjustifiable intellectual energy to your latest contribution to a social networking site doesn't mean that you are not in the interval between losing everything you take for granted and finding out that you have lost it. In the era of instant communication, that interval still exists. Even as you read this, someone, a police officer or a teacher or a colleague, the person playing the angel of death in the script you didn't know you were following, may be taking a deep breath, remembering the workshop on Sharing Bad News, as he or she prepares to dial your number and say the words we have all imagined, the words with which we torture ourselves, as if thinking about this possibility, admitting it to our minds, will keep it in the realm of nightmare and fantasy. *There's been an incident.* Imagining things does not stop them happening. Nor does not imagining them. People, mostly parents in the school playground which, of course, one of us still had to attend twice daily for Rose, said, 'I can't imagine what you and Emma must be going through.' It is exactly as you imagine it, I said. When you read accounts of ordinary lives disrupted by sudden disaster, by the ice on the road or the sleepy lorry driver or the plane falling from the sky or the angry young men with military hardware and nothing left to lose, when you shiver and turn the page, it is like that. You can imagine it. What you imagine is correct. This is not what they, the parents, wanted me to say.

There is no irony, either. The fact that you are turning your face to the spring sunshine dappling through a bluebell wood or heading out for a coffee you have awarded yourself in the middle of the afternoon for no reason other than your own pleasure does not mean that the angel of death will swoop. There is no angel. There is no script. Enjoy the bluebells when you can because they are not symbols, just flowers. They have no power.

I was not, as it happens, eating a sandwich, although it had begun to cross my mind that I would soon do so, and nor, for once, was I lingering on the internet over the floorplans of houses we might have been able to afford if we had joined the property market ten years earlier than we did. I was working, by which I mean that I had my laptop open on the kitchen table and I was reading a large book that was mostly pictures of the design and building of Coventry Cathedral. I was keeping laptop and book away from the puddle of jam Rose had left on the table when we set off for school, which I had promised myself not to wipe until I stopped for lunch, and from the cup of cold milky coffee that Emma had made and not drunk before the rest of us were up, which it was pos- sible that I would leave on the table until her after-bedtime return to make a point that I could not quite articulate even to myself. I had been for a run between dropping off the girls

9

and settling to work and I had to remember to keep moving around as my legs stiffened.

I wasn't thinking about the bombing of the old cathedral. That would be too neat. I was trying to think about the tapestry. I've heard the guides talking about the tapestry to herds of grey-haired people in cardigans and sensible shoes, the sort of people – fate willing, I will become one myself – who take guided tours of cathedrals on weekday afternoons. The tapestry, the guides say, is the biggest one in the world. It is foreshortened from where you stand, but if we took it down and spread it out, it would reach all the way past the choir stalls and the chairs. As if Graham Sutherland had been hoping to win a global competition for square metres woven. I was wondering how to say that the tapestry announces as you walk through the doors that despite its modernist garb the Cathedral, finished in 1967, is in the tradition of English Arts and Crafts. That while it looks unfamiliar, unecclesiastical, to eyes accustomed to stone floors and gothic windows, to marble effigies of local squires, this building is a more conservative reassertion of vernacular and even local tradition than most of its peers in France and Germany. Hand-made, artisanal, another articulation of the English suspicion of the machineries of mass-production which began in our green and pleasant land. It was one of the less pressing problems across Europe in the aftermath of that war, what to do about the smashed churches. To rebuild, as if there could be a return to the old ways, as if it were possible to resurrect what had been lost. Or to leave the broken ruins as a memorial, or memento mori, as if we could never return to and never forget what was lost, as if the condition of mourning were to be made permanent. I was experimenting with ways of explaining some of this without sounding pompous, and wondering how much I was allowed

10

to discuss beyond the material of the building and its contents. I was trying to remember not to write a book, and – suddenly, as how else? – my phone rang.

A mobile number, unknown to my phone. I went up the stairs as I answered. We always do, because there's not much reception on the ground floor, and so I was on the turn of the stairs, looking up towards the landing, just passing the photo of one-year-old Rose staggering into the outstretched arms of eight-year-old Miriam on the beach at Porthleven. This is Victoria Collier, she said, and it took me a moment to remember that she meant Mrs Collier, Miriam's headteacher. Still, nothing lurched. Miriam must have argued once too often with her dim English teacher or refused to tie her hair back, one of those venial sins invented by schools to forestall any real rebellion. She's forever getting detentions, courting them. There's been an incident, Mrs Collier said, with Miriam. An incident, we found her on the playing field. She got clobbered, I was thinking, someone hit her with a hockey stick or a lacrosse ball, I've always hated lacrosse with the balls at head-height, not that Mimi's given to co-operation with team games, but I could feel fear in my throat, in my ears. Miriam seems all right now, she said, she's conscious and stable, but she had some kind of faint or – well – collapse. We called an ambulance and she was out for quite a while, longer than they like, so they're taking her in, just to be on the safe side. In, out, I was thinking, like one of those weather-houses you used to see where the man comes out and the woman goes in when it's going to rain, or maybe the other way round, but while my mind was working on imagery my body already knew what to do and I was down the stairs, pushing my feet into my shoes, picking up my car keys and bleeping the doors while I unhooked my coat. Can they wait, I said, if she's conscious and stable can they wait ten minutes. It takes twenty,

11

normally, in the middle of the day with the traffic clear. I got there in eight.

She was all right. That was the first thing I saw. In the cavern of the ambulance she was flat on her back under one of those waffle blankets and there was mud on her face and wires coming out from under the blanket and a bleeping monitor like that of a very early computer parked between her feet like a small dog and she was very pale and her face oddly swollen under an oxygen mask but she was all right. She lifted the mask when she saw me. Hi Dad she said, and rolled her eyes the way she does when she can't be bothered to rise to Rose's teasing, as if the whole event were something of a farce. Sorry about the fuss. The mask hissed, like a leak, like an emergency. I looked at the paramedic who was watching the monitor, watching the blood-pressure cuff on Miriam's arm puffing itself up like a flotation device. In the event of a landing on water, pull the string, blow the whistle. She gets a bit wheezy, I said, she does have asthma. Her mum, my wife, she's a doctor, a GP. As if that were our excuse. As if having a doctor in the family means you're allowed to ignore your children's symptoms, their incidents, until someone else calls an ambulance. Yes, said the paramedic, her blond plait moving on her shoulder as she adjusted Miriam's blanket, that may be all it is. They'll just check her over at the hospital. We'll keep that mask on for now, please, Miriam. If you could sit down here, Dad. I'm not your dad, I thought, though later I would get used to it, to the way medics at the same time as being the deities of hospital life adopt the linguistic position of children. They're quite right, it doesn't matter what else I might be. Miriam's dad. I reached for her hand as I sat down and she smiled at me but she was remote under her blankets and wires, too far away to hold my hand.

It was only when they started the siren that I realised I was not as afraid as I should have been. I look back now and see a last moment of innocence, sitting in the back of an ambulance and believing that Miriam was all right.

There was a roomful, a team, of medics waiting for us, gathered around the bed in Resuscitation as if ready to perform a ritual, to transform bread into human flesh. To sacrifice a virgin.

'Here they come,' I heard someone say, and then, almost disappointed, 'Oh, she's conscious.'

Miriam had tried to sit up on the stretcher but the wires weren't long enough. She was craning her head to see where she was going and her face was still white and still puffy, her breathing still odd. There was mud in her hair and I wanted to brush it out, to set things right. Lie down for me now, they said, a little prick coming in your arm now, sorry. The fact that they seemed to know what they were doing, what would happen, both reassured and silenced me: there was, plainly, a narrative being followed, and it was only I who did not know what came next.

the arithmetic of staying alive

It was important to tell people. To let people know that this can happen: your child's body can stop. Stop breathing, stop beating. At any time, her lungs can close down, the wing-beat that began in her heart before her bones were formed, before the foetus-to-be-Miriam had a spinal cord or a skull, can pause and fall tumbling. And then blood pools in your child's veins. It stagnates. And your daughter's cells have no more oxygen, her muscles no more sugar. There is no more movement. No thinking. Where the body's metronome ticked, there is silence. She goes. She goes away. It can happen. It had happened. I needed to tell people that the world was not as they believed it to be.

I asked Miriam if she'd be all right while I made some calls. She was eating a pot of yogurt by then, sitting up in bed on the High Dependency Unit with the monitors' wires creeping through the ripped and muddy vestiges of her school uniform. Fasten your shirt, I wanted to say, pull up the blanket, we can see your bra. OK, she said, actually I might watch some TV, since it's here, since they seem to think we need it along with the oxygen and the intubation kits here on the High

Dependency Unit. Are you sure, I thought, because she never watches it at home, accuses her mother of being hooked on the opiate of the masses, stands about pointing out that costume dramas feed the English fetish for poshness, for the adulation of unearned wealth and privilege; that the news is hopelessly parochial and the cookery shows Emma enjoys glorify not only domestic labour but the consumption of exactly the ingredients we're all being told to avoid. It's an eating disorder on a national scale, she says, watching Emma watching people ice cakes with butter and cream and chocolate and fill pies with caramel and condensed milk, we're all obsessed with obesity and weight loss and *also fucking baking*. Shut up, darling, Emma says, I've been working with the obese and malnourished all day, have a biscuit and let me watch a little rubbish before I go to bed. Make your calls, Dad, Mim said, and she pressed a couple of buttons and filled the room with synthetic American laughter.

The nurse sitting on the other side of the room looked up and made a note. Patient watching television? The monitor began to bleep faster and I watched Miriam's heart-rate rise on its green-on-black screen, watched its scrawled notation rise and fall, erasing and rewriting itself after four or five beats. It's speeding up, I thought, her heart's speeding up, but the nurse was unconcerned. Her oxygen level dropped: 95, 94. 95 again. Dad, Miriam said, her eyes on the television, I'm OK, make your calls. I could see that she was OK, that the yogurt and her upright posture were out of place in this room where people were brought to be kept alive. I leant against the radiator. It was far too hot, burned through my trousers, and the discomfort felt correct.

I started with the department, where I was supposed to be teaching the next day. Art History 113: How to Look at a Building. I'm not an academic, not really, just among the unemployed with PhDs who get brought in to do first-year teaching on an hourly-paid contract every September when the University realises that half the faculty are on research leave and the other half consider themselves too important for introductory courses. Hannah the departmental secretary's phone rang and rang. Mostly I'm a stay-at-home dad. A full-time parent. 'A man of leisure', says Emma's dad, who is a surgeon and the kind of man who shrinks your new cashmere jumper so he's never asked to run another load of laundry, who has the brass neck to assert that although he can and does implant titanium replacements for worn-out knees and hips, the concept of a washing machine's spin speed is beyond his comprehension. He means to say that I'm a scrounger, a layabout, his daughter's feckless lodger. I'd forgive everything if he were nice to her, if he had ever let Emma imagine herself adequate as doctor, daughter or human being.

I left a message. It's Adam Goldschmidt, I'm sorry, I can't come in tomorrow, my daughter – my daughter is in hospital. She stopped breathing. Her heart stopped. Sorry.

I held the phone in my hand. I'd called Emma from the ambulance and she was on her way, had borrowed a colleague's car. Don't drive too fast, I thought, don't get arrested, don't have an accident. As if there were a plot summary set out somewhere that didn't include a car crash. You can't have a respiratory arrest and a car accident in the same family on the same day, Aristotle's rules don't allow it. Miriam had finished her yogurt and was watching the television and pleating her fingers in her lap, fiddling with the oxygen probe that was biting her left thumb. Her heart-rate rose as I watched, 73 beats a minute, 76, and then down again, 68, 66, 63. What if it goes on falling, I thought, where's the nurse, why isn't she doing something, maybe this is it happening again, 62,

61, is her heart meant to go down into the 50s? Quick. Find someone. 58.

'Mim?'

She looked up. The swelling had gone down and her colour was back. She seemed ordinary. Apart from the wires, the mud and the ripped clothes. Apart from being on the High Dependency Unit. 61, 63, 64.

'Yes?'

'You OK?'

She looked at the monitors, at the red button over her bed. 'Never better, Dad. Blooming. Can't you tell?'

'I meant—' I meant, are you going to die? Are you going to die again? I meant, are you still breathing?

'Is Mum coming?'

I nodded. 'She's on her way.'

'Good. Dad, have we still got my phone? I want to tell Sophie and Charlotte I'm OK.'

I stood there. On the screen, bronzed white teenagers in perpetual Hollywood sunshine massed beside a David Hockney pool. I used to worry that the girls would mistake this stuff for real life, that it would teach them to expect clear-skinned boys to ask them for 'dates' and to encounter small-scale moral dilemmas from which they could emerge victorious and virtuous in the course of forty-five minutes, but of course our children, better than us, recognise genre, know the difference between stories and real life. A girl jumped into the water fully clothed and bobbled there, crying, her face half-submerged. I could feel my own heart accelerating: she was going to drown, they were all going to stand there and let her drown, and then a boy who'd been talking seriously to another girl on the veranda noticed the girl in the pool and ran, beautifully dived. Ah.

'Oh Brad, you, like, saved me?' Miriam mocked. 'You're like, my hero? Only we're still not, like, going to have sex, because I'm, like, pure? And anyway, we like live in a country where they think contraception is, like, a sin, so, as you may have noticed from other imported teen shows, everyone who has sex gets, like, pregnant? Dad, did you bring a book for me?'

'No,' I said. 'Funnily enough, this time I didn't.'

The nurse made another note, as if sarcasm were one of the things they were looking for.

I wandered back to the window. I should phone more people, I thought. School, I should tell school that she's OK. That she appears to be OK. And we'll need someone to collect Rose, we're probably not going to be out of here in time for the school run. I hadn't taken the salmon for dinner out of the freezer, would need to cook something else instead, something quick because it was going to be a rush to do homework and dinner and bedtime by the time we got back. Pasta. There was a bag of spinach in the fridge, and I thought also a pot of ricotta. Rose would object. The window overlooked the car park, where people were queuing to buy parking tickets from the machines, opening the doors of their cars and leaning in to get their coats from the back seat, putting their keys in the ignition without thinking about it and fastening their seatbelts to set off home. As if they were safe, or safe enough. You worry, I thought, you worry about your children crossing the road. You worry, after a few days, that her fever might be meningitis not flu, especially when she starts a rash. You worry that bad boys will seduce her and she won't see what you can see. You worry that her own inexperience and the darkness of the world will harm her, even though you know that only experience of the darkness of the world will protect her, that you can't and shouldn't do it yourself for ever. You worry that she will go to the wrong sort of party and take the wrong sort of drugs, or board a plane on the same day as an angry person with nothing to lose. But you don't worry, it doesn't cross your mind, that one day she will simply stop breathing, go into cardiac arrest on the school playing fields, not because a car has crushed her or because a virus has made her sick or because a blade has made her bleed or fire has burnt her flesh, no because. How could you live if you worried about that?

I wandered back and watched the screen over her head while she watched the screen over her feet, I because it seemed to tell a truth and she because it seemed to tell a lie. Her oxygen saturation level was dipping, 95, 92, 89 and something began to chime, an urgent note like someone repeatedly ringing a doorbell, beginning to worry, to wonder if the person inside is lying at the bottom of the stairs. The numbers disappeared.

'Please—' I said, but the nurse was already there.

She reattached the probe to Miriam's finger. 'There,' she said. 'That was all. She's fine. We look at the patient, Dad, before the machines. She's a good colour.'

I sat in the shiny plastic chair plainly intended for the escort, the guardian, the witness. I watched the monitor as if, eventually, I would learn from it what plot we were following, and as I watched I remembered the last time I had followed the numbers of a beating heart, in another hospital when Rose was being born. We worried then because her heart was slowing with each contraction, not picking up again afterwards as fast as the midwives wanted it to. Oxygen deprivation, Emma hissed between groans. We're worried that she's crushing the cord. Even then, *we*. We medics. I remembered the first time I heard Miriam's heartbeat, before you could see from the outside that there was anyone else inside Emma's body, remembered the misshapen homunculus swimming into view on the black-and-white screen, a cinematic special effect, a primitive kind of CGI. After the scan, we got back in the car and when Emma started the engine, the radio came on. The afternoon play, I thought, an odd reprise of *War of the Worlds* in which the premise was that airliners had flown into sky-scrapers in New York. It wasn't very good and I turned it off so we could talk about the baby.

What was it like, Miriam asked recently, what was it like before the planes hit the World Trade Center? Innocent, I thought, although like all innocence, visible only in ret-rospect. There were different enemies, I told her, that was all. We'd barely stopped worrying about the Cold War and Mutually Assured Destruction, which was just as scary as faith-based terrorism and in some ways more so. Maybe there was a gap, in the late '90s, a break from fear, but if so I don't remember it. But I still do worry about Mutually Assured Destruction, Miriam said, it would be pretty stupid not to. Did you know that no-one knows where most of the weapons-grade plutonium in ex-USSR states has gone now? Well, someone does, obviously, and it's not hard to guess, but there's no official record. Oh Jesus, I said, tell me you haven't been looking up weapons-grade plutonium on the internet again, I thought we'd talked about that. Calm down, she said, I told you, no-one's going to think a white fifteen-year-old girl poses a terrorist threat. And I told you they bloody are, I said, and even if they weren't scrapping the Human Rights Bill, it doesn't apply to terror suspects, we'd never get you back, you have to stop doing things like that. This is not a free country, Miriam. You can't say anything that comes into your head, not when you're thinking about bombs and war. She'd shrugged, the way teenagers do when they know better. OK, Dad, but you know the iPad's registered to you, it's all coming from your account. Excellent, I said, I'll have to write a sodding book about terrorism so we can say it was my research and cover your tracks and even then they're unlikely to believe that a bloke with a background in the Arts and Crafts movement was suddenly called to research the movements of weapons-grade plutonium around disintegrating nation states. You have to stop it, Miriam. I knew she wouldn't, knew that the horror of the world she was inheriting represented for my daughter the adulthood we all crave at fifteen. A better parent would have worked out how to censor the internet for her. Better, I supposed, the arms trade than pornography. Maybe.

Her heart-rate was rising, 68, 71, 72, her oxygen levels variable but stable in the mid-90s, her blood pressure 108/72 at the last reading, the arithmetic of staying alive no longer to be taken for granted and writing its headlines above my daughter's bed.

The air moved. The nurse straightened her notes and her skirt. Even Miriam's eyes flicked towards the door. A doctor, I thought, a doctor is coming, and the doctor will tell us what happened. Or maybe why it happened, and perhaps what is to be done and when we can go home. Sit up, I wanted to tell Miriam, turn off the television and pay attention. The emergency doctor, I thought, the long-limbed one from the resuscitation room who knew what to do, but it was Emma. I saw her pause less than a second, saw her muscles and her skin, her hair and her clothes, arrange themselves. I saw her allow herself one glance at the monitor as she crossed the room to Miriam.

in hospital time

For days we drifted in hospital time, which is in some ways
not unlike toddler time, the weeks and months passed at home
while essentially waiting for the child to grow up enough to do
something else. The aim is to pass minutes without noticing
them, to be pleasantly surprised when you look at the clock. It
is an outing to walk down the corridor to refill the plastic jug
with fresh water, perhaps glimpsing a new arrival or exchang-
ing smiles with another parent on the way. It is a social event
to ask a nurse for a new box of tissues; if you are lucky, she
will have time to exchange sentences about the weather or the
traffic. Ward round, they say, will be at nine-thirty, and at
first you think this means that shortly after that hour someone
will come and tell you something you didn't already know,
will move the story along. You are wrong. No-one, it seemed,
knew why a healthy fifteen-year-old had gone into a field and
stopped breathing. I had, until then, vaguely imagined that
medical knowledge was more or less related to the seriousness
of the problem, that while doctors might not know why your
leg hurts a bit sometimes or you've been feeling nauseous for
a few days, there would be a good reason for a person to stop

22

breathing. To lie down on a field and die. It's hard to say, the doctor said when I tried to make her talk to me, there could be several reasons, we'll need to wait for the test results. It looks as if Miriam might have had some kind of reaction to something. Oh good, I thought, some kind of reaction, some response, there was some trigger or cause and when we know what it was we will be able to avoid it in future. She's right, Emma said, it's actually harder to tell when someone's previously healthy, especially given how fast she recovered. I mean, obviously the history of asthma is interesting and it does look as if she was reacting to something, but even if that's it, sometimes there's an underlying – well, let's wait and see, they're looking after her very well.

Looking *at*, I would have said, as much as *after*, although in hospital it is probably the same thing. Looking at every contraction of her heart muscle, reading every pull of her lungs. She was still wheezing intermittently, mostly at night, and sometimes her oxygen saturation fell to levels that brought the tapping steps of the doctor when it wasn't ward rounds. More nebs, they said, and someone would put a mask on Mimi's face and fill it with a hissing mist, the smell of it, almost floral, flitting briefly on the air.

So this is not toddler time, because the reason you are here is that Miriam's breathing stopped, and plainly it is expected to stop again. You are not going to get the fish out of the freezer or change the lightbulb in the hall and you have cancelled the plumber's visit to service the boiler and your meeting with a PhD student writing about women in the Arts and Crafts movement. Everything is paused, except that Rose still needs to go to school and to eat her meals, and the laundry must still be done and the bathroom cleaned, somehow, from the High Dependency Unit of a city fifteen miles from home. The monitors' bleeping fills the nights and days

23

the way your own breathing fills the nights and days, because the norm, the beating of the heart, is not to be trusted. Silence is no longer natural, or perhaps, what is natural is no longer silent, no longer to be taken for granted. Fear hammers along your veins, in your ears, behind your eyes, and fear, it turns out, gives meaning to time. Because the real fear is that time, Miriam's time, will run out.

I stayed the first two nights, lying on the fold-out chair at Miriam's bedside, in closer physical proximity than we had lain since she stopped coming into Emma's and my bed on weekend mornings. We need to swap, Emma said, it's my turn, Rose needs you and Mimi needs me too. Mimi doesn't need you the way she needs me, I thought, I'm the one who's always with her, I'm the one who saw her first steps and sat through every Nativity play, I'm the one they called. Yes, I said, I know, you're right, OK.

We were talking in the corridor, aligned so that we could see Miriam, in case we had to rush in, press the red button, in case I had to call for help while Emma began CPR, which is not resuscitation at all but only slowing down the rate at which cells die in hope that someone will bring adrenaline and a defibrillator and use them before the heart and the brain lose the ability to communicate with each other. We had ten minutes, before I needed to say goodbye to Miriam and go to collect Rose from school, take her home to change and eat something, pick up whatever Miriam wanted from her bedroom and then bring Rose back to see her sister. Emma, I wanted to say, tell me all the possibilities, let me in to your fear, to all the stories your expertise offers you, but also go away, don't infect me with horrors that may, after all, recede and fall away as if in a rear-view mirror, don't tell me a word that isn't twenty-four-carat truth. I'll go to Sainsbury's, I said instead, if I have time I'll make a batch of

24

dhal, leave it in the fridge. I think Rose might have a school trip this week. Our eyes met for the first time in the conversation: no. No, Rose doesn't go anywhere, not now we know that a healthy child can drop dying for no reason, not now we know that being well at any given moment is no indication that the next moment will not bring sudden death. I'll check, I said, there's no reason she shouldn't go if she wants to, not really, it's not as if she's any less safe on a trip than in the classroom, the distraction would probably be good for her. Yes, Emma said, I know, I know that. Behind her, Miriam was watching television with her eyes and writing on her phone with her fingers.

In forty-eight hours on the children's ward, the smell of the wind and the thought of driving a car become exotic. I wanted to leave, to have my share of outside air and fast roads, and I was afraid of what might happen when I left. As if my presence made any difference to what happened.

How was Rose at school yesterday, I asked, anything I need to know?

Emma shrugged. In the absence of the children, I could see her shrink and sag as if something in her back and neck and shoulders was deflating. I knew why she was planning to pick up some morning shifts again next week. Not, as I had allowed myself to allege in my head, because even now her commitment to her patients and to the NHS came before her commitment to us, but because she didn't dare to stop, to find herself one morning alone in a house that should be expecting four people and is expecting three. To find herself tidying the bedroom of a child who is not there and may not return.

'Mrs Wasley says she seems OK. A little subdued, maybe, but of course she's tired.'

Rose is not subdued when tired.

'At home? Has she said anything?'

Emma rubbed her neck and turned her head from side to side. Her neck gets stiff, bent always at the same concerned and sympathetic angle towards patients sitting always on her left. 'She keeps asking what's wrong with Mimi and when she's coming back. I keep telling her that Mim fainted and needed help to wake up again and she'll have to stay in hospital until we know why.' She looked up at me. 'It's not much good, is it?'

'It's true,' I said. 'Come here.' I turned her around and pressed my thumbs, dry from all the hospital disinfectant gel, into the warm muscle above her pale grey neckline. Cashmere, that jumper. Hand wash. I moved closer; the smell of her brought a momentary comfort.

I collected one plastic bag with Miriam's laundry in it and one with mine, the bag with my toothbrush, towel, and the tracksuit in which I'd been sleeping – you need to wear something in which you can talk confidently to medical staff in the middle of the night – and the bag of books and magazines and art supplies that Miriam didn't want. Miriam stopped watching a documentary about mountain gorillas long enough to make eye contact and allow me to kiss her hair, which I took, under the circumstances, as some provisional kind of good sign.

I left the High Dependency Unit, averting my eyes from the opposite bed in which a three-year-old with cerebral palsy was in such difficulties that the nurses kept the screens closed and spoke to the mother with terrible harmonies in their voices. Until I hear those notes, I thought, I'll know that they don't think Miriam's going to die. Not here and now, anyway.

I walked past the nurses' station, where one was on the computer and another, the smiley dark-haired one who seemed to have been on duty for at least thirty-six hours, holding a cup of tea in both hands and gazing out of the window, as if in temporary defeat. I passed the tank of bubbles and tropical fish and a toddler wearing only a nappy banging on the glass while his mother sat on a plastic chair and communed with her phone. I pressed the buzzer and simultaneously turned the high door handle to get through the first doors, paused in the no-man's-land of posters about hand hygiene and how to sneeze while I readjusted the plastic bags so I could turn both handles of the second door. I walked down the slanting corridor. I would like to know who chooses the pictures for hospital walls and if there is some reason why he or she thinks patients and visitors wish to be reminded that there are or were at the end of the nineteenth century lives in which people danced beside the Seine by candle-lanterns and lost themselves amid women in feathered hats in contemplation of steam trains bound for Venice and Seville. I passed a bed and a drip being wheeled the other way, its occupant a half-conscious man, bare-chested above the sheets, a man who should have been wearing a suit and offering a strong handshake. I overtook an elderly man pushing an elderly woman in a wheelchair with a pink blanket over her knees. I sped up. I passed the newsagent by the entrance where I had thought I might go to buy magazines and sweets for Miriam and had not gone because it would mean being away from her too long, because there would be time for her to die while I tried to remember if she preferred mint to orange in her chocolate, and then I was out, in the air, wholly unable to remember where in the outlying fields of tarmac Emma had left the car. I had to call her, in the end, to be reminded, and then after I had paid an outrageous sum for parking on my card because I had no cash and negotiated the maze of barriers, mini-roundabouts and one-way lanes to the exit I took a wrong turn and found myself in a housing estate of smug detached executive homes designed

hours over the sea

The house was a mess, of course. Emma has no gift for these things at the best of times, leaves clothes she intends to wear again stuffed over the towel rail in our bathroom, usually for days, until I wash them or put them away. She opens her post and then leaves it, pushed back into torn envelopes, on top of the shoe-cupboard in the hall (yes, the standard issue Swedish white shoe-cupboard found in all urban middle-class family homes since our generation discovered that life is easier and pleasanter when the tracking of dog shit and Saturday-night pavement-vomit is limited to the hall. Emma's parents, accustomed to larger and more secluded habitats, both disapprove, and separately make great drama of the hardship of removing shoes *at their age*; I remark that ageing seems to be less debilitating in both Japan and the Nordic countries, interestingly connected by the proscription of street shoes indoors – who knows, perhaps the frequent removing of shoes in fact slows ageing by maintaining flexibility? No, really I do not remark, not out loud, or at least not until they have gone away and I can tell Emma at no doubt tedious length what I would have said had I said it).

There were three cards from the Post Office saying that they'd tried to deliver parcels addressed to Miriam. Parcels from our friends, the friends I'd texted and emailed from the High Dependency Unit that first day when I still thought someone was going to come and tell us what had happened, give us a story and maybe some pills to make it all go away. Tomorrow, I would be able to take Miriam presents, offer her affection in material form.

The load of laundry that I had left washing while I went running before – well, before it happened – was still wet in the machine and now smelt fishy. The dishwasher was full of clean plates and cutlery, and the dirty ones, not many and not really dirty, as if Emma had been feeding Rose mostly on toast and apples and not eating herself, were piled on the counter. I'd been late, after all, to collect Rose, had had to apologise to her teacher, to mutter about the hospital and the traffic, but at least had avoided the gaze of curious parents who had heard what had happened, couldn't imagine what we must be going through and if there's anything they could do, anything. How was school, I'd said, the usual cue for the usual stream of detail about what Molly and Samira had said and who'd come top in spelling, a flow of information entirely compatible with our wholesale ignorance of events that to the adult mind appear more important. It says in the newsletter, I'd said a couple of Fridays ago, that cooking club is cancelled until the fire damage is repaired. Oh yes, she said, the fire brigade came, I think it was Tuesday, that was my class, actually, but anyway as I was saying Mrs Wasley says that if Phoebe doesn't stop playing with Fatima's hair she's going to move Phoebe but it's not fair because Fatima— Wait, I said, you set the kitchen on fire? Yes, she said, but Fatima's a crybaby and she's always telling—

So I didn't listen much. Our house is cheap modern in-fill,

built with ten others on land that was the orchard of a real house like the one where Emma grew up, but it's in one of those Victorian suburbs with wide roads and mature trees, the manifestation in red brick and horse-chestnut of a century and a half of the English bourgeoisie, and so despite living in a town, because of living in a town, we are intimate with the changing of the seasons. Nothing was different from before Miriam's incident. Her cardiac event. The lime leaves were still the colour of brown envelopes and falling from the sky like leaflets from a plane. The pavements were still lumpy with broken chestnuts, their auburn skulls smashed and the white matter crushed on the paving slabs, and the survivors still gleamed waxy from inside their grass-green carapaces. The day was neither bright nor rainy, only English grey, the sky pressing on the treetops, and I kept my hand on my phone in my pocket as if answering it fast would change anything. Emergency, I was in a state of emergency, except that there was nothing I could do.

Rose didn't ask about her sister. I sent her upstairs to change while I took a few things out of the washing machine, Miriam's T-shirts and jeans from the weekend. I sniffed their mouldy smell and put them back in, set the machine to run again on a higher temperature. She would come back and wear them again. Yes she would. I started to empty the dishwasher and then remembered that there was an alternative to my thoughts and turned on the radio. There had been more bombs in the places where there are bombs. Children had died. No-one had started CPR and called an ambulance, no-one had rushed to them with adrenaline and oxygen and a defibrillator, no-one was piecing together what had happened. There had been bombs and children had died.

The wind rustled through the trees outside. I called to Rose to come down for a snack. She gets beguiled by toys

31

and drawing and forgets that she is hungry until her blood-sugar level is so low that she is unable to decide whether to start with the apple or the biscuit, although on this occasion, I found, there were no apples, in fact no fruit at all, and I tried to summon the energy to persuade her to eat carrot sticks instead, to persuade myself to take out the chopping board and the knife. She needed normality. Dietary rules, after all, are there to give us the illusion of order and control, although I doubted that even an eight-year-old would find the imposition of carrot sticks any kind of counterweight to the discovery of sudden death. I was about to call Rose down again when my mind tripped over the word 'unresponsive' and I ran up the stairs to find her.

Emma, I supposed, would have called me if anything had happened. If Miriam's condition had deteriorated. Her not calling probably meant that things were no worse than I already knew.

I tested Rose on her six times table while I started to cook supper. The chicken I'd been planning to cook on Tuesday was now five days out of date and smelt unappetising, so with my ancestors chuntering in my ear I threw it away. The peppers were the kind that come sealed in plastic and last for a disturbingly long time so I fried them with onions, garlic and ginger and then added a tin of tomatoes and half a bag of red lentils and called it a kind of curry. Rose was using my laptop to watch a children's programme in which a fool-hardy Australian elicits violent reactions from carnivores in intemperate climates, but behind his excitable tones, behind the rustle of onions in the pan a size smaller than the one I'd usually use, behind the digestive noises of the washing machine, the house lay in silence around the absence on the top floor. It's not that she's always here, I reminded myself, it's not as if Rose and I are not often alone here with Emma at work and Mimi out with her friends or at drama or art club, but it was different.

I tried to talk to Rose at bedtime, after I'd insisted on washing her hair, taken turns reading paragraphs of a book about a boy on enviable terms with the classical gods, replaced her water glass and promised her overdue clean sheets in the morning. I'm going back to the hospital in the morning, I said, it will be Mum picking you up tomorrow because she's going in to work on Saturday, but she'll bring you over to see Mimi straight after school, maybe bring some dinner so we can all eat together on the ward, OK? She turned over, so I could see only her damp hair on the pillow and her shoulders in the pyjamas that Miriam also wore, for years, before she turned righteously against pink. Through the skylight over Rose's bed, the night was muffled with cloud and streetlights. No, she said, actually I'd rather stay here, actually I don't like that hospital. There was a plane crossing the sky, coming in to land. People up there looking down, picking out the motorway and the shopping centre, finding landmarks after hours over the sea.

I rested my hand on her shoulder. 'I don't like the hospital either. I don't think even Mum likes it and she used to work in one. But we do like Mimi, and she's stuck there and I want to see her. And she wants to see you.'

Rose shrugged off my hand. 'I'd just rather stay here, that's all.'

I took a deep breath. Mostly, I think, the girls get on well, for sisters either side of puberty. I don't have siblings so I have no real comparison, but there was more conflict between me and the two other boys at Bryher Farm than there is between Miriam and Rose. They had been playing companionably enough on Emma's iPad when Emma had brought Rose to the HDU on the evening of – that evening.

'Miriam would rather see you. And all of us. She's very bored there, Rose. She likes it when you go and play with her.'

She pulled her knees further up to her chest. 'If she's all that bored, she could just come home.'

'You know she can't. We talked about it. Didn't you and Mum talk about it? She has to stay there until we know what happened and how to stop it happening again.'

'It's taking ages.'

I risked patting her shoulder again. 'I know. It's really hard. It will be easier when we know, at least then we'll be able to make a plan.'

'And bring her home?'

'Yes. And bring her home.'

I heard the question hanging in the air: what if she never comes back? What if we never know what happened?

Rose uncurled enough to look over her shoulder. 'What did happen?'

Another plane began to bisect the window. I knew Emma had already told her this.

'Mimi was on the playing field. At school, at the end of lunchtime. She says she was running because she'd got all the way back to the classroom and then realised she'd left her phone under the tree where she'd been showing her friends some photos, so she rushed back to get it as the bell went. And while she was running she started to feel odd but she was in a big hurry and you know she's not supposed to have her phone out at school so she was probably worried about being caught. Mostly when people run, their muscles need more oxygen and more sugar so their breathing speeds up and their hearts beat faster and their body makes the chemicals it needs to move quickly, but very rarely that doesn't work, and then the person has to stop running and sometimes to lie down.

34

Miriam had to lie down, and Mr Stanton found her lying down and feeling very ill. He called an ambulance and while it came he had to help her with her breathing. So we're very grateful to Mr Stanton. And when the ambulance came, the paramedics were able to help Mimi's heart to work better so she felt well quite quickly and you know she's all right now, you've seen her. But we need to know why her body made the wrong chemicals and why her heart and her breathing went a bit wrong so we can make sure it doesn't happen again, because it's very unusual.'

I paused. She was still looking at me, as if I hadn't finished.

'That's all we know, love. At the moment. But she's all right now, and she's safe. They're looking after her very carefully, aren't they?'

She nodded and rolled over again. 'I just think she should come home.'

I swallowed. 'We all do, sweetie. She will. But meanwhile, we have to go and see her where she is.'

'I'll go, but I don't want to.'

I kissed her hair. 'That's very grown-up. Thank you.'

I went downstairs and put the radio on. The American police had shot another child for being black and outside, and the child had died, there on the pavement in the company only of his killers. Blood spreading across the tarmac, and in the child's head pain and fear and a final, wondering realisation that no-one was going to help him. And the parents, hours later: *there's been an incident.* I would kill my child's killers, I thought, I would go out and look them in the eye and kill them quite slowly and fuck all the consequences.

But of course I had no-one to kill. And of course Miriam was alive.

I took the damp laundry out of the machine and carried it

up to the bathroom, where I dumped it in the bath while I set up the two clothes-airers. I picked up each garment, shook and smoothed it and arranged them for maximum exposure to the radiator. Women's pants in three sizes, Miriam's unsuitable black nylon bra, thickly padded so that it looked like a surreal pair of breasts hanging off the white plastic rods, Emma's plain now-off-white cotton sprouting tendrils of elastic from its worn straps. Rose's purple flowery socks, previously worn by Mimi and going at the heels. My own boxer shorts, sombre flags among the pastel wisps of women's underwear. Miriam's T-shirt and cardigan, Emma's floppy grey top, Rose's striped leggings. A weekend wash. I pulled more clothes out of the laundry basket, leaning over the smell of feet and deodorant. My old tracksuit, now hospital pyjamas and smelling of hand sanitiser and plastic. Miriam's school uniform, the shirt muddy and missing buttons where they'd torn it open to position the defibrillator pads. No need, I thought, to mend it, they're cheap enough, let's just – I put it back, pushed it down to the bottom underneath Emma's hand-wash cardigan and a bathmat for which there was no hurry.

Downstairs, the radio had moved on to a lively discussion of the culinary habits of second-generation immigrants, featuring the sounds of wooden spoons beating eggs into flour and people enthusing with their mouths full. I could bake, I thought, if we still have eggs I could make some muesli muffins which would be portable and give Mimi and Emma some fibre and vitamins in an easy form. Sunflower seeds, dried apricots and flaked almonds, olive oil and wholemeal flour, use up the yogurt before it goes off and Rose can have one for breakfast as a treat. I turned up the radio to mask the silence. Emma, after all, would have called me if there was anything wrong. I'd had my phone in my pocket all evening.

*

36

I'd thought that after two nights on the fold-out chair beside Miriam's bed, I might sleep well in my own bed, might crash through all the levels of fear to oblivion, but I was wrong. I missed Emma. It was months since we'd last slept apart, not since she'd been in London for a GP training event early in the spring. I tried to spread out, to use the space, but that only reminded me that she wasn't there. I pulled her pillow into the place where she lies, so that it wasn't empty, and turned away. It would have been easier to be in the hospital, to be beside Mim and watching her breathe, watching the monitors scrawl the beating of the heart that could no longer be trusted to continue unheard and unseen. I thought for the first time of Emma at home that first night, lying where I lay now in the fresh knowledge that Miriam had been well at lunchtime and clinically dead half an hour later. And the second night too, I'd said I'll stay, you go home and get some rest, my stuff's already here and Rose is expecting it to be you at the school gates. Look, I had not said, this is where you pay the price, love. For fifteen years you go off every morning in your nice clothes and you get to say actually I'm a doctor and you come home late to find your clothes clean in your drawers, your dinner in the oven and the girls in their pyjamas with their homework done. I'm the primary carer, the one whose name and number are first on the forms. I'm the one they call when there's an incident and I'm the one who got here first so go home, Emma, go click your heels and earn your money. Our money. The money that pays for the roof over all of our heads and the food on all of our plates, the shoes on our feet and the books on our shelves. I am not, I hope, ungrateful. My resentment is occasional and not her fault. I should not have sent her away the second time. I was sorry. I turned over and brushed against the pillow impersonating my wife.

Outside, the sky was orange. Cars passed.

arts and crafts

I probably shouldn't really be doing the Coventry Cathedral project. It's probably no more than a distraction from the attempt I should be making to revive, or more truthfully to inaugurate, a serious academic career. But the truth is that it's too late for me to have a serious academic career, or indeed a serious career of any kind. Fifteen years out from my PhD, with one book and some odds and ends of hourly-paid teaching on my CV, geographically tethered to the West Midlands by Emma's job and the girls' schools, I still keep an eye on the adverts for permanent academic jobs but it's not going to happen. British higher education in general is running on casual labour, on people like me who ran themselves into debt doing PhDs and then found that the old-fashioned jobs with permanent contracts and time for research were all but gone and also that they were now too old and over-qualified for the things they might have done in their twenties, law conversion courses and management trainee schemes and internships in journalism and the arts. I know, what happened to working-class jobs a generation ago is now hitting the professions; I'm not claiming to deserve sympathy, or at least no more than anyone else in the mess of England today. So we go cap-in-hand to heads of department every summer: please sir, give us some work? Not much work, for me, just a couple of hours a week in the classroom, not so much that it interferes with the school run or the laundry or the baking of sourdough bread, with cycling to the next town where the wholefood shop sells the only kind of sunscreen to which Rose is not allergic, with taking the car to the garage and the girls to the dentist and Emma's suits to the dry-cleaners.

And they do give us work. Not in the summer, when they say no, there's nothing at the moment, the department generally aims to meet teaching needs with full-time staff, but in September. The academic awkward squad, which is about a third of the department, spends the summer arguing about what they will and won't do the following year. It's not fair, he's got more than me. I did that last year. But I'm special, I have a book to write. No, I'm special, I have mental health problems. (In academia, this does not make you special.) I'm even more special, I might leave and take my research funding with me if you don't give me what I want. I don't know what they pay the head of department but it should include danger money. He's a glorified dinner lady, arbitrating playground brawls and trying to forestall the worst outrages of bullying and provocation. When arguing time runs out, he calls on the likes of me, the unemployed with PhDs, to come in and mop up. First-year stuff, mostly, the introductory courses for which the awkward squad consider themselves too important, but occasionally someone's sabbatical leaves a more specialised option for one of us. I like both, I don't mind. If I'm not too important to wash pants and buy Christmas presents for nursery staff, I'm not too important to teach an eager eighteen-year-old how to look at a painting. It must, I sometimes think, be exhausting for the awkward squad, for

Professor Troublemaker and his henchmen, to maintain their relentless superiority at all times and in all places. They must long, sometimes, to sit on the grass or lick an ice-cream, to fall off something or to be able to offer a casual apology for unintended harm.

I looked up and saw myself reflected in the French doors of our one downstairs room. Hair on end, baggy old sweatshirt over pyjama bottoms with a hole in the knee, face lit by the screen in front of me. Cars passed outside, not often. The neighbours had left their landing light on. My heart lurched: Miriam. Miriam had nearly died. Miriam's heart had stopped. I met my own blurred gaze in the glass and looked away.

Anyway. My hourly-paid teaching is not research, and it's research that leads to jobs, when there are any jobs, which there aren't. It gets me out of the house, brings in pin-money, enough that I don't have to use Emma's earnings to buy her birthday presents, gives me people to talk to. It's not wholly implausible to suggest that the Cathedral project could lead to something else, since the ability to write audio-guides could be a skill with more applications than the ability to teach undergraduates to understand the role and limitations of the Arts and Crafts movement in shaping the nation, but I doubt that there is somewhere a recruitment website bursting with adverts for the writers of scripts for old buildings. Not audio-guides, sorry. Geolocative media apps, which are audio-guides in a higher-tech form that will defeat and annoy the generation who visit cathedrals. Not my idea, I'm just following my instructions, in this case from Prof. Simon Godnestone (pronounced Gunston, obviously), who has a research grant of half a million pounds contingent upon 'impact'. 'Impact' means that academic research has to be offered to the general public in a form believed by the Research Council to be accessible and engaging, which means dumbed-down and digital. You get extra points for using mobile phones and social media, regardless of the probable audience; there seems to be an idea that Young People Nowadays will flock to cathedrals if promised an experience involving the use of selfie-sticks and Twitter, and no awareness that the beige-clad pensioners who do in fact come off the tour buses and up the ramps two by two do not want a geolocative media app but a knowledgeable guide in a silly hat and a nice cup of tea in the café afterwards. Anyway, even geolocative media apps start, it appears, with words on a page, and that's what they're paying me for. Only carrying out orders, see?

flock of birds

I had begun by going to the Cathedral. I had been before, once accompanying Rose's Year 1 school trip – they like to have a father along so someone can take the boys to the loo – and once to a carol service, when Emma discovered that the girls didn't know any Christmas carols and were mildly disbelieving about her claim that the baby in the manger at Christmas was the same person as the man on the cross. We should Google it, Rose said, that doesn't sound right. This time I went alone, a daytime outing that felt mildly transgressive even though I knew it was work and I was being paid. You should go to the theatre, Emma always says, put Rose in after-school care and take yourself to a matinée at Stratford, you used to love live Shakespeare and here we are with it on our doorstep, you do know that I would actually like to think of you sitting there watching *Hamlet* while I'm at work, you do know that it would make me smile when I think about you during the day. A stay-at-home mum, she says, would do such a thing, would take the odd day off, so why don't you? Because I have something to prove, I think. Because despite the joint account and the rhetoric, it's not our money but hers, and even in the kindest version of the story of my unemployment, I'm supposed to be looking after the girls and the house and the laundry, not taking myself to matinées.

Emma had the car that day so I took the bus, and sat upstairs at the front; there is no need to outgrow small pleasures. I looked down into gardens where wet brown leaves stuck to bright grass and caught the occasional glimpse of unmade beds and open wardrobes, a student picking his nose while sitting at a desk in a first-floor bay window. Rose would like this, I thought, I should take her on buses, make sure she knows how it works before she has to get herself to the High School because Miriam won't always want to be looking after her. Although by then, if the government has its way which it will, the High School will be the Jobz-R-Us Academy specialising in hairdressing and mindless obedience, and Emma will overcome two sets of principles and allow her father to rescue his granddaughters from the consequences of her error of judgement in marrying me by paying private school fees which he has already more than once offered to do. It's only, he said, that one doesn't like to think of one's grandchildren facing greater disadvantages than one's children. Well then stop voting Tory, you prick, Emma did not say.

I remembered my own school bus. I'd been scared by the prospect of being the youngest in a lawless community of teenagers in transit, but in fact we were a deeply conservative bunch. Big bad boys sat upstairs at the back with big bad girls, the moral tone rising towards the seat in which I now sat. Younger bad boys sat at the back downstairs and the rest of us sorted ourselves nearer the driver, sole and unwilling representative of adulthood and the law. The bus was too big for the winding lanes and high hedges of West Cornwall, so that branches hurled themselves into the windows and it was impossible not to duck. We teetered around corners, were

44

often late because of stand-offs with on-coming tractors, once got stuck under a bridge. I was, at least in relation to school, where standards were lower than at Bryher Farm, a good boy, but I tended to sit in the middle and hope no-one noticed.

Coventry is not a planned city in the way that Milton Keynes and Letchworth are planned, but even so I had thought that from the top of a bus I might see a logic invisible from the streets. Much of the ring-road is set up on stilts like a spiral slide at an outdoor swimming pool. There are out-crops of medieval houses and shops, dwarfed and implausible as sandstone pebbles on a granite beach. They look fake, Tudorbethan, chip shops with slanting oak beams and white plaster walls leaning over the pavement, posters for pay-day loans in the slanting windows of buildings made of small red bricks, smoothed as if by the sea, where low timber doorways force overgrown humans to duck and shimmy. More fibre-glass heritage, you think, but it's real, poking up between disintegrating post-war concrete and 1980s brick facings, stained by exhaust smoke and graffiti. It is cheating to find beauty by picking out the old buildings and softening the focus on the rest. There is no obvious reason why older buildings should be more beautiful, although it seems that we have always thought so. Many contemporary poets and writers were horrified by the crescents and terraces of John Wood's eighteenth-century Bath, mourning the organic beauty of the ancient village houses demolished to make way for miles of uniform pale stone. Vulgar and ostentatious buildings for tasteless new money, hundreds of houses all the same, piled on top of each other with no gentlemanly privacy. Huge, brutal windows, all very well for those looking out but glaring and inhumanly geometric for passers-by. I used to tease my friends by suggesting that the domestic architecture of the '60s and

'70s would also have its day, and I was right, but it's still hard to imagine anyone wanting to venerate much built in British cities in the 1980s.

The Cathedral is strangely hard to find, hidden behind a building that looks like a Soviet-era Russian hotel and is a students' hall of residence. I approached it from the side, head down, wanting to see it first without any later clutter in the way, as if I could trick myself into an authentic experience of some past moment of the place, as if I might see it suddenly. I stopped in front of Epstein's St Michael and the Devil on the outside of the east wall; I had not yet discovered that one of the charms of Coventry Cathedral is that the geographical cardinal points are at odds with the ecclesiastical ones. The wall that faces the rising sun is called the south wall, because all altars are assumed to present themselves to the resurrection in the east, even when a compass would point north. I am reminded of an experiment once described to me by my friend Anna's husband Giles, an ornithologist, in which migratory birds are shut in a windowless dome set up so that researchers can change the magnetic field to make north become south, to see if the birds are navigating by the pull of the North Pole when they leave Africa for Europe.

I've heard the sculpture called 'St Michael Wrestling the Devil', but he's already triumphant, floating over prone Satan with his wings outstretched like those of eagles on church lecterns and his arms open. There's no pantomime about this devil, no pitchfork or tail. His face looks like a death mask. Green bronze against sandstone. The air smelt of rain and the flagstones underfoot were dark with damp, but the clouds were only silver grey and no drops fell. When Basil Spence, the Cathedral's architect, wanted to commission Epstein to make St Michael, the Reconstruction Committee objected – in 1957 – that Epstein was Jewish. So was Jesus, Spence said.

Epstein died just before St Michael and Satan were installed. I found myself nodding to St Michael, or Satan, or maybe Epstein, as I went up the stairs towards the forum between the ruins of the medieval cathedral and the soaring of the new one.

I'm not a believer. I trust that's already clear. The virgin birth, the miracles, the resurrection – no. But I've always liked churches. The community at Bryher Farm was in many ways a good place to grow up, and I'm glad Dad stayed there after my mother died, but it could be hard to find space for reading and writing. People join communes to be with other people, and often because they enjoy at least the idea of manual work. If they do want to be alone, it's outside, watching the sea or meditating on a tree, and a person, especially a young person, found alone and at ease indoors is assumed to be in need of an improving occupation. Come and knead the bread with me, Adam, take that mood out on the dough. We need some more wood chopping, just what you need after a day stuck inside at school. The onion bed's full of weeds. In a town, I'd probably have gone to the library, but even Porthleven was four miles along the coast path or six on the road, so I went to the church. It doesn't occur to anyone to look for a teenaged boy in a church. I used to pile up the tapestry kneelers along one of the pews at the back, take off my shoes and stretch out my legs, using the holders for prayer books to keep my notes and books to hand. School work, often, but I was fortunate in having a school library that had plenty of space if little money, so the collections acquired in the '60s and '70s were still there, full of dust and the occasional annotations of people who were by the early '90s settled in their jobs-for-life and industriously making untaxed repayments on six-bedroom houses bought for the cost of half a bin-shed on a modern estate now. In winter the church was already locked when the school bus reached the village, but from February to October I saw the fall of light through the stained glass windows lean, strengthen, and fade, heard the wind and rain on the roof, smelt the ghost of incense at Easter and the dying of roses after summer weddings. Sometimes, especially during the school holidays, the organist was there practising, or the ladies who cleaned and changed the flowers. You again, they said, just so you're doing no harm, and later sometimes they included me in their tea breaks. Must be hard, growing up without a mum, see why his dad stays up there with the hippies, could be right lonely else. I didn't often see the vicar, who was serving five churches across three parishes and probably regarded the sixteenth-century buildings in his care as nightmarish liabilities, all Grade I listed and apt at any moment to require impossibly costly repairs. Hello, Adam, he'd say, everything OK? As if it was my job to be in the church reading, the way it was other people's jobs to be dusting the pews and weeding the path. I rarely looked at the altar, fenced off and swathed in cloths, but I came to know all the epitaphs and to imagine the life stories and especially the funerals of those interred around me. Robert Hendrick and Elizabeth his wife, she dead thirty-four years before him, two days before a nameless 'infant son'. An assortment of young men killed in battle: Napoleon, various acts of imperial aggression, the Crimea, as well as the lists of those who didn't return from the big two. Nearly forty gone in two weeks in 1916; it was surprising that the village had anyone to send in 1939. On the west wall, the Pengillick family, who lost seven children between 1822 and 1826.

I stood inside the Cathedral and turned to the north-facing West Screen, the Screen of Saints and Angels. On both of my previous visits, I'd wanted to stand before it, to let it dwarf me, and to read both the intricacies of each figure and the sails of light and space between them. There are upright saints, angular, emaciated, bearing fairy-tale symbols of their particular lives and deaths, summoning from memory the stilted saints in the medieval windows smashed and melted by bombs in November 1940. They are human figures but there is no pretence of life. They look like the risen dead, flesh falling away, gazes averted. Between their ranks, angels rise and descend like a flock of birds, like rooks. A host of angels, a murder of crows. A parliament of rooks. John Hutton is said to have made his angels in the image of those liberated from Nazi concentration camps.

the rumble of the approaching train

Take the train, the friendly Welsh nurse had said to Emma.
It's cheaper than parking and probably quicker from where
you live anyway, and frankly, Mum, you don't really look
as if you ought to be driving. That's a shame, I didn't say,
considering that she's planning to go into work and practise
medicine the day after tomorrow, but the next day I took the
train so that Emma wouldn't have to drive home.

I stood on the platform and closed my eyes. Tiredness was
a stone in my head, a weight on my throat, but it was also an
anaesthetic of a kind, a small mercy. What if Rose had an
emergency at school while Emma and I were a train journey
away at the hospital, what if the trains were running late or
cancelled and we needed to get back to Rose? I do not want
to be here, I thought. I do not want to be doing this. I do not
want to be the father of a critically ill child. I do not want
to be the tragic figure at the school gates. The departure
board showed trains to London, Glasgow and the airport; I
had time, still, to go back through the underpass and come
up on the other platform for Oxenholme, Penrith, Carlisle,
Motherwell and Glasgow Queen Street, for the sour smell of

the overheated red trains and the flashing of mountains and coast in the windows, the growing space between me and the High Dependency Unit.

I leant against one of the girders supporting the roof of our rather charming Victorian station and let my head tip back, felt the rumble of the approaching train in my skull.

here, already

My feet were learning the corridors the way they know my running routes, navigating by the announcements of realised fear on the walls. Children's Wing: oncology, neurology, cardiology, ICU, and the unnameable misfortunes, the Bluebell Ward and the Rainbow Suite. Even the corridors were too hot and the hospital radio jabbered and jingled day and night. Jesus Christ, Miriam had said, do you think they're playing that stuff to prevent bed-blocking, tip people over the edge one way or the other, imagine if you were dying and the last thing you heard was that addled twerp, he sounds like a crap teacher about to lose control of Year 1.

Up the stairs, lined with posters telling me how much energy I was using by assailing two flights of stairs rather than taking the lift, as if calories were an enemy to be outwitted at every turn. Through the heavy double doors at the top, past the posters warning of the consequences of smoking around babies, and past the chapel – more posters about the evils of fizzy drinks and crisps – to the HDU. No-one has ever smoked near our kids, I thought. We do not buy crisps or sweet drinks and I make sure the girls get at least five portions of fruit and vegetables every day, remembering that fruit disrupts blood-sugar levels and that the widest range of colours approximates the widest range of nutrients. I remembered weaning Miriam, buying organic vegetables, steaming them because boiling removed too many vitamins, rubbing them through a strainer with a spoon because liquidising merely chopped up the indigestible fibre, blending them with organic baby rice and Emma's expressed breastmilk. Remembered Miriam rubbing the resulting elixir through her hair, which was blond then, remembered her dropping it off the spoon onto the floor and pointing and beaming in triumph. Why don't you, Emma said, give her food out of a jar to put in her hair while you spoon the good stuff in? All those years this was waiting to happen, lying in her future.

I pressed the bell outside the first set of doors and waited. It takes time. Of course answering the door is not the first priority for the nurses on the paediatric HDU, where the resus trolley wanders the hallway like a hopeful dog and several children a week are transferred to Intensive Care and not expected to return. How do you do it, I wanted to ask the nurses, how do you return every day to this place where families have fallen into ruin, how do you live in a world where it is normal for children to die and parents to grieve? Except that we all live in that world, don't we, only some of us, most of us in Britain today, are able to pretend otherwise. It is normal for children to die. Look at Syria, at Palestine, at Eritrea and Somalia. Look at the tidelines of beaches in Italy and Greece. Look, while we are on the subject, at certain parts of Chicago and Los Angeles. The nurses' world, the hospital version of normality, is true and what most of us here and now regard as ordinary life is a lie. Perhaps that is why we don't pay them very much. I read the posters about vegetables and not smoking and tried not to ring the bell again. I peered through the wired glass panels in the door, making sure that things were only normally busy, that there wasn't someone lying on the floor or a red emergency light flashing over one of the doors. I caught the eye of another parent watching her four-year-old watching the fish, but she was quite right not to move, parents are not allowed to answer the door, to admit strangers. I read the poster about fizzy drinks and exercise and tried to imagine a future in which I would leave Miriam alone in the house and go out running again. I failed. I rang the bell again and this time someone came to let me in.

There were curtains drawn around her bed.

No.

'Mim?'

She was sitting up, leaning forward with Emma on one side of her and a nurse on the other, the mask over her face. She waved a hand.

Emma glanced around. 'She's been wheezing again. Her sats were a bit low, we're just giving her some more nebs.'

Miriam reached round the plastic thing to push her hair aside and give me the kind of pissed-off expression I used to think she over-used. Not everything, I used to say, needs your best sarcasm. I blew her a kiss and she closed her eyes. Stop *embarrassing* me, Dad.

I put the parcels down at Miriam's feet. 'Look, people have been sending you things. Quite heavy things. And I made muffins for you. Rose had a couple for breakfast. I picked up a smoothie from that place outside the station, blueberry and banana. And your *New Internationalist* came.'

I'd wondered whether to bring the *New Internationalist*, which is a monthly digest of reasons why civilised human beings should despair of their species and their planet, but Miriam likes such despair, uses it as the foundation stone of her teenage identity.

54

The nurse stepped back so I could see the monitors. Her heart was going faster than usual, high 70s, and her O^2 was only 92. 'All right, darling, we're nearly done here. I'll just ask you to keep that probe on your finger for a bit, all right?'

Miriam handed the plastic thing, the nebuliser, back to the nurse. 'I need the loo.'

Emma and the nurse exchanged glances.

Emma cleared her throat. 'Could you wait a few minutes? Just while we see how that's worked?'

Mimi swung her legs out of the bed. She was still in her pyjamas, as if she was ill. 'No, actually. I had three cups of tea.'

'Oh.'

The nurse took over. 'All right then, darling, we'll take you off the monitors but I'm going to ask you to keep talking to me, all right?'

Miriam was unclipping the oxygen probe and reaching into her top to detach the heart monitor's wires from the pads stuck to her chest. 'I'll sing, OK? Save you making conversation.'

They left, Mim defenceless in her gingham pyjamas and the Chinese black velvet Mary Janes she affects as slippers, the nurse tired in her pastel tunic and trousers and the trainers they all wear as if about to enter a fun run dressed as a nurse.

Emma sagged as if someone had cut her string. I should have stridden across the room and taken her in my arms but I didn't feel like it.

'So?' I said.

She bowed her head. There was dandruff on her shoulders and her hair needed a wash.

'She started wheezing a bit around midnight. I'd tried to get her to settle down but she hadn't gone to sleep. It wasn't too bad at first, the inhaler seemed to work, but then her sats kept going down and we ended up with the nebs again. This is the second lot. She's going to end up on oxygen at this rate.'

I fiddled with the tape on one of the parcels. It was franked by the University of Glasgow, where my friend Anna works. 'And what does it mean?'

Emma shrugged. 'Either it's a coincidence and she arrested because of something else, or it was a reaction to something and it's still rumbling.'

'A reaction?'

'Anaphylaxis. I've been reading her notes. But we need a proper eye-witness account. Mrs Collier's talking to Mr Stanton.'

'But she's not allergic to anything.'

I could hear the words in Emma's head. *She is now, stupid.*

'We'll see,' she said. 'It's too early to say.'

Stop being such a fucking doctor, I wanted to say.

They came back. Mim sat on the bed, on the NHS blanket like cotton chicken-wire, and held out her hand for the probe's bite. Stop it, I thought, stop making her sick, let me just take her home and we'll start again.

'Lift your top for me, darling, and I'll just pop you back on the monitor.'

'I can do it myself.'

I stepped out through the screens, met the eyes of the mother of the spindly blond boy in the next bed. He'd been there when we arrived, propped up on pillows with a drawing pad on his lap, the bed covered in felt-tip pens and his torso scoured with surgical scars, old silver lines intersecting and overwritten by newer red ones. He was still drawing and she was just sitting there, large and pale and unwashed, her hands drooping in her lap.

'She had a bad night, your girl.'

'Yes,' I said. 'Sorry. I hope we didn't disturb you.'

She shook her head. 'You don't come in here for a rest, do you?'

The nurse pulled back Miriam's curtains and the ward got bigger. 'All done for now, Dad. I'll pop along and check on her in a little bit.'

Sats at 94, heart-rate 69, 66, 67. She lay back and watched her own monitors. Emma was at the window, watching rain fall on cars.

I went in and sat on the bed. 'Have you had breakfast?'

Mimi shook her head. 'You know what it's like. I experimented, that bread really is waterproof. And the cereals are all full of crap. You have to wonder how many of the people in here've just got malnutrition from being in hospital.'

Emma leant against the wall. 'There's been research. You're right. But the money's not there and most people aren't in long enough for it to make a difference.'

Mim pleated her blanket. 'How long am I going to be here?'

'Until we know what happened,' Emma said. 'Until we know how to stop it happening again. Believe me, no-one's going to keep you on the HDU any longer than they have to, these beds cost hundreds of pounds a day.'

I held out the first parcel. 'Here, see what Glasgow's sending you. And I'll get a plate for those muffins.'

She looked up. 'Can I have a coffee?'

Darling girl, you can have anything in this world. 'Yes. Emma, why don't you go get a proper coffee for her and one for you, get off the ward for a bit?'

She shrugged. 'Whatever you say.'

I opened the blind all the way and turned off the bright white light over Miriam's bed, turned the monitor so that we couldn't see it so easily. I picked up the books sliding across

57

the plastic armchair where Emma had spent the night and piled them on the plastic table at the end of the bed. Miriam watched me.

'Shall we send some of these home with Mum and ask her to bring some new ones when she comes back with Rose?'

Miriam let her head fall back on the pillow. 'Dad, how long am I going to be here? Really?'

I sat down and rested my hand on her knee under the blanket. 'Really, I don't know. I suppose there are two things: are you well enough to leave hospital now, and do we know what happened well enough to know how to stop it happening again? And I'd guess that mostly you are well enough, though the wheezing thing isn't great, but we don't yet know that we can keep you safe at home. Or school, or wherever. So for now, you're here, and distraction's probably your best bet.'

She closed her eyes. 'Dad?'

'Yes.'

'Who decides where I have to be? I mean, can I leave if I want to?'

I took a deep breath. Here, already. 'Legally, we decide. Mum and I. If the hospital thought we were acting against your interests, I think they could get a court order to overrule us, but I'm fairly sure that as long as we and your doctors are in accord, our word prevails. Mum probably knows the detail.'

She didn't open her eyes. 'So what about me? What if I decided to leave?'

I reached for her hand. 'I'd ask you not to make that decision. Not to put any of us in that situation. I'd remind you how much you have to gain by staying. The rest of your life, potentially. University and work and marriage and kids if you want them, and all the places you'll go and the things you'll do. Later on, you'll see that being bored and miserable and undignified for a few days when you're fifteen is a price worth paying even if it's horrible at the time.'

'If I still wanted to leave?'

'Open your parcel,' I said. 'I'm getting you a muffin.'

I went and stood in the kitchen and looked out at cars parking in puddles, at people taking umbrellas to the pay-stations. I thought of nothing at all.

When I went back in, there was the smell of coffee and Miriam had put a jumper over her pyjamas and was sitting cross-legged on the bed with her phone in her hands. I didn't look at the monitor.

She put the phone down and moved a torn padded envelope over something on the bed. 'Guess what was in the parcel?'

I had carried the parcel around. 'Books.'

'Yeah, but which books?'

'Erm, *The Second Sex*? *The Beauty Myth*? Though she knows you've read those. *Das Kapital* in parallel text.'

'Nope.'

'Tell me.'

'Giles's latest.'

I handed her a plate holding two muffins. 'That's kind.'

'No, Dad, that's monstrously egotistical. Oh, sorry you nearly died, you'd better read my book. My monstrously egotistical book about how when I go for a walk it's a profound moral and spiritual experience that makes me a better person than you, but when you go to the same place you're just a tourist messing things up. I read the extract in the *Guardian*, it's a pile of bullshit about how he's weighed down by sorrow for my generation, only not like normal adults are because we're being badly educated for jobs that don't exist in an economy that condemns us to poverty and homelessness at levels not seen since before the First World War but because we can't tell the difference between the lesser marshwort and the – the flowering marsh grass which all goes to show that we're losing our vital and precious sense of being at one with the natural world, rather than for example showing that the world's moved on and by the time we're grown up two-thirds of the global population will be living in cities and not actually giving a fuck about the lesser marshwort and it doesn't seem to have crossed his sorrowful little mind that if we all went and joined him communing with the fauna of furthest outer Scotland it would in fact be full of people and he'd have to find somewhere else to be superior which—'

Emma handed her a coffee. 'You know we were planning to go see them this summer?'

Mim took a sip. 'Thanks, Mum. Well, Giles and I might have a full and frank exchange of views. Do him good to hear from young people nowadays. I'm not going to let him talk crap just because he's a posh bloke who writes books.'

I looked at my fifteen-year-old daughter. Wouldn't England be an utterly different country if we didn't let people talk crap just because they're posh blokes who write books?

'He does hear from young people nowadays,' I said. 'He's got Raph and Tim.'

She started on the muffin. 'I like Raph but you can't really call him a representative of teenagers everywhere. He only talks about engineering. And Tim probably does know all about the lesser marshwort, it's not as if he's got anything else to do up there.'

I took a muffin myself. Speaking as a posh bloke who writes books, I thought, as long as we can get the patriarchy in here to piss her off, we're going to be OK.

a parent whose mind

On the children's ward, parents' sadness comes out at night. During the day, friends text to tell you *you're doing so well* and *being heroic* and they *don't know how you keep going*, which is kind but makes you feel even further from ordinary life than the fact that your daughter's breathing stopped and no-one seems to know why it stopped or when it might stop again. You keep going as everyone always keeps going, because an alternative has not been offered. You play Scrabble and chess and Monopoly with your daughter when other diversions fail, using the set of board games (bored games, Miriam always insisted) that usually come out only at Christmas. Miriam is predictably good at Monopoly. You carry plates of nauseating hospital food out of the room and work your way through the pots and packets you bought at Waitrose yesterday, when you were in the grey light of the outside world where there is weather and movement. You persuade her to turn off the television and walk up and down the ward when she's been sitting in her bed for two hours. You try, courting sarcasm, to interest her in the fish, with which you increasingly identify. You invite her to make up stories about the people seen foreshortened in the car park below, live in hope of seeing some of them argue or lose their keys or get a parking ticket. You try to ration the number of times you look at the clock. You offer another game of Scrabble, a cup of nasty orange tea from the kitchenette, which children are not allowed to enter for fear of burns and knives or maybe contamination, even fifteen-year-old children long accustomed to cooking soup, eggs and the occasional pasta dish all on their own. You let her watch television again, and then it's probably time to eat something. In a while, your wife will arrive, or maybe a doctor will look in, raising your hopes that soon someone will tell you what is happening.

But at night, eventually, the children go to sleep. It takes a long time. There will be a television playing somewhere on the ward, even though the rules say they should be switched off or used with headphones after 9 p.m. The lights are always on. The telephone at the nurses' station continues to ring. There is always someone crying on the children's ward, but at night there are fewer other sounds to mask the noise. Pain. Fear. Boredom. Sorrow. Young children can cry for hours while their parents reason or pat or sing or walk up and down with the weight of bone and muscle and blood in their arms. Nurses, I observed, by and large, lose patience with tears after about twenty minutes. They know what it is to have something to cry about.

At home, Miriam had slept with the light off, her curtains drawn and door closed since Rose's birth ('this baby is too loud and I will not have it'). She often gets up in the night to turn off the landing light that Rose requires. I draped towels and my coat over a chair and positioned it so the shade fell on her face. I offered her ear-plugs and an eye-shade from our flight to New York four years ago. (I couldn't imagine that we would ever fly again, either, or hazard her to an unfamiliar medical system.) Already tethered by the monitors' wires, her skin red and itchy under the glue on the pads and her finger in the grip of the oxygen saturation monitor, the last thing Miriam wanted was more objects attached to her. Stop, Dad, with the shadow theatre, it's no use, I can't sleep and I don't see how anyone else can either, I don't see how anyone ever gets better from anything in hospitals where the food is not food and they shine lights in your eyes and let the phone ring all night, I'd have thought it was a good way of making people ill. It takes more, sweetie, than crap food and broken nights to make people ill, I did not say, or most of the adult population would be sick, you'll learn if you have your own kids that there is a difference between being tired and real illness, you'll learn that humans are tough. Most humans. When we don't stop in a field and die for no reason. I should go away, I thought, I should take myself off and let her feel sad and go to sleep on her own, the way everyone does. I sat at her bedside, in the chair that would fold out into an approximate bed for me, held a book in front of me and pretended not to watch her go to sleep.

I heard the undertone of the ward at night, like the running of an aeroplane's engine when the passengers settle into half-sleep in simulated night, surrounded by drooling strangers, wearers of glasses bare-faced with the grooves on their noses indecently exposed, the smell of feet and bad breath and private shame recirculating in everyone's lungs. I heard the rhythm of all the monitors, now syncopated, now together, as the chambers of the children's hearts sang to each other. I heard the repeating chime of a bradycardia, the burr of a low oxygen saturation, the stirring of a parent whose mind could now translate her child's monitor in her sleep. Miriam turned her head, spreading her hair across the pillow. Hair

63

like Emma's, light brown and so fine it drops through your fingers like silk. Her eyes closed. I remembered all the times I'd watched her go to sleep as a baby and a toddler, my finger in her grasp and my desire for a cup of coffee, a phone call, a crap, in attendance. I had to wait a while after her eyes closed, then, or she'd wake and cry as I took my finger back and crept towards the door and I'd have to return to the cot and begin again. All that time this was coming. All those years she was going to stop breathing.

I put the book down, marking my place although I didn't remember from one day to the next which book it was, and eased myself to my feet. I wanted a cup of coffee and a crap.

The mother of the blond boy was in the kitchenette. She was blonde too, though dark at the roots, and everything about her was fallen. She had been crying. She raised her head, as if it was too heavy for her neck.

'Kettle's on,' she said. 'Though I'll be lucky to get a cuppa before he wakes up again.'

'They should keep gin in here,' I said. 'Something that works faster than coffee.'

I didn't mean it. I was never going to drink again, because what if I was needed, to call an ambulance or to drive fast or to start CPR, which I needed to learn?

She peered into a mug. They were rarely clean. One said Property of Dr Whyte, Ward 15, in black marker pen, and I avoided it in case Dr Whyte should appear and accuse me of theft.

'I'd settle for chocolate,' she said. 'Or a bit of weed. No, don't worry, I'm joking.'

I hadn't been worried. None of us was going to start on psychotropic substances. Where would you stop?

'You're the big girl's dad, aren't you? I noticed her, reading and that. She's very good. Must be hard for a teenager, in here with all the little ones.'

It's like being in prison, you don't ask why the other person's here.

'Oh, she has her moments. She's not in pain. Your son was doing some lovely drawings a couple of days ago.'

The kettle boiled.

'It's his seventh operation. He wasn't two weeks old, the first time.' She poured water into her mug. I watched the colour of tea swirl like smoke from the teabag. 'He hates coming in here.' Her hand shook. 'My husband had to carry him onto the ward this time. Kicking and screaming.'

Is it worth it, I wanted to ask, is our violence towards our sick children justified? Could there be healing without harm?

'Miriam's older,' I said. 'It's probably easier when you can talk about why you're here and explain the risks and benefits.'

She opened one of the plastic pots of fake milk. 'Yes, well, I just hope we get that far.'

We're very lucky, I found myself wanting to say. We're lucky that we didn't know about this world until now. We're lucky that we went to Colsay and to New York and Paris and some Greek islands without thinking that there are hospital wards where children die by inches and their loving parents have to force them back into places of terror and then compel them to get out of bed and walk about when they are cold and hurting and afraid and do not want to expose their fresh wounds to the gaze of strangers. We're lucky that we had eight years of having two healthy children. And heaven knows, we're lucky that we have them both still.

'I hope you do too,' I said.

I went back to Miriam's bedside and sat down. I held my

coffee. I did not think about my daughters. I did not think about the blonde woman, or about her son's prognosis, or about the nurse I could overhear trying to get a bed in Intensive Care for a child who'd arrived on our ward that afternoon. I thought about the Coventry project.

present. A woman met her fiancé to end the engagement and return the ring. An engineer built shutters to protect his windows but took away his family's gas masks on the grounds that 'when life degenerated to such an extent that men gassed each other then life was no longer worth living'. Many prosperous families had abandoned homes in Coventry and rented cottages in the surrounding countryside or moved in with relatives in neighbouring towns months earlier, and many of those who remained were 'trekking', leaving the city in cars, buses, trucks or on foot to sleep in their vehicles, in outbuildings or under the hedges each night, returning for work in the mornings. The danger was not sudden. Nor was the fear.

For politicians and military leaders, little is sudden. The Nazis had a navigational system that I found oddly fascinating, the *knickebein*. Knickebein means 'bent leg', but is also the name of a magic raven and fairy-tale guide, which seems a more likely origin. It was a navigational technology for night bombing, involving the broadcast of interlocking radio beams over England from antennae on the other side of the Channel. Pilots could fly along a radio beam, hearing a steady tone as long as they were accurately positioned and 'dots' from one side of the line and 'dashes' from the other if they veered off course. Cross-signals told them when to prepare the bombs and, allowing for the speed of travel, when to drop them. The knickebein made the German air raids in the early years of the war much more accurate than the British raids on Germany, which relied on navigating by the stars. I remembered the diagrams of the beams forming a grid over Britain, intersecting at major targets, at cities. It's hard to look at a map of one's own country without superimposing an autobiographical map. There in the far south-west I grew up; there, right in the middle of the fat bit, I went to university; there we lived not-exactly-in London while Emma was training; there we live now. Put it like that and I haven't gone far, an adulthood spent in the major targets of the Luftwaffe. There is Emma's sister in Cheshire, there's her aunt's cottage on the Norfolk coast, wide beaches and big waves and the wind straight from Siberia. There are mountains: Peaks, Lakes, Trossachs, Cairngorms, memories of sandwiches eaten part-frozen with gloved hands and moments of exhilaration approaching a summit. There, too small for this map, is Anna and Giles's island, where Miriam was conceived and where we attempted an ill-advised holiday the following year.

A young Oxford physicist called Reginald Jones was the first scientist to work in British military intelligence. He theorised the existence of the magic raven, found it and developed ways of jamming the broadcasts, which was easy at first but became harder as the wartime arms race gathered speed. Just before the Coventry raid, Enigma communications deciphered at Bletchley Park suggested that Wolverhampton, Birmingham or Coventry would be the target of a moonlit raid in the next few days. By 3 p.m. on November 14th, Jones knew that the first beams were intersecting over Moreton-in-Marsh – a Cotswold town now so blatantly wealthy and pretty that passing drivers of perfectly moderate political inclinations and some respect for English vernacular architecture long to spray anarchist slogans on its honeyed walls – the second over Kenilworth Castle, where I accompany school trips in my role as token penis-owner, and the third over the centre of Coventry. Jones had to guess what frequency the Nazis would be using, in order to set the jammers to the same one, and 'spent a distinctly unhappy night realising that if I had guessed wrong there were going to be some hundreds of people dead the following morning'. He had guessed right, but most urgent case in the hospital, it means they think you're safe. Not, she'd said, when the only people who get treatment are the ones who aren't safe. Not when you realise that there is in fact a steady supply of emergencies.

In our heads, lying beside each other, her in the bed and I on my slippery plastic chair, we had made the next step: only when Miriam was again in danger would someone give us the next part of the story, show us the path we were on. Don't you dare, I thought, somehow on the High Dependency Unit of the Children's Wing find a way to risk your life. It's like the bloody Garden of Eden, isn't it, she said, today's NHS, the price of knowledge is death, they'll only investigate you if you're actually visibly dying. Nonsense, I said, you're not dead and if you were we would have been largely ignorant about why, that's the point, that's why it's taking so long, people don't just go into the middle of a field and stop breathing and if they do they're not being sarcastic about it less than a week later, it's not surprising the NHS isn't set up for it. All right, Dad, she said, chill, get some sleep, I was joking. Jesus. And then she had gone to sleep and I lay there listening to the ward, to the toddler at the other end crying and then suddenly, cheerfully, demanding pink yogurt, to the blond boy's whimpering in his sleep, to the discordant orchestra of heart and breathing monitors, and worried now that Mimi would try to find some way of harming herself, making an emergency. I was too hot. I heard one of the nurses telling the others that her cousin was making more money per hour being one of Santa's elves in the mall down the road than they were, working the night shift in the children's High Dependency Unit. I heard the moment's silence while they all looked at this injustice, at the fact that we are all in a country that pays young women more to impersonate elves in a shop than to give expert care to critically ill children, and then spoke again of weddings. What can you do? The plastic chair was too slippery and plastic-smelling. Outside had been impossibly far away, like the memory of a country before the revolution.

Miriam looked round. 'Have you noticed that most of the paramedics are women?'

I watched two green-clad women manoeuvring a stretcher down a ramp and under the canopy of A and E. 'I hadn't. But I suppose it's low-paid, caring shift-work. You can work all night, come home and take the kids to school and then sleep fast for six hours before you pick them up, cook the tea, put them to bed and go back to work. Like Simran does.'

Simran is the mother of one of Rose's friends and a midwife; I often end up looking after Molly during half-terms and holidays because this cunning routine collapses entirely when school is closed.

'Simran likes it, Dad. You make it sound like martyrdom but she's perfectly cheerful. Anyway, I'd have thought blokes would be into the blue lights and adrenaline. I've yet to see a female firefighter.'

'There might not be enough blue lights and adrenaline for that sort of bloke,' I said. 'More picking up puking drunks from the pavements late at night and collecting little old ladies with kidney infections from their care homes.'

She turned back to the window. 'Did I get blue lights?'

She didn't remember, I knew that. Her memories ended when she realised she'd left her phone under the tree and began again in resus, even though she'd been conscious and responsive for at least twenty minutes of that time. Her brain, short of oxygen and unable to do everything, appeared to have prioritised communication over memory. It didn't matter, I reminded myself. Other people were taking care of her by then. She didn't need to remember, and I couldn't remember because I hadn't been there. The centre of the story was lost to both of us.

I raised my hand to touch her shoulder and then let it fall again. 'Yes, you had blue lights. That was when I realised it was serious.'

'The blue lights rather than the not-breathing?'

'I didn't know about that then. You were breathing when I saw you. Mrs Collier just said you'd had an incident.'

I saw her shoulders lift in a sigh. 'When will I go back to school? I'm missing loads, it's going to take for ever to catch up.'

'Soon. I hope. Shall I ask them to send some work?'

Her back shrugged. 'Don't mind. Up to you.'

I heard, amid the babble of the ward behind us, the Welsh nurse approaching. 'Don't panic, Mum, look, there they are, in the playroom.'

Small running feet. Rose. Behind her, Emma. Rose coming too fast. I braced myself and swung her up. She wrapped her arms around my neck and her legs around my waist.

'Hands-free hug. Let go, Dad.'

I held my arms out and she hung on, as if she were a koala and I a tree. Emma walked towards us. She was wearing work clothes, black trousers and a grey shirt she must have ironed herself, with a silver necklace I gave her a few years ago, a reproduction of one of Ashbee's designs. Her hair was up and she'd made up her eyes as well as her face, the full mask and costume, but it wasn't working. In the shirt's opening, you could almost see all the way round her collar bones. Her cheeks had fallen away. She looked sick, much more so than Miriam. Rose tightened her grip, rubbed her cheek on my shoulder.

'Sorry we're late,' Emma said. 'I got caught at work.'

It's her version of 'hello'.

I patted Rose and tried to put her down. 'Never mind, you're here now.'

Miriam hadn't turned. Emma went and stood next to her. 'Hello, love. How are you?'

Miriam shrugged. 'Most paramedics are female.'

'I'm not sure that's right. You'd have to watch for a very long time to be sure.'

'I do watch for a very long time. There isn't anything else to do.'

Rose slid down. 'At least you don't have to go to school. I wish I didn't have to go to school. We've got some cards for you and Mrs Wasley said to give you her love and she remembers teaching you. Yucky.'

'I'd rather be at school,' Miriam said. 'I'd rather be anywhere at all.'

Rose looked incredulously at Miriam's back. 'What, even Forest Lake?'

Forest Lake, as Mimi never misses a chance to point out, is neither a forest nor a lake, nor indeed constructed on the site of either, but the biggest shopping mall in the Midlands, also known round here as a temple to late capitalist decadence and the local epicentre of global practices of exploitative labour, environmental destruction, misogynistic marketing and other fashionable sins. Some of the girls in Miriam's class worship there more than once a week, giving Mimi and her friends the pleasures of moral superiority as well as themselves the joys of shopping.

'Anywhere. Heathrow. McDonald's. The Tube at rush hour. At least you know when you're going to leave. Even prisoners know that.'

Don't be ridiculous, I thought, don't you dare compare a hospital where people are trying to take care of you and make sure you are safe and well with a prison where—

I reached out to touch Emma. She didn't look at me. It was as if she wasn't there, as if the woman in the doctor had gone away.

'How was work?' I asked.

She, too, was watching the rain. A couple who couldn't find a parking place were sitting in their car, arguing.

'Bit grim, really. Fourteen-year-old self-harmer, didn't want her parents to know. In a bad state. Had to get hold of the emergency psych.'

The NHS works on the assumption that all of us want to stay alive, although you would think the healthy eating and anti-smoking posters covering every vertical surface sufficient evidence to the contrary. Many of us, given the choice, knowing how to be well, choose sickness, which does not stop overweight drinkers despising those who write their self-destruction in blood.

The woman got out of the car and slammed the door. The man set off too fast, stalled the engine and pounded the steering wheel with his fist. Quite a lot of people, Emma says, have heart attacks in hospital car parks; I wonder if the revenue generated by the astonishing parking fees covers the cost of the treatments required by the resulting stress. Actually, the fees probably go to some private company while the rest of us continue to pay for the hospital. They should have taken the train. Right, I thought, we should generate some normality for the girls. Keep their relationship going. Let Rose see that Miriam is OK.

'Who wants to play Cheat?'

Rose took my hand. 'Me. I'm going to win again.'

'Mimi?'

She shook her head.

'Come on. It will distract you. Pass some time at least.'

'No.'

I looked at Emma. I saw her sigh, square her shoulders. 'Play with your sister, Mimi. Please.'

Rose touched Miriam's hand. 'Come on. It's fun. I'll even help you if you like.'

Miriam let Rose lead her down the hall to the bed which had become her world. Emma and I fell into step behind them, a procession of no significance. I did not reach for her hand.

Emma went straight to Miriam's file, which lived in a metal holder on which I banged my head every time I unfolded the chair-bed. She carried it over to the window, as if the fluorescent light overhead were inadequate, and her hand reached to push away hair that had not fallen down. Rose was rummaging in her school-bag.

'Look, Mim, here are the cards. And my class made gingerbread. I brought you mine, I didn't even taste a corner. Mrs Wasley wrapped it up for you.'

Miriam put the envelopes and the foil package on her bedside cupboard, between the plastic water-jug and the pink roses sent by Emma's colleagues and the colouring book from someone who'd forgotten how old she was.

Rose leant against Miriam. 'Aren't you going to try it? I made a cat. Because you like them. Snowy came in the kitchen again and Mummy roared at him.'

Snowy is next door's cat. Every time he invades our house, Rose returns to her cat campaign. They kill birds, Emma says. They spread parasites. Dad and I have enough responsibilities. Get it off that counter!

'Thanks, Rose. I'll save it till later.'

The pack of cards was under Miriam's clean clothes and my sweater at the foot of her bed.

'Here you are, girls. Mimi, can you shuffle?'

I went over to Emma.

77

'There's nothing here,' she said. 'Everything's completely normal. It's just the wheezing.'

'They did the scan this morning,' I said. 'They said someone would come and talk to us later.'

She put down the papers. From this window, we could see a section of another building clad in pale concrete, an emergency exit where sometimes two nurses met for a cigarette, and a curtained window in the opposite wall. It was still raining. The gutter across the way was blocked and the trickle from it blew out through the grey air.

'Do you want me to tell you what I think? I've been reading about it.'

No, I thought. No, let's cherish our ignorance. Let's, at least, wait until the consultant tells what he knows. We will have the rest of our lives to live with the story that is about to begin.

'Can we see if Dr Chalcott comes today? I mean, he might be able to tell us something for sure.'

She tapped the papers straight on the windowsill. 'If you want. But there's really only one set of possibilities now. It wasn't just a freak event, Adam. This isn't going to go away.'

I wanted to put my fingers in my ears. Stop it. Go away. For now, in that moment, I did not have to know what Emma was trying to tell me.

'Now you're here,' I said, 'I can make tea. And I'm going to do you some toast. You need to eat.'

Rose looked up. She was winning. 'Can I have some toast?'

'No,' said Emma. 'You had a snack on the train and Dad will be making your dinner as soon as you get home. Adam?'

I looked up from the bag of groceries she'd brought. A box of sushi for Miriam, a pot of cut fruit for Miriam, a pot of layered yogurt and muesli for Miriam's breakfast. Nothing for herself. 'What?'

'Your dad called. Left a message on the machine. You haven't told him, have you?'

'Haven't had time,' I said.

The blond boy's mother was in the kitchenette, opening a foil package. Her hands were shaking. 'He's not well. We're going over to the ICU. Soon as there's a bed. His dad brought these in. Pancakes. But I don't think.' She stopped. Her hands stopped. 'I don't think he's going to eat them now.'

I didn't touch her. I didn't smile. Because she was holding herself together by the smallest cobweb and anything could have made her break.

I called my father that night. I'd bought a magazine for Rose at the station, which kept her absorbed until we got off the train, and then I'd let her play on my computer while I cooked stand-by pasta again (onions, garlic, tinned tomatoes, tinned chickpeas). I'd sat on the edge of the bath and done the voices for her while the mummy and daddy plastic horses taught the baby plastic pigs how to swim, and agreed that hair-washing could be postponed for another night. I'd read two chapters of a book about a misunderstood child who finds comfort in friendship with a talking badger and sung Bridge Over Troubled Water and Scarborough Fair, diminuendo until her eyes closed. I'd gone back upstairs half an hour later to provide a fresh glass of a water and again five minutes after that because Owl was missing and my superior skills were required to find him at the bottom of the bed. I'd put on a load of laundry and hung the damp-smelling clothes I found wet in the washing machine. I'd paid two bills and checked that Emma's salary had come in and nothing unexpected had gone out of our bank account. I still needed to make Rose's packed lunch – maybe stand-by pasta salad, given the emptiness of the fridge – assemble her PE kit and clean at least the kitchen and bathroom, but it was already getting late. I hadn't, I realised, seen enough of my father recently to know what time he might go to bed.

He moved back to Cornwall a few years ago, after a long time in Vermont. It took me longer than it should have done to realise that after my mother died, he'd stayed in England only for me, only until I finished school. The community at Bryher Farm had disbanded not long after he left, selling the land and buildings to someone setting up an outdoor activities centre. I'd thought that after so many decades in intentional communities, he'd find another for his later years, a place where he'd have company and support and eventually care, but he'd had enough. Time to be alone, he said. Time to eat when I'm hungry and sleep when I'm tired, to hear my own music. Lord knows, I can meet my own needs. When he said that, I badly wanted that time too. I wanted his house on the edge of Porthleven, with its view of the blue water where the English Channel becomes the Atlantic Ocean. I wanted his stone-walled vegetable plot, barely sheltered from the salt wind, and the two-hundred-year-old mining tower keeping watch on the headland to the east. I wanted his quiet, and the assurance of his carpenter's hands, his farming hands, his mechanic's hands. What does your father do, people used to ask. It is perhaps hereditary, not to have an answer to that question. Everything, he does everything.

His phone rang. Landline, he doesn't use a mobile. I found a clean cloth and wiped the kitchen counter with my other hand.

'Adam?'

He always knows. I don't know how. My lungs took a deep breath.

'Dad. How are you?'

'Very well. Just been out to look at the stars. Wonderful clear night.'

'Good.' I dropped the cloth in the sink. Not the moment to run water. 'Dad, I have to tell you something. First, the important thing is that we're all still here. And unimpaired.'

Two hundred miles away, I heard the intake of breath, heard my father pull in starlit air with the smell of the sea on it and hold it inside him, ready.

burning

The obliteration of Coventry began as an ordinary air raid. At that time and in that place, there were ordinary air raids; if there is a hierarchy in these matters, there were and are worse ordinarinesses elsewhere. Several families were accustomed to play Monopoly as the bombs fell, putting imaginary hotels in central London as the real ones were destroyed. One such household waited for the arrival of two elderly sisters living next door who, believing that anything white was visible to the enemy pilots above, went out at night with colanders on their grey heads. (Enamel colanders, perhaps? All the colanders of my acquaintance are steel and much shinier than a blue rinse, although I could see that reason was not the ruling principle in this case.) I read of other instances of this belief; one woman, living in a village outside Coventry, responded to every siren by running outside to take white laundry off the line, as if the Luftwaffe had crossed the Channel to bomb clean sheets. In the same village, an elderly man went around with shears chopping white blossom off fruit trees. I found these acts of superstition in some way reassuring. Not everyone, then, gathered with Spam sandwiches and a stiff upper lip for a sing-song until the All Clear. I found myself looking for evidence of fear and brokenness, anything to counteract the 'Blitz Experience' that my children seemed to 'do' repeatedly by way of primary school history. Please send your child to school in shorts, shirt and flat cap (for boys)/cotton dress with socks and sandals (for girls). We will be trying out some wartime recipes and Make Do and Mend! As if war were all about accessories and baking. Miriam was told off for asking about the Holocaust.

The eyewitness accounts speak of the bombs as a kind of weather. One man, leaving work on his bike, looked at the sky and decided he could make it most of the way home before anything started, was waiting at a red light when the first planes came over. A bus-driver on the Leamington to Birmingham route decided to serve the Coventry stops according to the timetable despite the sounding sirens, because his passengers were mostly wives and mothers who'd been shopping in Leamington and needed to get home to cook the tea and put the kids to bed, bombs or no bombs. Reaching the central bus station in Coventry on time, having driven around a couple of incendiary bombs falling into the road in front of him, he saw that 'no-one was about' and so left for Birmingham at the timetabled 8.08 p.m. The first bombs were already falling on the Cathedral. Domestic routine takes priority over political violence until the very last minute; this is one reason why some wealthy Jewish families were still in Berlin and Prague and Innsbruck when the Final Solution was ratified. Who can believe that his wife will die while cooking dinner in her own kitchen, that his children, tonight, won't survive bathtime? Perhaps more importantly, how can we live once we have understood that any or all of us may be killed while tying our shoelaces or going up the stairs? While reading a novel, or writing one? Two children died in the

Coventry raid because the older one had left their Anderson shelter to take her younger brother back to the house to use the toilet. A man survived because he'd left a shelter to pee in a neighbour's garden and the shelter received a direct hit while he did so.

I looked up from my books, stroked the handle of the blue cowslip mug that Miriam and Rose gave me for my birthday. I remembered my mother's father, whom I rarely saw after my mother's death; he had other, more amenable children who gave him other, more amenable, grandchildren. We didn't 'do' that war in primary school in the 1980s. It wasn't history then. But I did once ask him what he remembered about it, after Dad had been telling me about my other grand-father's journey from Austria to Bristol and then to Brooklyn. Nothing, Grandad said, it was very dull. I was in the Navy and I saw an awful lot of waves. You should ask your grand-mother, she was fire-watching in London all the way through the Blitz. But I'd forgotten about it by the next time I saw her. Surely, I thought, what shaped that generation, and even more so their parents, who were young in 1914 and almost old in 1939, was not knowing how to make jam out of marrows and wedding dresses out of parachute silk, reusing wrapping paper and, as I remember my grandmother doing, washing used paper towels so she could use them as handkerchiefs, but living with the knowledge of death. And, worse than mortal-ity, deliberate harm.

There were four men protecting the Cathedral that night. The Provost, two young men, and an elderly mason who knew every stone in the medieval building. They stood on the roof, where moonlight on frosted lead must have made it and them visible from miles above. Quietly shining to the quiet moon, my mind murmured, as if all moonlit frost belongs to Coleridge, but many of the people in Coventry that night remembered not only the bright moon and the embossing of frost but the glamour of the flames. A man twenty miles away was reminded of the aurora borealis, which he had seen from the North Atlantic during the First World War. Those working on the streets of the city thought of fireworks on a previously unimagined scale, of forests of flame and huge chandeliers. Buildings leapt and shimmered.

People were crushed and burnt.

There were no defences. Four hundred and forty-nine Nazi planes reached Coventry and almost all returned to their bases before morning.

Men and women hurried around the streets pouring sand over incendiary devices and water over burning buildings, escorting people from bombed and burning shelters to not-yet bombed and burning shelters, and the sky was bright as day but red.

The four men could not control the fires in the Cathedral. A Victorian restoration had put in steel roof beams, which conducted heat through the ancient timbers. Melting lead dripped from the roof. Flames wrapped the organ.

Coventry's water mains broke. Bombs blew deep holes in the roads. Vehicles burned. The telephone lines melted. In Manchester, they sent fire engines to Stoke so that Stoke could send fire engines to Birmingham and Birmingham could send fire engines to Coventry, but the roads were broken and there was no more water.

Coventry burned. The Cathedral ended.

I was tempted to pass on to my imagined audience the small comedies, the man whose superior told him not to smoke while wearing his uniform as the air around them both glittered with sparks and burning filled the air like rain; the workers at the engineering plant who took the opportunity to

85

test their new water-pumps using water from the canal after the fire brigade gave up for lack of mains water; the man who sat under a table eating an entire box of Dairy Milk chocolates because he wasn't going to die and leave them unfinished. Maybe later, I thought, and I began to write about the three-year-old holding his dead mother's hand all night, and the family who survived a direct hit on their house because they were sheltering in the cellar, but could not get out when the mains burst and the cellar filled with water.

echolocation

Mostly, the parents in the playground had stopped speaking to me. I do not know, even now, that I would know what to say to a father whose daughter was being indefinitely detained in hospital. Word had spread; we had become a tragic family, one to whom terrible things happen. Rose ran off to play with her friends, a game involving pawing their feet like horses and pretending to hide behind a netball post. I took out my phone and read the news, so that no-one would have to acknowledge me. I did not care about the news – let politicians rage, no-one was giving the hospital enough money to feed the children adequately or run MRI scans within a week of being ordered – and at the same time the news had become unbearable as it does when you have a newborn baby. The sacred buildings of ancient civilisations which had stood for thousands of years were being obliterated by men who didn't like them. In Palestine, children were cowering through the night in schools and hospitals while bombs landed around them. Body parts flew, there was blood on the walls. Glass shattered and blew into the heads of children, into little girls' plaits. In the morning, fathers ran open-mouthed, howling, through the ruins with small misshapen bodies in their arms, small heads drooping at appalling angles.

The bell rang. Rose hurtled towards me and clung on hard.

'I don't want to go to school. Don't make me go. It's not fair, Mimi gets to spend all day lying around playing and watching TV. Just because she's so lazy she lay down and went to sleep in the field.'

I stroked her hair. Her pony-tail was off-centre and I should have brushed it better.

'Sweetheart, Mimi would so much rather be at school. She's bored there. She misses you and all her friends. And Rose, she didn't go to sleep. Not like that. It wasn't her fault at all.'

The children had all lined up.

'Can we talk about this later? Or at least, with Mummy, because it's my night to stay with Mim?'

Rose butted my stomach with her head. 'No. It's not fair. Mimi always gets everything, all those presents you keep giving her, and you always make me go to school.'

She kicked at my shoes. Her class began to file in. The other parents were watching. I'd been hoping to get the 9.15 train and I needed to call at the post office on the way to the station, for more of Miriam's parcels.

'OK. Do you want me to ask Mrs Wasley if she can find us somewhere to have a talk about all this now? It's not us giving Miriam presents, you know that. They're all coming in the post. And there have been some for you.'

Almost as many as for Miriam, in fact, and Miriam was passing on the puzzles and colouring books from Emma's aunt, who seemed to have forgotten which child was which. Not that any of this was about presents.

She pushed me and began to run across the playground after the last of her line. She turned back to shout. 'No. I have to go now. I don't want a kiss and I'm not saying goodbye to you.'

I could feel the other parents' gaze. It was like a TV show, they'd say later, Adam and poor little Rose yelling at each other across the tarmac. I kept my eyes on Rose as she disappeared through the double doors. What if she died before I saw her again, what if anger was the last thing to pass between us, what if I had to remember this miserable interaction for the rest of my life as our last? My hands clenched in my pockets.

'Adam.' It was Martha, Phoebe's mum, late as usual, a twin still clinging to each hand. 'You OK?'

I nodded. I didn't speak.

'Adam, it's not you she's angry with. You must be doing pretty well for her to be able to tell you how she's feeling at all just now. She feels safe enough to shout at you. Look, I have to take these two to nursery now, but shall I have Rose after school? Give you and Emma a bit more time? It's no trouble, you know that, four's not much different from three and I did the shopping yesterday, we've more food than we can eat.'

Martha used to be a psychologist, before the twins were born.

Four is different from three when the fourth is Rose. Especially furious Rose. But if Dr Chalcott was finally able to see us today, I wanted Emma to be there too. Or I wanted Emma to have a little time between leaving Miriam and collecting Rose, to eat something or catch up with her email or replace the tights she'd laddered while folding up the chair-bed. Though I didn't want Rose to feel any more neglected than she already did.

Tom and Lily pulled on Martha's hands, one one way, one the other, pulling her in two. They do that. 'Mummy, we're late again and you're making us even later.'

'Shush a minute. Adam, I'll make a fuss of her, make her feel special. I'll paint their nails or something.'

I remembered teaching Phoebe to swim and helping her cut out gingerbread when she was upset about the new babies and Martha as overwhelmed as any sane person would be when left in sole charge of infant twins and an angry three-year-old. 'OK. Thanks, Martha. It really helps. I'll get Emma to text you when she's on the train. Won't be too late.'

Can you feed Emma too, I wanted to ask, can you stick a plateful of something in front of her and distract her while she eats it. Because I don't know what we're going to do, what I'm going to do, if she gets sick too.

I had a book to read on the train, a memoir about sailing along the coast of the Pacific Northwest which I'd read before and remembered as absorbing. I was finding it as hard to read as Emma was to eat: nothing was what I wanted. Books that mattered were too demanding and books that didn't were too trivial for the new reality in which death stood in the corner of every room and came to breathe over my shoulder whenever I took my eye off him. This one, at least, was too demanding. I let it close. The city spreads a long way and all of it is ugly, but the first part of the journey crosses fields and canals, the half-heartedly rural landscape of my runs and bike rides. Four unkempt horses stood in a field with a coil of rusty barbed wire and something under a flapping blue tarpaulin. I watched the back gardens of houses as meanly miniature as our own, faded plastic toys crowding around faded plastic conservatories. A stand of trees, fenced with Keep Off notices, and a bird of prey hanging in the damp sky above. The canal, a runner on the towpath. I had not run since that day. Sheep grazing as if the motorway bordering their field were a sparkling river. Lorries in full spate, flashing overhead signs above the carriageways. Slow down, accident ahead.

I opened the book again. Forest and quiet water, the sounds not of the roaring Pacific but of small inlets, backwaters. Light refracted from ripples dances on the sail, on the cabin roof. Wind stirs the trees, pulls across the water like breath on glass. Our narrator remembers the people who used to live here, who could take all this for granted as he and I cannot. He resists our Romantic impulses. He thinks about the paintings and carvings those people made, the way the reflections and the movement of the sea came to live in their eyes and in their minds. Everything, he says, they saw everything as if lit by dancing water. Our narrator's father, I remembered from my first reading, is dying, but at this point in the book our narrator does not know that, or at least – since by the time the author wrote the book his father was dead – he is pretending not to know what will happen before the ending.

So am I. So, perhaps, are you.

Rain spattered the window. We were entering the city now, via an avenue of derelict industrial buildings interspersed with expanses of concrete and rubble. Victorian hubris hung around ornate brickwork between smashed windows and rooftop turrets through which shrubs grew towards the grubby sky. The streets here were malevolently quiet and there was no-one walking.

The inchoate shapes of the city centre neared, the bulbous shopping arcade and the skyscrapers dwarfing the nineteenth-century pomp and circumstance at street level. Whatever the embarrassing ambitions of Victorian architecture, it was at least designed to speak to pedestrians, to catch the eye of the man on foot. Most of this city's more recent buildings would appear to address people in airliners. We passed the first of the two derelict churches, its windows boarded and its graveyard clipped by a dual carriageway, willow trees pushing their way through its chain-link fence. Knock them down, launch wrecking balls at traceries and Gothic stone and marble memorial slabs meant to last for ever? Convert them, mildly haunted flats or self-consciously iconoclastic clubs and cafés? Resurrect some gods and give them a home.

I hurried from the station. Christmas was coming and people were shopping, people whose children were not in hospital. Look, Adam, I know you don't want to think about this but you need to know that this wasn't just a freak event, that there's an ongoing risk and always will be. It may well happen again. Christmas, I thought, what if she's still on the ward at Christmas? I stepped around a puddle. Rain was coming through my hair and through the shoulders of my coat. I tried to push Miriam's packages further into their plastic bag, shifted the weight of the holdall on my shoulder. Past the Magistrates' Court, another Victorian brick building where realities change with the telling of a tale, where people walk up those stone steps, through those heavy wooden doors, with one story about themselves and leave, some other way, with another. A bus passed and splashed my trousers. I found myself almost running, the bags hammering my back and legs.

Miriam was still in bed, hair tousled and face blurred, hands beneath the covers, doing nothing. Above the hospital sheets and blankets we could see the deep neckline of the red silk pyjamas she had bought herself the week before it happened, and upon which she was now insisting. A protest against infantilisation, a way of making everyone who came in to listen to her chest feel as uncomfortable as she was. The silk pyjamas meant we couldn't pretend we weren't violating her, all of us. I could hear a whistle on her breath again, a breezy descant to her breathing, but knew now not to comment. Emma had refolded the chair-bed and was sitting on it, dressed as if for work, feet neatly beside each other, doing something on her iPad. It is the saving grace of general practice that very little work can be brought home, or indeed to your daughter's hospital bed, but Emma finds exceptions when she needs them.

She looked up. 'Oh, is it raining?'

Miriam sighed. 'No, Mum, it's not raining, Dad just decided to pour water all over himself on the train. Probably because it's more interesting than sitting here waiting for me to stop breathing again.'

Emma and I exchanged glances.

'And stop looking at each other like that, I'm not stupid.'

I went around the other side of the bed to kiss Miriam.

'Wash your hands, Dad. Haven't you seen all the signs?'

I put the holdall down on the floor, where it would get in the way when the nurse came to make her two-hourly observations of Miriam's pulse, blood pressure and temperature. I started moving things around on the table, as if I'd be able to make room for the parcels, and then dumped them on Mimi's bed while I went to wash my hands. When I came back, Mimi had folded her hands behind her head and was gazing at the ceiling. The whistle was still there, singing in her ribcage. Her eyes rested on some cracks in the plaster. Above her hung fluorescent strip lights, one a paler shade of aluminium than the others. Emma shook her head at me.

'Don't you want to get up, Mim? Have you had breakfast?'

Emma swiped something on her screen. 'She says she's not hungry. I offered to phone you and ask you to bring a croissant but she said not to bother.'

You should have done, I thought. As if, its name once uttered, a croissant might have significant properties. As if I could have bought or brought something that would make a difference.

'Would you feel better for a shower?' I asked Miriam.

She closed her eyes. At least she's angry, I thought, at least she's telling us how it feels. Isn't that what Martha said?

Emma stood up. 'Adam, is it OK if I go for a walk? Just around the corridors. I've got my phone.'

'Get yourself a coffee,' I said. 'Go over the road for a croissant, if you like.'

She shook her head. 'I'll be back in ten minutes. Bye, Mimi. It would be lovely if you were out of that bed when I come back.'

Miriam and I listened to her clipped footsteps retreating down the ward. Poor Mimi, having us come and go like the figures in a weather-house while she lay immured and shackled by stickers and wires. The child in the next bed, behind the curtain which Emma had kept half closed, began to whimper.

'Let's look at your parcels,' I said. 'Maybe there's something to cheer you up a bit.'

I was peeling off sticky tape and enthusing to myself while Miriam lay with her eyes closed when I heard the high voice of the Family Liaison Nurse at the nurses' station. Her footsteps approached. Most of the nurses wear the kind of shoes you'd expect a person to wear for standing and moving round for a thirteen-hour shift, but the others, and the women doctors, make a kind of percussion in the ballet of hospital life. Castanets. The opposite of echolocation. Miriam kept her eyes closed. She had retreated, I thought, she had gone away.

'Good morning. Miriam, are you not feeling well? A bit wheezy again?' She looked at me. 'She's usually up by now, isn't she?'

Yes, I thought, she's usually at school, hanging out with her friends during morning break.

'She's well,' I said. 'Miriam, Erica asked you a question.'

Allowances, yes, but not rudeness.

Miriam opened her eyes but didn't look at us. 'I heard. I'm perfectly well, thank you. Never better.'

Erica nodded. 'OK. Well, the doctor's going to talk to your mum and dad in a little while, and then maybe we can make a plan.'

Miriam looked at her. 'Do you mean he's going to say I can go home?'

Erica's eyes widened. Family Liaison Nurse, she should have seen that coming. She's used, of course, to younger children, less alert children, sicker children. 'I mean we can start planning for when you will go home. When we all know you'll be safe there.'

'When?'

Erica looked at me. 'When Dr Chalcott and Mum and Dad are all happy with the plan. I know it's hard but I can't tell you when, Miriam. This is going to take a bit longer. But it will feel better, won't it, to have a plan?'

To have a story. A plan is a story about the future.

a room for telling bad news

The Family Liaison Nurse led us past the fish, out of the ward, into the corridor where the air was spiced with the promise of external doors and people in coats and gloves. It did not feel right, for Emma and me to be in each other's presence and not with Miriam. We'll look after her, the nurse had said. I hesitated; I had heard children whose parents were not there crying until other parents took charge, and while I knew Miriam wouldn't cry, she might stop breathing. You can go, Dad, said Mimi, I promise not to die until you come back. I know that she needs to say these words, needs to hold them to our throats like a blade to see if we flinch. I do flinch, which is, it occurs to me, what she hopes to see.

I did not take Emma's hand. We walked as if we had met so recently that the silence was awkward. You got here all right, then, I might have said. Any plans for Christmas? Erica took us through a waiting room where couples looked up as we passed, ready to hope for news or to resent other people's movement, and toddlers drooled and sneezed over plastic toys on low plastic tables. She led us down another corridor, narrow so I fell in behind Emma, full of central heating and second-hand air. Doors marked in the NHS font stood half open, showing plastic desks and patterned screens around examining couches. They think that cartoon characters comfort, or perhaps only quiet, children who may be going to die.

The room at the end was octagonal, the windows too high to see through, and it was pink. Old-lady pink, salmon pink; it is dead salmon that are salmon pink. There was a grubby pink plastic sofa and a low plastic table supporting a box of tissues which was among the most sinister things I have ever seen. It was a room for telling bad news, such bad news that the posters about the evils of obesity and smoking were not here. There was no need, really, to tell people anything once you had brought them to that room. Perhaps the idea was that any prognosis would be better than you would come to expect after being left there for fifteen minutes waiting for the consultant, especially in the company of a frightened GP who knew a whole lot more about rare kinds of anaphylaxis than she had done ten days earlier. I told you, Emma said, this isn't going to go away. There's no diagnosis that means everything will be OK.

Shut up shut up shut up shut up. I am afraid I put my fingers in my ears. I am afraid I threatened to leave her there and wait in the corridor outside if she said one more word on the subject, if she continued to steal the closing minutes in which I could not know what I very much did not want to know.

We heard footsteps, and Erica's voice. Erica and Dr Chalcott came in together, as if he needed a henchman for this conversation, someone who could hold us back or pass the tissues. I stopped myself standing up as they came in, bracing myself. Why do all conversations with doctors in hospitals feel like a confrontation? Because they want to get away, because they fear that you will lie on the floor and grab their ankles, claw at their white coats, allow them to drag you along the corridor behind them as you implore them to tell you a story. There was, of course, a clock on the wall of the room for bad news. A clock and nothing else. I saw Emma straighten herself, pull the mask back over her face. Doctor.

her body made a mistake

Dr Chalcott and Erica had come to tell us a story. To tell us a diagnosis, if you prefer, although a diagnosis is a story, brings a story's promise of safe conduct through time and place to an anticipated ending.

Once upon a time there was a clever girl. She lived with her father and her mother and her little sister, in a town in the centre of England. The town had two fine parks, given to the townspeople by a Victorian entrepreneur turned philanthropist, doubtless in expiation of the kind of sins that end in the ownership of land, but the magnolia flowers there were no less like expensive paper, the roses no less heavy-headed, for that. There was a river where swans glided, where moorhens and ducks presented the town with charming infants in due season, and a canal where wooden boats painted like Christmas tree ornaments lay serenely moored. Perhaps, the townspeople would say on their Sunday walks, perhaps we should buy one of those, perhaps if we lived on a boat we would be happier and more free. Not that there was any reason for unhappiness.

Not that they were not already, by any global or historical standard, free.

The girl's family were not poor, but, like most families, they rarely felt rich. Her mother was a doctor who worked mostly with those in a neighbouring town who were poor and often also unhappy and afraid, and her father made it his work to care for his wife and his two daughters. They lived in a small house where there were more books than bookshelf space, more toys than cupboard space, more coats than coat-hooks, and so they were not always comfortable but they were not unhappy: the man loved his wife and had not, in twenty years, cast a covetous eye on another woman. He loved his daughters and had never in their lives wished that they were different from the way they were, never wanted them in any way muted or diminished. The time would come when he would remember his faith in his girls and be comforted that he had always felt it.

For fifteen years, the family thought they had been blessed with two healthy children. Or perhaps, for fifteen years they had been blessed with two healthy children. The girls began to breathe at birth, within a minute of the cutting of the cord, and went on doing so, day and night, waking and sleeping. Their hearts continued to beat, faster for running, for fear and for joy, and slower for resting and growing. Their mouths received food and drink, their digestive systems took what was good and eliminated what needed elimination, and the girls grew in strength and sense as the seasons passed. They were well. There was nothing wrong. And their parents, who for one reason and another already understood that to have children who are well is to be in a state of grace, knew their blessings. Their luck. Their blind, undeserved good fortune. This is important. They were not complacent, not heading for a fall.

And then one autumn day when the wind was wild in the trees and the last leaves filling the air, the girl ate her lunch at school (pizza which she would later describe, when asked by her doctor, as 'ersatz'; an apple, later characterised as 'red and powdery', and half of her friend's cereal bar, brand name and ingredients forgotten and the subject of extensive research and speculation in the following weeks). After lunch, she and her two friends went out onto the playing fields, where they found it too cold to sit under the trees as they had been doing earlier in the autumn and so walked around, circling the field as they chatted. We talked about the usual stuff, she said later, not that it was relevant, not that anyone really thought that what happened next was caused by conversation. Parents and their comparative iniquities. Boys, and specifically whether Will in 10H returned Charlotte's interest. Next week's Geography test. The likely outcome of the next election, what might have motivated or driven a girl of their own age at a neighbouring school to make her way to Syria with the intention of marrying a fundamentalist fighter. We were saying, the girl would report to her doctor, that your generation has pretty much taken our future, that unless we happen to have parents with at least cultural capital and equity in their houses if not actual surplus in the bank, our generation has no reason to expect to have jobs or houses when we grow up however hard we work, so why wouldn't you bugger off to a war zone if you're desperate or gullible enough to believe it offers more opportunities; we were saying that if the grown-ups want to stop teenage girls going off to be terrorist brides they should be thinking about what the girls are running away from as well as towards. Stuff like that, we were saying. Yes, her doctor would say, I understand that, and then what happened, Miriam?

Then she took out her phone to show her friends the pictures of her play at the weekend, and then they started taking close-ups of the leaves. They found a drift of skeleton leaves, holly and beech, and became fascinated, dusting off the fragments of loam and soil as if from ancient remains, holding the leaf-bones up to the watery sky, trying black-and-white photos. Playing. The bell rang and they hurried in for Maths, but at the door the girl felt for her phone, which was allowed on school premises only if it remained switched off and in her bag throughout the school day, and thought that she had left it under the trees, on the far side of the field. I'll catch you up, she said, cover for me if I'm a bit late, and she ran.

And somewhere deep inside the girl's blood, in her bones, molecules began to tell the wrong story as she ran. They perceived, from somewhere, a threat. Her immune system acted fast, as immune systems need to do. She became, she would think later, profoundly afraid; a 'sense of impending doom' is invariably listed as a diagnostic sign although it is also, as she would observe, a reasonable and indeed obvious reaction to the other symptoms, which on this occasion followed in rapid succession. Her skin reddened, her face and then her throat swelled. Her blood left her belly, her lungs and her heart and filled her skin. It became hard to breathe. Her heart-rate accelerated, and went on accelerating. Her blood-pressure fell and went on falling. And then there was no more oxygen for her blood, no more energy for her arms and her legs and then for her guts and at last for her heart and her brain and her movement. Her sight and hearing and then her thoughts and finally her heart ran out of fuel. Her heart's chambers, its portals, fluttered frantic, struggled, slowed. Stopped.

Once upon a time, her body made a mistake and ended itself. And her doctor did not know why, but he did know that the event, the incident, was likely to happen again. To repeat itself, he said, as if the incident were an agent, the subject of a reflexive verb, capable of eternal motion. As if the story of her dying, of her anaphylaxis, were a form of mutually assured destruction between her blood and the world, a pact that by its nature could not be undone. This is called exercise-induced anaphylaxis, he said, and it means that when Miriam exercises shortly after eating whatever the trigger food turns out to be, or after being stung by a particular insect or taking a particular drug or in some cases feeling cold, her breathing will shut down and then her heart will stop. Usually, he said, there is a cause, usually there is an agent that we eventually identify, but sometimes, especially if it doesn't happen again, we never know. Sometimes the body keeps its counsel. And sometimes the anaphylaxis is not induced by exercise or any other known cause, and then we call it idiopathic, which means—

I know, I said, it's the same root as 'idiot' or 'idiolect', it means we don't know, it means that sometimes these things just happen. It means that death can occur spontaneously for no reason.

He nodded. One thing I will say, he said, as if he had not said the other things, or had said them involuntarily, one thing I will say, Mr Goldschmidt, is that Miriam was down, she was without oxygen, for quite a while, for several minutes and I know she seems normal so far but sometimes you see changes, sometimes you start to notice things, when someone goes home.

I looked at Emma and saw that she already knew that, had thought of it at the beginning, that there had even been conversations, among medics, when I was not there.

I saw that I had not given her permission to tell me what I did not want to know, and that in refusing I had left her to know it alone.

I was sorry.

But I did not say so.

103

unforgivable lists

My father came, the first of our magi. He took the train, coming out of the depths of the Cornish winter where the stars shine brutal through the long nights and the rest of the world seems very far away, aborting the Cornish hibernation to hasten along the blood-red coast of Devon, through the sullen marshes of the Somerset Levels, past the strange earthworks and jealously guarded military installations of Wiltshire, into the magnetic field of London and out again, pulling away north, to us. I thought, he said on the phone, I thought I'd get a hotel room by the hospital, give you some kind of base there, be on hand where you don't have your friends round the corner. Unless I'd be more use at your house? No, I said, you're right about the hotel. If that's OK, if you can afford it. I mean, we could help with that, if you like? I am never sure how much money he has. The house, yes, bought with his mother's legacy, saved, it turned out, for decades because he had never intended to see out his days at any of the communes where he'd spent his adult life, but income? Odd jobs for neighbours, a run of evening classes in woodcraft, a few things on a friend's stall at the craft market in summer. Enough, apparently, to pay the bills. No, he said, Adam, there is no need.

Miriam slept late again that day. The child in the next bed had had a bad night, pain and crying, and somewhere around 4 a.m. there had been some kind of emergency at the far end of the ward, bells, running feet, urgent talking, a senior voice angry on the phone and the rush and squeak of a bed being rolled away to Intensive Care. I have not seen Intensive Care and do not want to; let there be some bitterness I don't taste, something left for other people. I wanted coffee but I didn't want Miriam to wake up alone, to think that I leave her when she sleeps. I needed the bathroom, needed cold water on my face. No-one in a hospital is fully awake and in the world. Hospitals have their own gravitational field, their own atmosphere; you can feel it from the car parks.

I stood by the window, tasting the sourness of my own mouth, aware of my own smell after a night on a plastic chair-bed under a synthetic blanket. It was raining again, and since we had been moved across the ward, Miriam's priority dropping now she had a diagnosis of sorts and medication, we had a new view. The canopy of the hospital entrance, the end of the police station, an oddly quiet four-lane highway beyond, and office tower-blocks filling the sky. You could watch people approaching the hospital's maw, see them lower their heads or set their shoulders, and you could see people going away, parents leaving without children. I did not look very often.

I scanned what I could see for organic forms, for leaves or flowers or anything at all that had not been built or dumped by humans. There is always the sky. There was rain. There was moss in the hospital's gutters and some rosebay willow herb growing out of one of the disused chimneys. I craned further. There were a few dead leaves along the windscreen wipers of one of the cars parked in the named bays for senior managers, passengers betraying a garden at home, another life. Although it was six months since we had last been there, although all the time my father was in America I never crossed the Tamar, I sickened for Cornwall, for my father's house, for the gorse and rocks of Bryher Farm and all those years when I did not know that this was going to happen.

It could be worse, I knew that. On the ward, I was surrounded by parents and children for whom it was worse. I leant my head against the cold window and closed my eyes. In the darkness of my head, I made unforgivable lists of parents who might reasonably envy me. Auschwitz, Belsen. The massacre of the innocents. When Yugoslavia came apart, there were villages where people nailed their neighbours' children to their own front doors. Those whose children's dying cries were recorded by their murderers. The toddler whom no-one saved from the boys with bricks. The children under falling bombs in places where bombs fall, in the sea in the places where boats sink. At least no-one had deliberately harmed Miriam, no-one had seen her going about in the world and decided to take her body and kill it. Inexcusable, I was inexcusable.

'Adam?'

Suddenly, Dad.

I found myself in his arms.

For a long time.

He stood back, tipped his head towards Miriam. 'How is she?'

'Well. Stable. Very bored.'

'Out soon?'

'Once they've tested her for reactions to some of the less obvious things. As long as she doesn't start wheezing again. A few more days.'

106

He nodded. I didn't tell him the other bit of the story: once I have been properly trained in CPR, and once we have all been trained to use the adrenaline injections she will need to carry for the rest of her life.

'I'll fold up the bed,' I said. 'Then you can sit down. It's time she was waking up anyway.'

Dad had brought saffron buns from the village bakery for Miriam, and one of those supermarket plastic pots of cut-up tropical fruit that we all kept offering her as some kind of synecdoche of everything from which she was debarred: sunlight, trees, choices. Go out, Adam, he said. Take a turn around the block, buy a newspaper, get yourself a proper coffee, take my hotel key and go have a long hot shower. You've only just got here, I said, I haven't seen you for months. But I meant, what if she stops breathing and you don't push the red button before you start CPR, what if you don't know how to start CPR, or if you do know but turn out to be one of those people immobilised by an emergency, what if you think I don't mean it when I say you must stay with her, what if you decide it's OK to go down to the hospital shop or if you let her go wander the corridors on her own because she wants to and she's fifteen, what if even in the children's hospital my presence is all that can keep my daughter alive? As if it had been I who saved her in the first place, as if we had not, in fact, learnt that we could and must trust the wider world to look after her. I'll be here for a while, he said, we'll have time to talk. Anyway, I came to see Miriam, didn't I, Mimi? Go, he said. Look, I've bought a phone and turned it on specially, and I won't take my eyes off her, I've even already been to the loo. Miriam watched us talk, back and forth as words bounced like a tennis ball across her bed. Her breath sang in her chest again. God knows, I thought, she has her own fear, let me not give her mine. I went out, into the rainy streets, and walked unseeing the avenues of Christmas pop music and overheated air billowing from the doors of shops, the red and green and white lights bouncing in the wind, dyeing the rain as it fell. I found myself at the railings around a city church, whatever God's acre it once had long eaten by stone and concrete. A jumble of uprooted gravestones leant against its wall, under stained glass windows caged against the casual rage of passers-by. In memoriam, in loving memory, here lies, near this place are deposited the mortal remains. What, I thought, what would we have done for Miriam, how would it have been to stand at a graveside, to see a coffin lowered and know that she was in it, how could we not throw ourselves on top of it, how could we not return, how could we not track day by day, month by month, the imagined fall of flesh from bone, the

how can you bear

sometimes something he later thought

My father leant back in his chair, surveyed the curtains around the bed, which were printed with rocking-horses in red and green and blue, and the bulbous cartoon fish painted on the walls in parody of those confined in the tank at the entrance. Once upon a time, my father said, a boy was born to a couple living in Brooklyn, New York. Theirs was a common story, you've read it before, often and in many voices. Before they met, the couple had crossed the seas to escape bad times, because they had seen their friends and neighbours and cousins killed on the streets and in their homes and had seen that there was no future for people of their blood, for people with their cast of face, in the countries they had always thought to be their own. So at opposite ends of Europe the parents had left their towns by night, scurried across unfamiliar lands under cover of dusk and dawn, sleeping in barns and under hedges, sometimes helped and sometimes hunted by those whose blood and cast of face kept them safe in that time and place. And at last they'd come to the sea, these ancestors, where they had used the end of their gold to take passage for America, and had woken one morning a few weeks later to see the Statue of Liberty on the horizon and a new life waiting for them at her feet. They found refuge, and began again.

But the boy, growing up, knew little of this tale, would piece it together later from other versions. Better, the parents thought, not to tell such stories, better their children and grandchildren should bear new names to walk new roads, although no-one, they thought, no-one of their blood should ever again imagine himself safe, imagine that his passport and his prosperity came with any guarantee that he would not some day be grateful to find himself able to escape the streets where he had always lived. Among themselves, the ancestors spoke something that was probably Yiddish. You don't need to know, they said. You concentrate on your studies. You make yourself American. So the boy learnt French at school, for no particular reason, and not much. He had many of the rites of passage you've seen in films: summers at summer camp, dates with girls for which he borrowed his father's car, a prom before which he presented his date with a corsage planned to match her dress, and by and large he enjoyed these things.

Mimi had closed her eyes, was perhaps pretending not to listen, thinking that her grandfather had forgotten that she was nearly grown up, was reading books with bibliographies and footnotes and brutal accounts of genocide and civil war. She was too old for once upon a time, but also too old to tell my father to stop talking because she wasn't interested in his story, in the cliché of a young man's journey to the west where he was probably going to *find himself* or something. But she heard him. It's not as if she had anything else to do.

The boy, my father went on, loved to read, but did not associate reading with schoolwork, and was happy enough when a friend of his parents offered him a year's work in a city bank to make some money before he went off to college. His mother bought him two new suits that made him look like a little boy stuffed into silly clothes for a wedding. The girl he'd taken to the prom – a nice Jewish girl, dark hair, good figure, who was going to work in her aunt's floristry business rather than going to college – gave him a tie, amber to match his eyes. He went off to Manhattan every morning, feeling, truth be told, a little superior to his father and his uncle who were walking across town to the factory where the boy used to work summer jobs.

And then, my father said, shifting a little on the chair, which was really as poor a chair for sitting as a bed for sleeping, watching the rise and fall of Miriam's chest under the red silk pyjamas, going on talking before she could begin to instruct him in the evils of banks and factories, then the boy, who had almost proposed to the girl at the flower shop before he left, went to college, and then the story changed. Or perhaps, then it became a story, because the one where the son grows up in lower-middle-class Jewish respectability and stays there, marries his childhood sweetheart and settles down near where they both grew up, is arguably not a story at all, and anyway you already know some of what is to come because you, dear girl, would not be here if the boy had stayed in Brooklyn.

As you probably know, the mid-'60s were an interesting time in which to begin college in upstate New York. Of course the boy had seen hippies before, and like most of his contemporaries he wore his hair long and his pants – trousers – wide. He'd kept reading, mostly on the subway as he travelled to and from the bank, and covered what was fashionable: Camus (in translation), di Lampedusa (in translation), Salinger. He'd read *The Feminine Mystique*, and tried to liberate his mother,

111

and when *The Group* came out he read that too. He was not thoughtless, or unwilling to learn. He could see, even as he benefited from it, even as he enjoyed big beefsteaks and big cars and hoped one day to own a big house where he could raise big sons, that there were things wrong with America, and after a couple of years spent reflecting on what these things were, he dropped out, left college before he had finished his degree. He wrote to his parents, a letter of which he would later be ashamed, telling them that he couldn't live the way they wanted him to, and taking only a canvas haversack containing a couple of books and a change of clothes, he set out towards California, not so much to seek his fortune as to lose his fortune. The fortune for which his parents had left Europe, just in time.

The young man hitch-hiked, which was not safe then and would not be safe now. He thought that having almost no possessions meant he would be all right, because no-one would see any reason to hurt him, but he had been well cared for all his life and despite his family history had not understood that there are people who have their own reasons for hurting others. His parents did not tell their stories, not to him. He met one or two of these people as he made his way west, but he also met a great many kind and interesting people, some of them young and also questioning the world and looking for new ways to live, others older, wiser, more cautious.

There were communes forming across America, groups of young people who rejected the nuclear family and saw that living collectively meant less work for everyone and fewer demands on the environment. It's easy now for you to laugh at the body hair and the naïveté, but theirs are the ideas inherited by all the radical groups and protesters of the last fifty years. My generation screwed up all right, just like the one before, but we had ideas. Yes, also like the one before.

112

Radicals and revolutionaries in every generation, Mimi, don't forget that, don't blame your parents or even your grandparents for the ways of the world. Anyway, I can't say our young man had always wanted to see America, because for most of his life he'd thought that the only reason to leave New York would be to go to Europe, which he imagined as more of an art museum than a continent. But when he started out west, he wanted to keep going. One day you'll see the big skies of the American west, and prairies so flat you can see a cloud-shadow coming from miles away, and grass rippling like a sunlit lake. Real lakes reflected in the clouds, earth and sky mirroring each other and so far apart – not like here. I'll always miss it, my father said. The big sky.

The boy, the young man, stayed on communes, making his way from one to another, half hoping to find the place he wanted to stay but half-hoping to keep on travelling, because travel is addictive. Never having to solve anything, never having to plan more than a few days or weeks ahead. The places all had different rules, different ideas about how to live. Buddhism was popular, there was a lot of chanting and meditation. Most communities – though frankly they weren't really stable enough to be called communities – were vegetarian, made their own bread, didn't eat sugar, but usually there was beer. Often there were drugs, too, a lot of pot and a little LSD – well, you don't need to know about that. OK, you do know about that. In which case I don't need to tell you. They were all dirty. Communal living doesn't have to be dirty, but if it's cleaner than the dirtiest person there it's usually a sign that someone's being exploited. The young man didn't see it at the time and I'm not sure the women did either, but looking back, the women were being exploited. We talked a lot about freedom and equality but we never thought to do the washing up, and we talked about raising kids communally but I never changed a nappy until your father was born. Every time you hear a man talking politics, Miriam, listen to what he says about his wife.

The young man kept going, and came to the mountains just as winter was closing in. He'd picked up a truck, what you'd call a lorry, going clear through to Portland, a grand high view from the cab and a driver not much older than himself and curious about the young man's life, the places he'd seen. Never met a Jew before, he said, and the young man felt his ancestors at his shoulder, asking if he knew what they'd given up, what they'd done, back in the old country so that he could be here now. They passed before his eyes, briefly haunting the dying grasses and the open road, the truck stop ten miles ahead, the women shawled and hollow-eyed, the men bearded and dressed in long black coats. What are you doing here, they asked, how can you forget the price that was paid? He shook his head, shook them out of his ears like water. His father's ghosts. The haunted genes of European Jewry murmuring in his blood and bones and brain. Look, the truck driver said, there's snow falling up there. And on the mountains ahead, bounding the horizon and pressing closer, rising higher, with every new mile, there was already a dusting of white.

at the hearth

The young man had heard there was a good place on the mountain, a group who owned a real house and were seriously working towards self-sufficiency. He arrived at dusk, having hiked the last few miles from the town knowing that if his directions were wrong, if there was nobody there, he'd have to make his way down the road in the dark and persuade the owner of the diner where he'd drunk a sour coffee to give him a bed for the night. The snow hadn't yet settled here, but an angry wind lashed the remaining leaves from the trees and low cloud moved fast across the darkening sky. A track led off the road. He followed it through the trees and saw a stone farmhouse in a clearing on the shoulder of the hill. There was a light in the window. A thin man whose bushy hair spread over his shoulders opened the door an inch to the young man's knock, and the others didn't let him in but came out into the yard to stand around him. The last few weeks, they said, had been a bad trip. They'd split over whether it was legitimate to ask people to leave, whether the principles of the commune meant they shouldn't exclude anyone even for stealing and fighting. People needed to steal and fight, a woman said,

115

because bad things had happened to them, and treating them as bad people wouldn't help. Morality, she said, was a bourgeois idea, a way of passing off responsibility for injustice and harm. Maybe, the hairy man said, but that didn't mean Bear Mountain Ridge could hold all the anger and pain in America. It didn't mean the children had to watch a grown man banging a woman's head on a wall, or that one person was allowed to take the group's stereo and sell it for drugs. The young man knew that the conversation was really about whether he could stay, whether they could risk another voice and another pair of hands in the house. Winter coming on. His feet were numb with cold. C'mon, guys, he said. Just one night. My ride's gone, I walked up here, I won't find anywhere else tonight. I'll be gone before sunrise if you want me to go. He didn't know why he wanted to stay, before he'd even seen inside the house. Something about the way it settled on the mountainside, looking down over the plain like a sentry for the mountain range behind. Something about the tidiness of the garden, plants cut and staked, wrapped in sacking against the frost. Something about the woman.

She cooked that night, and he went to help her. He chopped onions – he'd got good at chopping onions – grated a block of orange cheese bought with food stamps. The garden was doing OK, she said, the beans were from the vegetable patch, and also the onions and the herbs drying in bunches in the window, but they wouldn't get through the winter on that alone. She stepped around him where he stood uncomfortably bowed at the table, chopping. He liked the way she moved, and the smart swirl of her hair as she turned. She used to be Rachel, she said, she'd grown up in Boston, finished her degree at Wellesley before she broke up with her fiancé and headed out west with another man, a man who'd left her back in Illinois last year. She'd been saying these sentences

116

all summer, he thought, to men who came and watched her cook and ate her food, used the bathroom she cleaned and the sheets she washed and then split when they got bored. He began to wash up while Rainbow stirred the inevitable bean stew.

Watch out, my father told Miriam, for the man who's learnt that the way to a woman's heart is through the kitchen sink. You will find that most men, most young men, have an ulterior motive. And how do you know, Miriam said, that women don't have an ulterior motive, how do you know that women don't actually want to sleep with the man who does the washing up? Hush, he said, listen to the story.

After not-quite-adequate servings of beans and onions, Eagle lit a fire in the sitting room and they sat on the batik floor cushions representing furniture. The young man listened, didn't impose his questions, didn't want to remind them that he was a stranger. He stretched his feet to the fire but his back was cold. A child squatted at the hearth, intent on the flames. The woman who wasn't Rainbow took out brown knitting and one of the men began to whittle something, maybe a toy for the child. Some of the places he'd stayed had been huddles of hand-made sheds and wigwams, semi-legally built on cheap farmland. Other people were building domes, following the blueprint of a famous group in New Mexico, dropped-out architects and engineers who'd designed a structure made almost entirely of old car windshields and recycled timber, but at Bear Mountain Ridge, he gathered, they'd pooled legacies and parental gifts and bought the house. (Aha, you are thinking, capital and property ownership after all. Yes, indeed, but maybe in a new way.) Off-grid, leaky, with an outdoor privy and a private water supply that had run out in summer and was expected to freeze in winter, but a house nonetheless, and they thought they'd make it through

117

the winter. There was an air of relief, he thought, about the changing season, because the coming snow brought safety from visitors, allowed the group to concentrate on each other and on the life they were trying to create. It wasn't clear to the young man when they said 'make it' whether they meant that everyone would still be alive in the spring or that everyone would still be here, whether the alternative was death or dropping back in to the lives their parents had built for them. The ancestors muttered at his elbow.

You can sleep by the fire, Rainbow said, if you like. The single people usually do. He hung back: some of the places he'd stayed, physical modesty was bourgeois, a sign of hang-ups and repressions. Rainbow disappeared and the three men, Scott, River and the small one whose name he hadn't caught, pulled sleeping bags and blankets from a pile in the corner, arranged cushions into approximate beds, stripped to their underwear – firelight flickering over limbs and torsos – and settled down. Standing in the shadows, he did the same, lay in the stranger's place furthest from the hearth. Behind the woodsmoke and the comforting memory of onions and herbs, he could smell something older and darker trickling around the leaky window, under the tattered curtain. Winter. He lay on his back, feeling beneath the big cushion and the wooden floor the bulk of the mountain, thinking about the creatures of the hills burying food and building up fat to see them through the days ahead. River and the short one were talking quietly, looked over at him. You any good in a garden, Eli? We'll be lifting the last of the vegetables tomorrow. Sure, he said, whatever needs doing. The door opened, its shadow leaning over the firelight, and Rainbow came in wearing paisley flannelette pyjamas, pink and white, worn at the knees, and a pair of brown hand-knitted socks that made something in him soften and dissolve. She pulled two cushions into a

118

space at the fireside that he saw had been left for her, unrolled a red sleeping bag. She climbed into it standing, pulled it up around her shoulders and then sat a moment on her cushion watching the fire sink to a glow. A moment's peace, he saw, a time at the end of the day when everything has been done. He would have liked to know what she was thinking about.

the year pauses, turns

By Christmas, life beyond and before Bear Mountain Ridge seemed like a story he'd once heard. Even the child, Indigo, slept late every morning. Rainbow woke first, slipped out of her bag as if the frost were not seizing her heels and snapping around her neck, moved almost leisurely towards the bundle of clothes she'd left by the dying fire the previous night, as if they might hold the memory of flame through the silence and deathly cold of the early hours. She knew he watched her, would let a small smile flicker towards him as she went out into the snow to the privy. When he heard her come back and light the stove, he'd force himself out of his sleeping bag and find her already busy in the kitchen, spooning leaves – not always what he would recognise as tea-leaves – into the pot, adding milk powder and water to a pan of oatmeal. Her face was pink from the outside air. Wind and frost clung in her clothes and sometimes she'd pause long enough for him to wrap her in his sleep-warm arms, to blow his warm breath on her chilled ears while she stirred oatmeal, peered into the cauldron of water heating for washing. When he heard Joan on the stairs, coming down from the room where she and

Eagle and Indigo slept huddled like bears on an old mattress, he too would step outside, following Rainbow's footsteps over a fresh snowfall. The house, he noticed, grew warmer as the snow rose. He had begun to wonder if the day might come when they needed a tunnel.

There were no rules about mealtimes, they hadn't gone that far, but everyone gathered for breakfast. Oatmeal, tea. Hot and filling, plenty of both, and a little cinnamon on the oatmeal doing duty for stewed fruit or honey or syrup, all of which he imagined every morning. They discussed the day ahead. They'd agreed on consensus government, which in Eli's experience meant that the loudest person won, but in practice they pretty much did what Eagle said and in practice, at least now with few people and not so much to do, that worked well enough. Once a fortnight, someone hiked down the hill to the road where they kept Joan and Eagle's old truck, and drove six miles into town for the food stamps and a haul of canned goods. There was washing, cooking, chopping and stacking wood, filling the water buckets with snow because the pipes were indeed frozen, the daily work of getting eight people from dawn to dusk. Eagle took Indigo out every day, to build snow forts or climb trees or track animals. Joan made sourdough bread. Scott tried to teach Indigo his letters. It was the child, Eli thought, who held them together. Where there is a child, there are needs to be met, and things you cannot say.

It's nearly the solstice, Joan said. I know we agreed none of that Christian shit, big daddy God, but this is Mother Earth, the turning point of the year, the hinge. And kids need festivals. You could tell she had to get herself ready to say 'shit', especially so near 'God'. Sure, said Eagle, we did Midsummer. Scott looked up; something shifted in the room. Joan fiddled with a hole in her sweater. Not like that, she said. That wasn't what I meant. Rainbow stood up and began to gather the bowls. No, she said, you're right, everyone in the northern hemisphere marks the turning of the year, we should do it. He remembered Hanukkah, the candles in the window. It was never a big thing, his mother said every year, only we had to make it into our version of Christmas, and now look where we are. We should light candles, he said. We could make ice lanterns. Bring in a tree, said River, nothing Christian about that. Do you think we could have candy, asked Indigo, just for once? Sugar's cheap, Rainbow said, we have milk, I'll make fudge.

He and River had wanted to make a bonfire, a big one that they could dance around in the snow, but Eagle was right, really, that they didn't have enough wood to be burning it for fun. They compromised, took Indigo into the woods to gather fallen sticks and twigs for a child-size fire, and Scott came back from town with marshmallows for him to toast. The child should have friends, the young man thought, he should not be only the plaything of all of us, should not be living out the lost childhoods of seven young adults. He showed Indigo how to jump off a stump and land outstretched, to make a snow angel. He should come into the woods more often, should come alone sometime and listen to the deep silence of winter trees, note as Eagle did the movements of the remaining birds and the footprints of small creatures. Before they went back to the house, the two men and the little boy stood looking through the scribble of black twigs to the blue sky, feeling the dark earth beneath the white snow under their feet, hearing the blood bounding in their ears and the quiet of tree and hill as the year paused, turned, inclined once more towards the light.

Later, after they had linked hands and danced around the knee-high fire, after they had sharpened sticks and toasted marshmallows, the smell of sugar rising into the darkest winter night, after they had tasted the fudge – their appetites for sugar flagging now, their eyes flickering towards the box in the corner, because if the child can have sugar on this one day then the adults can also get a little high – after they had repaired the latest snowman and given him stick arms and a paper hat, they returned to the real fire, the one in the hearth. Indigo curled up in his mother's arms and she bowed her head over his, smelling his hair, rubbing her cheek on him, feeling his growing weight against her shoulder. He saw her arms tighten, saw her thinking that the child would not always be hers as he was that night, saw her wanting to stop the spinning of the world just for a short while.

For this night.

Later, he led Rainbow away from the fire, up the creaking stairs to the old, cold room at the back of the house, where he had left sleeping bags and cushions earlier in the day. Later, for the first time, in the darkest hours of the longest night, they gave each other warmth.

I found myself running back up the stairs to the ward, thinking as I always did about all the feet that had hurried up and down those steps in the hospital's fifty years. Nurses in starched caps and nylon stockings, doctors in tweed suits, five decades of parents out of their minds with fear, bargaining furiously with God for this not to be happening. Make Miriam be all right, I'd said, and I'll give up anything else, I'll never read another book in my life, I'll never climb another mountain, but of course I continue to read, because there is no connection between Miriam's immune system and my reading, because our lives are not furnished with such contingencies. I banged through the doors at the top, had to hold my hands behind my back not to ring the ward's bell

the way out

Suddenly, they let her go. An ordinary Sunday afternoon, inasmuch as the idea of ordinariness is intelligible on the children's ward. Sundays were always quiet, the list of names on the board at the nurses' station as short as they could make it; some children even went home on Saturdays and returned on Mondays, as if the weekend had some protective quality that made it safe for them to go out. Yes, Emma said, it does, but it's the relative not the absolute risk that changes, everyone knows that hospital outcomes are better during the working week. It's not safer at home on a Sunday, it's less safe in hospital. Well done Mimi for arresting at lunchtime on a Tuesday. Yep, said Mimi, I thought you'd be pleased.

It was a bright winter day and Dad had taken Rose out to catch the last of the afternoon light. Can't have you getting rickets, he said, children need to photosynthesise, there must be some kind of park or playground around here. I saw Miriam's gaze follow Rose down the ward and through the first set of doors and realised that even in her imagination she could not follow her sister down the vinyl stairway, under the boards painted with the names of previous matrons and physicians, because she had not left the unit since arriving on a trolley twelve days earlier. She did not know that the hospital chapel, the black hole in the institution's geography, lay below her bed. At that time, it seemed to me that the visitors' book in the chapel was the most terrible thing I had ever read, a minute catalogue of parental fear and grief whose exact specificity made it harder to bear than accounts of greater suffering. People wrote notes to God there, as if he might pop by at a quiet moment and be moved to grant the life of a particular child whose mother made her petitions in blue biro with old-fashioned 's's. As if there were things that might not be allowed to happen. Emma and I had ventured there almost as tourists, asserting our interest in architecture and history, as if we expected the hospital chapel to be a simulacrum of the village churches where we used to potter. I did not wish to go there ever again, and at the same time felt drawn to it every time I passed.

Emma's sister Clare had sent knitting wool and needles and Emma was trying to remember how to knit so that she could show Miriam. It's an ancient women's craft, Emma said, it's sisterhood in material form. No, said Mim, fuck that, it's time-wasting for girls, it's to keep women's hands busy so they don't go out and man the barricades, next you're going to have me doing macramé or cutting pictures out of magazines and sticking them into scrapbooks like some under-occupied Victorian waiting to get married. OK, said Emma, fine, but another way of seeing it would be that you're rejecting the garment industry and investing in your own skills instead, come the apocalypse you might be glad if you could make warm clothes. Come the apocalypse, Mimi said, we're not going to be knitting, sister, but meanwhile she allowed Emma to put the needles into her hands and show her what to do with her fingers. Teach her anatomy instead, I thought, show her how to read an ECG, explain calculus or the table of elements. She still has her future. I started tidying up, picking up the three books Mimi had left open-winged on her bed, folding the newspaper through which my father had been flicking, fishing a pair of socks from under the bed so I could take them home to wash. My turn, now, to sleep in my own bed, take a long hot shower and try to answer Rose's questions. Why did Mimi stop breathing? Why did she lie down in the field? What if it happens again? Why do I have to go to school when she gets to lie in bed playing all the time?

'Hello, Miriam, Mum.'

Janet, the only nurse apparently over the age of forty. Short, steel-grey hair, brisk and silent on her feet. I trusted her.

'Mum and Dad, the doctor wants to have a word, if that's OK? He'll be up in a minute.'

On a Sunday afternoon? Emma and I looked at each other. Bad news, I thought, worse than we already know. I remembered Erica saying things could be much worse, that sometimes paediatricians have to tell people that their child's condition is degenerative and there is nothing they can do. Probably not, though, on a Sunday. They would wait until all the henchmen were there.

Emma gave a tiny shrug. 'That's it, Mim. Now slide the next stitch along.'

Miriam put the knitting down in her lap. 'Is there some reason why the doctor can't talk to me?'

'I don't know,' said Emma. 'We don't know what he's going to say.'

He appeared at the end of the bed like anyone else, wearing jeans and a rugby shirt. He must have come in on a Sunday, I thought, to see a few special patients, and I could feel unwelcome gratitude spreading in my chest. Come in, doubtless, leaving his partner alone with the children again, perhaps when his parents had come for the weekend, and at that low point on a Sunday when homework collides with cooking and the late revelation of dinosaur costumes and unusual items of sporting equipment required by tomorrow morning. Miss Khalil said we'd get an *after school detention* if we didn't bring in goggles this time.

'How are you doing, Miriam? Knitting, is it?'

She didn't look up. 'It's a sign of despair.'

He glanced at me. 'Well, your sats have been good for two days now. How would you like to go home instead?'

She flicked him a glance. 'Obviously I'd like to go home. Or anywhere, frankly. Are you saying I can leave?'

'Mim—' I said. Don't be rude. Don't rock the boat. Don't offend the gods, or the doctors.

I met Emma's eyes. No, not now. Not today. Keep her safe here a little longer, with the resus trolley waiting at the door and the emergency bell above the bed. Of course we can't take her home.

Dr Chalcott looked at us. 'Mum? Dad?'

I felt my head shaking. 'No. Not tonight. I'm sorry, Mim, but we can't just do that. In the morning. We can get everything ready.'

As if I'd slapped her. 'What ready? What do you mean?'

I mean no. I mean I'd rather you were safe than happy.

Emma leant forward, pulled the ball of wool from under the bed. 'What if we all go out, Mim? For dinner, if you like? And then have one last night here, no monitors, no wires, but we'll all know that we've still got the call button if we need it. And then home tomorrow. When we're all a bit more used to the idea. And we've had another night without wheezing.'

'Good plan,' said Dr Chalcott. 'I'll sort it out with the

nurses. Maybe ask them to go through the epipen with you one last time?'

Miriam looked from one adult to another. Her mouth opened. Fuck you, I heard her think, fuck the whole lot of you. 'Mim,' I said. 'Mim, it's one night. Twelve hours. We'll take you out to dinner.'

Dr Chalcott looked from Emma to me and back. 'I'll leave you to it. You're good to go in the morning. I'm off to a conference tonight but we'll send you a follow-up in about six weeks. After Christmas.'

Rose and my dad came back and we persuaded Miriam to get out of bed, have a shower and put on street clothes. There's no point, she said, if you're only going to bring me back here afterwards, you're trying to buy me off with dinner. Yes we are, I said, so go put your clothes on so you can make the most of it. Go on, the pyjamas have done their work, we get the message, now you can exploit our guilt. Come on. Any restaurant in town, whatever you want from the menu. She eyed me. Well OK, I said, not L'Auberge aux Jardins, not that they'd have a table at an hour's notice. Come on, Mim. Emma had her phone out. There's a branch of Zucchini, she said, or there's Spanish or Thai or a new Japanese place, you choose, Mimi. Miriam rose, at last, from her bed. Thai, she said, I'm sick of bland food, and she stalked off to the bathroom, past the other families who had heard every word and who wouldn't be going to restaurants any time soon. Rose was fiddling with the buttons that made the bed go up and down. I don't like all that spicy stuff, she said, and before Emma could speak I said I know, don't worry, we'll get lots of prawn crackers, you can have those deep-fried dumpling things, ice-cream, anything.

Miriam, it turned out, didn't have a coat, someone had taken it off her somewhere between beginning CPR and removing the defibrillator pads and it had vanished into the world, had only black school shoes which she didn't want to wear with her jeans. They're too small, she said, I must have grown in here, I can't wear them. I think you'll find, I thought, that you can, but I said they won't damage your feet in a couple of hours, Mim, and you can't have grown that much in ten days. Twelve days, she said, twelve days and counting. Wear my coat, said Emma, and I'll borrow your cardigan, getting cold can trigger asthma. No, thanks, said Miriam, I wouldn't be seen dead in your coat, and annoyance fuelled her off the ward, past the fish and through the double doors to the corridor where she hesitated because she was, now, at the boundary of her known world, as far as she'd been since she was wheeled on the trolley from Resuscitation. I felt my dad's hand on my shoulder. It's going to be OK, Adam, he said.

No-one knows that. It's just a prayer. I know it in my bones, they say, but your bones, your blood and your marrow, have a different script, and it will not be OK, not in the end, not for any of us. It is the one thing we know, that it will not be OK.

Rose hurried to Miriam and took her arm. It's this way, she said, the way out, and I watched them, arm in arm, hair moving on their backs, leaving the hospital.

with paper umbrellas and sparklers

The restaurant was in a restored warehouse at the back of the old industrial quarter, which has now been regenerated by boardwalks along the canal and plane trees still spindly on 'piazzas' where once bales of cotton and silk lay piled. There were box hedges and outbursts of bamboo into which people had pushed crisp packets and ketchup-smeared polystyrene trays. The water lay flat in the darkness, too dirty to reflect clearly the Christmas lights swinging in the wind: like much post-industrial regeneration, it was all set up for a party that wasn't happening. The restaurant was empty and bright as a stage-set, two waiters lounging like extras against the bar, looking at a phone. I saw Emma feeling in her bag for the epipen. We'd have to get a proper handbag for Miriam, and see that she carried it; the epipen would end up in the washing machine if she kept it in her pocket. And a medical alert bracelet, Erica had said, so that if Mimi 'became unwell' in public, the paramedics would know what they were dealing with. The windows were covered with plastic transfers of elephants and onion domes. My father accepted a table by the window, where we would be mannequins if there were anyone out there to see us, and the girls claimed the banquette. Seafood, peanuts, eggs, sesame – what if – but they had tested her for all the obvious things, all the substances known to antagonise the blood, and found nothing. City centre, I thought, Sunday evening, the ambulance response time should be well inside ten minutes. Miriam gazed out at the dark-windowed Party Boat moored to the quay opposite, at the outline of the city against the brown sky.

She sighed, as if letting something go. 'OK. It does feel amazing to be out. I'm going to remember this. Just the sky and the filthy canal and the lights in the wind. It's all really weird. Like, extraordinary.'

I caught Emma's eye. 'Ordinary extraordinary,' I said.

May we forget. It is a pity that the things we learn in crisis are all to be found on fridge magnets and greetings cards: seize the day, savour the moment, tell your love— May we live long enough to despise the clichés again, may we heal enough to take for granted sky and water and light, because the state of blind gratitude for breath and blood is not a position of intelligence.

Mimi had picked up the menu. 'Can we have the mixed starter? And seaweed? And then can I have the squid thing?'

'Anything,' Emma said.

Rose raised her eyebrows. 'Even Coke?'

'Yep.'

The girls looked at each other, as if we were breaking their rules, as if something had gone wrong.

'Not the sugary one,' I amended, for reassurance rather than because sugar seemed important.

'What about champagne?' asked Dad. 'On me, of course?'

Emma and I exchanged glances. One day soon, I thought, we would be able to talk again, would not be always with a

132

child or a nurse or my father and would be able to use words. Not for me, I said, thanks, Dad. No, said Emma, but it's a kind thought. Hey, what about mocktails all round? With paper umbrellas? I bet they have them here. I'll go ask at the bar if they have little sparklers, the girls would love them.

Rose and I needed to get the train home because she had school the next day. Miriam, despite her epiphany, soon fell silent and seemed tired or somehow absent. But before that, in an ersatz Thai restaurant at the back of the business district, overlooking a canal that was once the main artery of English manufacturing and is now brimming with stolen bikes and shopping trolleys, it was good. The drinks came, with paper umbrellas and sparklers and tinsel tassels, and nobody minded when Rose set fire to her umbrella. The girls ate so many rice crackers and prawn toasts that they hardly touched the real food but then found room for ice-cream. Miriam, who used to fold piles of paper into cranes for Hiroshima Day every year, as if they might make things better, produced a family of napkin birds for Rose, who had them talking to each other and squabbling over the menu. Dad talked to Emma about American healthcare and its reforms, which is what Dad and Emma always talk about, and I sat there and watched them all breathing and eating, their hearts and lungs and digestive systems working to keep them alive.

When we left, hurrying for the train, leaving Emma to take Miriam back into the hospital for her last night's confinement – last for now, there will probably be more – Dad touched my arm.

'Adam? Do you think I could come back with you? Sleep on your sofa, just tonight? I think there's something we need to talk about. Once Rose is in bed.'

He must have seen my face change in the darkness, or sensed my blood brace for some further pain. 'It's nothing

133

new, Adam. No news. You asked me if anyone on my side of the family had any major health issues, do you remember? I've been thinking about it. That's all.'

That's all. More bad news, more of the story of my sperm and Emma's egg.

'Sure,' I said. 'OK. But I want to get things ready for Mimi too. Clean her room. Maybe bake a cake. We should have eggs. Unless Emma ate them.'

'Yes,' he said. 'Emma's not looking well, is she?'

'I had noticed. I can't be cooking for her while I'm with Mim in hospital. I can't make her eat.'

'I know,' he said. 'I wasn't blaming you. Let me help, that's why I came. I can put Rose to bed. I'd like to spend some time with her too.'

Emma, of course, had been working again, and had not done much with the house again. She had run the dishwasher but there were dirty plates on the counter waiting to go in, and the washing machine was full of wet clothes including the school uniform Rose needed for morning. The skirts are made of some kind of carcinogenic Teflon and dry overnight on a radiator even when the radiators are off, and the blouses can be ironed dry. Another late night. There were crumbs on the kitchen floor and the prints of wet shoes in the hall. I stood there, listening to Rose splashing in the bath and to my father's voice talking to her, to the rumble of next door's television, the passing of cars on the main road. People going places, a sound I thought I missed all my teenage years in Cornwall but which I now categorise as a distraction. It doesn't matter where they are going. You are here. I listened to the silence in Miriam's room and imagined how it would be the next day, and the next, how we would always now be listening for her breathing, how we would be stealing in to touch her skin to know it was not cold and grey. We've tested her pretty thoroughly, Dr Chalcott said, of course we'll follow up in Outpatients but whatever she was reacting to, it's not coming up, I did tell you that sometimes you never know what it was.

I left the dishes and the laundry and went up to see Rose.

She wanted to go through the story of what happened to Miriam again. People breathe in air and their lungs pass oxygen into their blood so that the blood can take energy to their eyes to see and their ears to hear and their legs to run and their hands to draw and paint and cook, and also to their hearts to pump the blood so that it reaches the muscles and the brain. But in some people, if the body thinks something dangerous has got in, the lungs narrow and the throat and skin swell up so that air can't get through, and quite quickly everything runs out of oxygen and stops, which is why we have the epipen, so that we can put adrenaline into Mimi's blood and get everything started again, before it stops. Yes, it does hurt to have a needle pushed into you, but not much and not for long and Mimi would rather we did it than not. I stroked her hair, kissed her, sang Scarborough Fair, sang Amazing Grace, started to sing Swing Low, Sweet Chariot, and stopped because I no longer liked the words, sang Summertime instead. Good night, Rosie-pose, sleep well, see you in the morning. I did not say, see you several times between now and morning as I look in to make sure that you are still there.

Dad had emptied the dishwasher and washed the dirty dishes by hand, found the drying rack folded behind the bathroom door and set it up in the bath for the wet clothes. He was sweeping the kitchen floor. Thank you, Dad, I said, you didn't need to do that. Tea? Wine? I opened the fridge; we did have eggs, and butter. Sugar, cocoa powder, self-raising flour. I had not baked since before— I'll get the cake in the oven, I said, and then iron Rose's clothes for tomorrow while it bakes. Do you think I can iron tights? They won't dry by morning otherwise.

Adam, he said, Adam, I need to talk to you. About your mother.

I know, I said, you don't need to tell me. I think I know.

stop swimming in the autumn, and even then she made it a tradition for most of the people at Bryher Farm to swim at least a few strokes every Boxing Day. There is a sequence of photos of her, from the days when photos were often blurry and unfocused, rising from the waves with a cold grey sky behind her and, one year, a dusting of snow on the headland to the west. She was slim and curvy, a 1950s shape, and she wore a businesslike black swimsuit and bundled long hair on top of her head. There aren't many other photos, because the people living there weren't much interested in documenting their daily lives, but her husband took a few on the day the boy was born in their bedroom overlooking the sea, the white walls glowing in the light of the long summer afternoon. Her hair was shorter then, her face bowed over the new person whose head was still bloodied but whose eyes are wide and already steady on his mother's face.

She died, as the beautiful young wives in stories are wont to do. One summer morning, when white light glittered so bright on the sea that you couldn't look at it, she left her gardening tools lying beside the tomato plants in the vegetable plot, went up to her bedroom to put on her swimsuit, put her shoes back on and threw a pink towel over her shoulder. She put her head round the kitchen door on the way out, telling Ian, who was making a big salad for lunch, that she'd be back in time to eat it and remember the olives in the fridge. She walked down the track towards the beach, pausing to talk to Mr Trelawney when he stopped the tractor to say hello, lovely weather at last, getting the hay in while we can, could do with a good year after the last two, oh, and the missus said to tell you she saw a fox in the yard the other morning, you'll want to keep an eye on those hens with the dawn so early. The tide was high, though going out, and she left the towel spread out on one of the big granite lumps at the top of the beach, so it would be warm when she came back to it. More evidence, the coroner observed, that she had every intention of returning.

She did not return.

The boy was still at the village school then, being not quite ten, and he and his friends heard the helicopter come and go and then come back again. Visitors, probably, grockles, the sort of people who go to sleep on an inflatable mattress on the beach at low tide and wake up to find themselves half a mile out and caught in a current, or who start exploring the caves and don't notice the turn of the water. Probably. A few of those children had dads who still tended the lobster pots in small boats. The helicopter wasn't going away, but the boy didn't think of his own parents. The classroom faced away from the sea, across the playing field and towards the road out of the village. Good visibility, the children thought, not much wind, but several of them knew well enough that the sea is dangerous however pretty the day.

There was a police car in the drive when he and James and Petroc turned up it. None of them thought about the helicopter, which had retreated somewhere up the coast but was still audible, almost unnoticed, like the sound of a distant woodman in an alpine forest. Cor, said James, do you think they'll let us see inside it? They ran up the drive, past the hedges now covered in fuchsia, the chamomile smell of cow parsley too sweet in their heads. The driver's window of the police car was open and they peered in, wondering which button made the lights and sirens go. The radio chattered, nothing that made any sense. Then the boy's dad, the beautiful young woman's husband, came around the house. You could see from the angle of his neck, from the way he breathed in and

139

out, that something was wrong. Then the boy remembered the helicopter. Adam, his father said, Adam, I need to tell you something. Come.

Two days passed before walkers on the coast path reported a body in the water, floating in a small inlet near where the boy and his mother had once stopped to watch a pod of whales passing out into the Atlantic. In those two days, the adults learnt the difference between knowing that someone must be dead and knowing that someone is dead. The boy, who was almost old enough to know better but probably just young enough to pretend otherwise, remembered the selkie stories his mother read to him, folk tales in which men living on the edge of the sea fall in love with strange women who come out of the waves at night. The women slip away from their sleeping fishermen before dawn, until one night a man finds his love's smooth pelt on the floor and locks it away so she can't return to the sea. Then a seal-husband and two seal-children rise from the water, calling and crying for their lost wife and mother, but without her pelt she cannot return. After some months, she seems to settle into life in a house, and eventually bears human children. But still, when the man of the house is belated on the road one night, she finds her true skin and goes straight back to her first family, bound to spend the rest of her days mourning one set of children or the other. The boy did not quite tell himself that his mother was, after all, a selkie, that she had read him these tales and delighted in the tidal zone and especially in the strange singing of the seals over on the north coast because she was never at home on the land. He was nearly ten, and he knew that no-one is too young for the truth when the truth comes to your house. But he remembered the stories. Since he did not have to go to school, he sat on the broad windowsill of the half-landing, overlooking the drive so he could see as soon as police cars turned up it, and held the selkie book open on his lap. He looked especially at the last picture of the selkie-mother, after her return to the sea, creeping back to the cots of her land-bound children to watch them while they slept and to cry.

No-one had hurt her. The marks on her body came from the waves and the rocks, afterwards. The pathologist thought she hadn't drowned. There was no alcohol in her blood, nor any kind of drug. Not much stomach contents, but she was known to have eaten a bowl of the same porridge as her son and the two other children at half-past seven that morning. She was an excellent swimmer, had won races and represented her school and then her university, and was not in the habit of swimming far out. Death by misadventure. An accident of some kind, of the kind that will happen when land-dwelling mammals enter the water, and perhaps, I see now, the accident was in her own body, in, for example, the betrayal of her blood.

history with ethics

Is it genetic, I'd asked Dr Chalcott, do we need to worry about Rose too? Probably not, he'd said, not if she has no allergies, it seems to be at least as much environmental as genetic. But she does, I'd said, she is allergic to certain sunscreens, or at least she develops a rash if they are applied to her skin. And my daughers, after all, share an environment as well as genes. And Miriam had no allergies, not until suddenly she did, and if we don't know what caused her anaphylaxis, how can we know that it wouldn't have the same effect on Rose? We can't, he said, not for sure, there are only probabilities. I'm sorry, Adam, but we can't always give answers, make sure she carries her pen and Miriam will be as safe as she can be. If Rose has no symptoms, there is no reason to expect any trouble. But there was no *reason*, I did not say, to expect trouble for Miriam either. Reason is not, under these circumstances, reassuring. What about my mother, I said, you're not telling me that's a coincidence? He met my eyes; he is, I believe, a good man and a good doctor, one who has time to tell the truth. I'm afraid I'm not telling you anything, he said, I'm afraid we don't always know as much as we would like, as much as we one day will.

I'm sorry, uncertainty is hard, but sometimes that's how it is.

And he could not tell me, of course, how safe Miriam could be. I could log into the university library and read the medical journals, but they couldn't tell me either. Very few people go into cardiac arrest as a result of idiopathic or exercise-induced anaphylaxis, so few that there's no meaningful data about their families. Bad luck. Medical science wasn't giving me a way forward and I went back to history.

Because the cables had melted and there was no electricity, the All Clear couldn't sound. Most people stayed underground well past dawn, waiting for someone to tell them it was safe to come out.

The city had gone. There were no landmarks. There were no streets. There were flames and craters, littered with unexploded ordnance. There were some body parts and pieces of clothing among the rubble.

I stopped. I don't know how to do this so that it sounds new. It looked, I wanted to write, like Gaza in 2014. It looked like Damascus in 2016. It looked, for the matter of that, like Dresden in 1945. It looked like a city full of people that had been bombed from the air for several hours. We know how it looked. It smelt of smoke. Where there had been tobacconists, the smoke smelt reassuringly familiar. (I remembered the sweet smell of my father's pipe-smoke drifting in from the garden on summer evenings.) Where there had been butchers, it smelt, to those people in that place, appetising. It was pretty quiet. No traffic, because there were no roads. Near the food warehouse, you could hear the tins popping as they burned.

Most people went to look for their houses. Many people found that they had no houses. Many people found that they had missing walls, blown-out windows, half a roof. Some people found that their friends and extended families had already gathered in the ashes to mourn them. Being English, many people would recall with particular distress the number of singed cats pacing the sites of destroyed houses.

It is an old problem that it's hard to care about 'many people' and 'most people'. The stories in the hospital visitors' book of the slow sickness and loss of individual children, of Jack and Kayla and Milly, are more upsetting than the news of another bomb at another market far away. It is a newer problem that we incline to treat the historical past as a mood board. I didn't want to tell endearing little stories about Blighty in the Blitz. Fiction is the enemy of history. Fiction makes us believe in structure, in beginnings and middles and endings, in tragedy and comedy. There is neither tragedy nor comedy in war, only disorder and harm. I've heard lectures on Ethics for Historians, which are sermons on amorality for historians. It is unprofessional to judge. Historians who make moral judgements are recreating the past as a sequence of fairy tales, not practising an academic discipline. Noble princes, wicked queens, young men brave in a lost cause: nursery tales, imperial self-justification. Interesting, the equation of ethics with fiction, the rejection of both as fairy tales. Fiction is history with ethics: discuss.

The most immediate difficulty appears to have been the lack of water. I found this surprising in England in November – surely cold was more urgent than thirst? No shortage of fire, I suppose. And it wasn't water people wanted but tea. Without mains water, they dipped kettles in rain butts and boiled them over smouldering ruins. (Where did the tea come from? Wasn't the water full of ash and debris? Don't ask awkward questions.) Several men were seen shaving, using fragments of mirrors propped over cracked bowls of rain-water. (Did they carry razors in their pockets, did people take bags of toiletries to the bomb shelters? Well, you would, wouldn't you?) There were no shops, and so no food for those without houses; people whose kitchens had survived found themselves running impromptu feeding stations. Supplies ran low, and one woman remembers her father telling her to open the tin of salmon saved in the pantry since before the war. But we're keeping that for an emergency, she objected. Yes, he said, this is the emergency. A man was told off by a police officer for making porridge over a burning incendiary bomb. A boy found a piece of tram track on his bed, blown through the wall.

There were heads. There were bodies. People made piles.

It was hard for anyone who had not spent the night in the city to enter it. The roads were gone, and the terrain now impossible for bicycles as well as buses and cars. Many people tried to turn up for work in the usual way, walking and carrying bicycles over the rubble, some because it seemed like the right thing to do and others because Friday was payday and they needed their wages, then usually handed out in cash in brown envelopes. The banks were closed and even businesses whose premises were physically intact were rarely able to lay hands on record books and accounts. Some workers wanted to get their money and get the hell out of town and there were ugly scenes when this was not possible.

People left. They piled their remaining belongings onto handcarts and prams and walked out of the city into the Warwickshire countryside with no destination and no means of support. They were hungry and thirsty and dirty and in some cases their children had given up crying. They went on walking as darkness fell. Refugees. You know what they look like. Unlike the ones you're seeing in the news or perhaps even walking along a nearby motorway, these people found refuge. Many, turning up in the villages from which residents had watched the city burn the previous night, were offered beds in strangers' houses. Some communities set up 'rest stations' in schools and church halls, sharing rationed food and loaning bedding, inviting strangers to take baths in their bathrooms. There were residential nurseries during the war, set up for the children of parents working irregular shifts or deployed abroad, and the Coventry nursery evacuated its infant inmates to the Canadian Military Hospital at Marston Green, a village now consumed by the city but then still far enough out to seem safe. That first night, each wounded soldier lay with two babies in his bed.

That first night, there were fewer people sleeping in Coventry than there had been for centuries.

A city ruined.

a matter of mitigation

I had not driven much since it happened, and every time
I started the car I remembered speeding to the field. Even
now, the big roundabout and the slip-road on which that day
I overtook three cars before joining the dual carriageway far
too fast, remind me of our loss like the ghosts of hanged men
at crossroads. I negotiated it slowly this time, ceremonially, as
if I were driving a bride to church (get lost, Dad, if I ever feel
the need for state sanction of my sex life I doubt I'll need you to
take me to the registry office). Rose, perhaps, Rose in a white
dress. Emma might enjoy that. There was no reason, really,
not to bring Miriam home on the train, but we didn't. It was
like having a new-born again, a new-born with a news habit
and red silk pyjamas. She seemed too fragile, too precious, to
expose to the proximity of strangers, to the smells and noises of
the railway. And I would not have been surprised to find that
after two weeks' confinement, the mile's walk home from the
station tired her, and it now seemed important that Miriam
should not get tired. And that she should not risk being jostled
among Christmas shoppers, or catching a cold. You must work
towards making your lives as ordinary as possible, Dr Chalcott

said. She is not an invalid. We used to climb mountains, Emma said. Climbing mountains is one of few things enjoyed by all four of us. We used to like small islands and remote paths. Carry her pen, he said, and keep climbing, there are probably fewer allergens at seven hundred metres than at school. Though maybe stay where you have phone coverage, at least for the next few months. I could not imagine taking her even across the fields again, or along the canal, where we are often ten or fifteen minutes' walk from the nearest road. I thought perhaps we might go sit quietly on a bench in the park adjacent to our local hospital, which still has a twenty-four-hour Accident and Emergency unit. Not for long, Emma says, not unless our MP turns out to have some mysterious hold over the Minister for Health.

I joined the motorway and turned on the radio, not wanting my own thoughts. I had not attended to the news since (I still do not have a word for it; 'my daughter's cardiac arrest' dynamites any sentence and several surrounding paragraphs), but of course it was *Woman's Hour*, a discussion of menopause in the workplace which I didn't think would have been any less puzzling if I hadn't been negotiating traffic at the same time. Not that I would know much about the menopause or the workplace. I am, after all, the second generation not to enter what would conventionally be regarded as a workplace. A historical quirk, 'the office', a creature of industrialisation, along with 'working hours' and 'leisure time'. I preferred C.R. Ashbee's Cotswold Utopianism, in which people co-operate to do what needs doing until it's done, whereupon they go off to swim or make music or write letters or make love until something else needs doing. Although doctors, of course, would never stop, but then doctors never do stop anyway. There is always more suffering. I checked the road ahead and switched to Radio 3.

Miriam was quiet, as if she, too, couldn't quite believe they were letting us take her home. She walked out with nothing in her hands, Emma following her clasping the duvet we'd brought from Miriam's own bed a week ago, I laden with bags of books and knitting wool and clothes, more than I remembered ever bringing. I stifled an urge to run like a bank robber as we reached the car park, where a traffic warden was already hovering beside the pick-up bay. Just in time, mate, he said, you're right on the fifteen minutes. I opened my mouth and closed it again. But we're special. But my daughter nearly died. Can there be no mercy, right outside the children's hospital? I dare say, said Emma, but she's been on the HDU for the last two weeks and sometimes it takes more than fifteen minutes to discharge a patient and get back to the car. Well then, he said, you should park somewhere else, shouldn't you, love? I could see her rising on the balls of her feet, could see the Do You Know Who I Am forming in her head, could see Mim gazing into the distance because she knew her mother was about to make a scene. Come on, I said. Mim, do you want to sit in the front? Mum won't mind going in the back today.

I opened the boot, positioning myself between Emma and the traffic warden. The epipen, I thought, in the little bag, let's keep it on the back seat, save two minutes running round the car. I would have kept it in my hands if I could, its point poised over Miriam's jeans, except that if I could, I would have taken her off to climb Ben Nevis the next morning, to prove to her and anyone else that she was exactly the person she had been a month earlier, undiminished. What if we lose it, I'd asked Erica, what if we forget to take it with us? I don't think you will, she said, people don't, not after the kind of shock you've had. I know it sounds odd, but the research suggests that having several pens makes patients less likely to have one when they need it.

I'll drive, said Emma. I need to feel in control of something.

So, I thought, do I, but our marriage is built on me not being the kind of arsehole who can't sit in the passenger seat while his wife drives so I passed her the keys, and managed to last almost as far as the motorway before leaning forward to ask Miriam if she was all right. I sat behind her, watching her shoulders move as she breathed. You do understand, Dr Chalcott had said, that this is for the rest of your life, Miriam. You do understand that we are all trusting you to keep yourself safe, that whether you are dancing at a club or swimming in the ocean you must have your pen always on hand now. You do understand that because we don't know what caused your anaphylaxis, we don't know how you can avoid it.

Don't think about it. I would have liked to have been driving. I sat forward. What would you like to do this weekend, Miriam? Grandpa's going to come over this evening and I'm making that stir-fry you like from the Chinese cookbook, start getting some fresh vegetables into your diet again, but you can choose anything you like tomorrow. Help me cook? I don't mind, she said. Whatever you want to make. And I don't really feel like going anywhere at the moment.

When we got home, she stood at the front door, waiting for me to unlock it. Inside, she slipped off her shoes, dropped her cardigan over them on the floor and went straight up the stairs to her bedroom. Two floors up, we heard the door shut. Leave her, Emma said, she's had no privacy for weeks. What if she stops breathing, I wanted to say, when she's alone in her room— I know, I said, I'll bring the rest of the bags.

It was coming up to lunchtime. The sky was grey. I stuffed the contents of Miriam's laundry bag into the washing machine and set it going. I turned on the oven to heat up a quiche Lorraine, Miriam's favourite. I took lettuce and cucumber from the fridge. Emma, having spent the previous night on the ward, was taking a shower, had already muttered

150

something about looking in at work on the way to pick up Rose, just to have a chance of getting home for dinner tomorrow. The dialogue we never exchanged hung in the air like a bad smell: *Even now, you can't make it home to have dinner with your daughters?*

Not while I earn all the money, no, not while the continuing existence of dinner depends entirely on my career.

They don't pay you extra for missing dinner, you know. There's no-one tabulating all the times you don't see the girls and rewarding you for each one.

You have no idea what it's like. You've never had a real job and you've never even lived with anyone who had a real job until you met me. Your idea of what's normal is completely fantastical.

My idea of what's normal is based on the priority of love over work. That was one of your reasons for marrying me, remember? Most people, you know, most people put family first, and if you're not going to do it, I will.

The next line was never going to lead towards happily ever after. Civilisation, after all, survives on repression: probably all marriages, all families, require the silencing of words that, once spoken, could not be unsaid. *Someone before you was better in bed. I thought you would change. You do exactly the thing for which you always criticise your parents.* Hush. More reason than ever, now, to stay together, because how could we subject Miriam and Rose to divorce as well as death? No, I thought, immersing my hands with the lettuce in cold water, no, our cards are played now. From now on, life is a matter of mitigation. With luck, and good medicine.

or maybe like

Rose ran across the playground, shedding a glove and two pieces of paper. She doesn't run into my arms, not at school with her friends watching, and she came to a halt a wary metre away.

'Mimi's home,' I said. 'She's home right now, waiting for you.'

Rose looked away. 'I got a numbers star. For doing my sevens.'

'That's excellent,' I said. 'Well done. Sevens are tricky.'

She stood on one leg and rubbed the other, muddy shoe on her tights. 'They're easy for me.'

'Good,' I said. 'I'll just get your glove, shall I?'

She stalked off, leaving me to follow her across the tarmac and through the gate, pressing the button at the pedestrian crossing and beginning to cross before I caught up with her.

'Mimi's back,' I said again.

The last leaves were coming down. Autumn seemed to have lasted a long time.

'Joey's got a new cat. Not a kitten, a rescue cat. Why can't we ever have a cat?'

'Because the house is too small.' And because it might get run over or sick and we don't need any more hostages to fortune, and I do not miss the shit-shovelling aspects of caring for babies and toddlers.

'That's silly. Cats hardly take up any room.'

'Rose, lots of things take up hardly any room but lots of your life. Babies. Money. Spatial volume isn't a good indicator of cost or benefit.'

'Yes, but you said the house was too small for a cat. Anyway, they're not loud.'

'Not that kind of volume. So today I drove to the hospital and brought Miriam back. And I iced that chocolate cake I made yesterday.'

Rose climbed onto the low wall outside the flats and began to balance along it. 'I don't like chocolate cake. It looks like poo. Why can't we have a cat?'

Miriam wasn't there when I unlocked the front door. My father and Emma came out of the kitchen, and I held back 'where's Mimi?' and said, 'Rose got a numbers star!'

'Brilliant,' said Dad. 'Clever Rose. Miriam's been down, Adam.'

Emma helped Rose take off her coat. 'Shoes off, darling. She's just taken an apple back up to her room. Did Dad tell you Mim's back?'

'I did my sevens in less than a minute and I got all of them right.'

Emma tried to put her arm around Rose. 'That's great. Sevens are hard, too.'

Rose shrugged her off and started to stamp up the stairs. 'Only for really stupid people. Only for people who don't even go to school because they're lying in a bed all day watching television.'

153

We listened to her crashing up the stairs, slamming the bathroom door. Emma bit her lip.

Dad put his hand on her shoulder. 'It's just change,' he said. 'It's just stuff we don't control.'

I saw Emma hold herself still, not push him away. 'I know. I'm going to go up there. Tidy up a bit. I can't face them fighting. Not today. I thought Rose would be pleased.'

I went into the kitchen and put the kettle on. Rose, despite an avowed preference for school lunches over my cooking, is always hungry when she gets home, usually hungry enough to accept cheese, crackers and fruit.

Dad followed me. 'Would it be better if I cleared off? Gave the four of you some space to rearrange yourselves? I don't have to stay for dinner.'

I opened a packet of oatcakes and tipped them onto a plate. 'I don't know, Dad. We've never done this before.' I remembered that he had left his house, taken three trains, was paying for a hotel. I remembered that the city is not one where anyone goes for fun, and that he especially dislikes crowds and dirt and noise and never leaves Cornwall by choice. 'Sorry. I didn't mean that. Please stay.'

'Only if it's what you need. What Miriam and Rose need.'

I rinsed the teapot. 'They need attention. And the more of us can give it to them, the better. Anyway, I think Emma's working tomorrow morning.'

He took an oatcake and frowned at it. 'When's Miriam back in school?'

I shook my head. 'Once they have a proper care plan. It might take a while.'

We were going to have to trust them to look after her. To save her life. It was, after all, they and not we who had done the right things last time; I had not brought myself to see Mr Stanton, to tell him that we were grateful and would

154

now for ever owe him everything because he had saved our child and we had not. Emma had sent a card, because there is no reciprocation for a life, no wine or flowers or pot of gold to pay the price. So now we depend sometimes on the kindness of strangers, I thought, we trust the world. That is how it is.

He nodded and turned over his oatcake. 'You used to have saffron buns after school, do you remember? Ian made them every week with the bread.'

'They eat enough refined carbs at school,' I said. 'If the school lunches were better, I'd be more relaxed about snacks.'

Yes, I am controlling, and look, my children have perfect teeth and healthy weights and no, they don't get as much exercise or as much freedom as I did and so we do have to be more careful about what they eat and yes, these facts doubtless represent a decline in quality of life since the good old days of the 1980s. I looked at him: go on then.

He shook his head and smiled at me. 'I wasn't criticising you, Adam. Well, not much. I wish you could be more relaxed, that's all.'

What the actual fuck, I thought, is there to be relaxed about?

I heard Emma on the stairs. I saw her glance at me, scent tension. She came and touched my shoulder, leant her head briefly against me.

I patted her. 'I made tea.'

'In a minute. Come and look. Quietly.'

I crept behind her up the stairs, stairs I learnt to tread silently when Rose was a restless baby. Emma beckoned, motioned me forward to the door of Miriam's room, where the girls stood at the window tight in each other's arms, Rose's face crushed against Miriam's chest where Miriam's heartbeat would echo in her ear, Rose's arms around Miriam's waist and Miriam's around Rose's shoulders. Their hair mingled, the same light brown, the wrist-bones under their sleeves the same shape. They were silent, relearning their shared blood, the codes in their marrow and their veins. We made them, I thought. We do not possess them but our bodies formed them. I clasped Emma's hand, stepped away from the doorway and pressed her against me. Her flesh too would one day fall away, her bones be committed to earth or fire, but for now we were there. Here.

Rose had spellings to learn but we ignored them. I diced pork belly and stir-fried it brown before adding a lot of green peppers and onions with dried black beans and not-too-much-chilli. Rice steamed, and the smells filled the house.

Dad peered over my shoulder. 'Pork.'

'Are you not eating it at the moment?'

His Judaism comes and goes. Well, no, his Judaism runs in his veins, inescapable. His mother was Jewish and therefore he is Jewish, as surely as my mother was not and therefore I am not. His observance comes and goes.

'It looks delicious. Of course I'll eat it.'

I always have tahini and tinned chickpeas. There was pitta in the freezer. I could have made hummus for him, which is what I do when I'm feeling accommodating and Rose decides five minutes before I put dinner on the table that she doesn't like the main dish. I didn't offer.

I turned the heat up a little. Real food, again, after all the grey and beige hospital slops. Anatomically identifiable meat and eye-watering onions, peppers that crunched between Rose's teeth when she came down to help and found a few still on the chopping board. You didn't cook for me, she said, all the time Miriam was gone you didn't cook for me, and beans on toast doesn't count. I didn't cook for anyone, I said, over the hiss of the wok. But I'm cooking now. Can you tell Mimi it's nearly ready? She's reading, Rose said, just sitting on her bedroom floor reading and reading and it's very boring. Well, I said, it's dinner time now, she'll have to stop for a bit.

We had to move the sofa to fit an extra chair for Dad at the table. I stopped myself telling Miriam not to exert herself as we lifted it, and almost stopped myself thinking of larger houses. There is probably no very direct correlation between the floor area of a person's house and his happiness, assuming happiness to be measurable. Rose said that since the pork recipe came from the Chinese cookbook, we should use chopsticks to eat, and then, glancing at Miriam, took out the patterned lacquer chopsticks that sit in the drawer from one month to the next, partly because the last time we'd used them Miriam had said that we were being pretentious at best and racist at worst, that it was ridiculous for an English family in England to sit at their table on their chairs and play at being Chinese because the person who wrote the cookbook had been to China before doing so. But they're pretty, Rose had said, I like the gold patterns. Yeah, said Mimi, so did Elgin like the pretty patterns on the Parthenon. But – I'd said – but Mim, you can't say – that doesn't work—

This time she didn't say. She just sat there with her hands in her lap and her eyes lowered like a Victorian girl waiting to get married, or maybe like someone with neurological impairment following oxygen deprivation.

places where our feet cannot walk

I didn't want her to close her bedroom door. I didn't want her to go to sleep up there alone in the dark, where no-one would hear if she – if she became unwell. I propped our bedroom door wide open, as if smaller sounds could come through a bigger gap, as if you can't in this house hear people turning over in bed on the floor above however the doors are arranged. I know, said Emma, I kind of want to sit outside her door all night, but you do know that it's actually silence we're listening for, that a respiratory arrest isn't going to make a lot of noise? You'd go mad, Adam, listening for silence, you have to trust her to keep breathing.

Emma took off her trousers and then the clip that was holding her hair in a knot on the back of her head.

I did, I thought, trust her to keep breathing, it never crossed my mind that she would stop breathing, and I was wrong. I was wrong and we were lucky and we might not be lucky again. I stood in the doorway, listening. I thought I heard a page turn in the room above.

Do we still have the baby monitor, I asked. They make

higher-tech ones now, I did not say, with breathing monitors you can attach to a mattress, one of the school-gate mums was talking about hers.

No, said Emma, I gave it to Siobhan when she was having Jonny, and anyway you can't do that, Adam. She's fifteen. She's going to be going to university in three years. She knows what the signs are now, she knows what to do, and even if there are allergens in her room she's not going to be exerting herself at night. Go up and say good night, tell her to turn that light off and go to sleep, and then come to bed. It's the new normal, remember?

No, I thought, I don't care, I don't want the new normal, I want the old one back, or if I can't have that I want Mim on the monitors for the rest of her life or at least the rest of mine and she is not going away in three years, she can live here with us where I can listen to her breathing and she can attend one of the five excellent universities within an hour's journey, to which I will happily drive her, outside whose lecture theatres I will happily wait. I need to go running, I thought, I need to go now, but I can't leave Mim because Emma's going to go to sleep and she won't know if Mim needs her and anyway if she needs to take Mim to A and E what about Rose, there wouldn't be room for all three of them in an ambulance so Mim would have to go alone.

Adam, said Emma, this is the new reality, love. This is what we live with now. We have to live with it, and we have to let Mim and Rose live with it. Don't make things worse for the girls than they have to be.

I know, I said, I'm sorry, I know. I think I'm going to go do a bit of work on the project, I don't feel like going to bed.

She folded her work trousers over the chair, which was already piled high with clothes that she'll wear again before washing but doesn't want to return to the wardrobe with the clean stuff. All right, she said, do what you need to do, but stay downstairs, OK? Don't go and sit outside Mim's door.

I know, I said, I did think about it but I wasn't going to do it.

Good, she said, don't stay up too late.

There were ghost cathedrals, never to be built, the first one imagined before the end of the war, even before the last bombs fell on Coventry in 1944. The Provost and the new bishop wanted a cathedral that would symbolise or even enact the imagined post-war Church of England's commitment to social justice. Bishop Gorton had in mind something that would bring the rising generation back to church, 'a People's Cathedral'. He didn't want anything invoking 'Gothic memory', no decoration or fuss, but a building in conversation with Coventry's industrial present and modern future. It's hard to imagine what material forms he saw in his mind, but whatever they were, Sir Giles Gilbert Scott, the appointed architect, rebuilder of the House of Commons in its Gothic form, failed to realise them. Scott departed, remarking presciently that 'you will find that it is not the extremists (who are always more vocal) who will decide the amount of financial support, but the older people, who have more money'.

Seven years passed in appointing committees, canvassing public opinion and arguing about the wording of the brief for an open competition for a new architect. During those seven years, the war ended and the rebuilding of Britain began. My father remembers that the rebuilding was incomplete when he first arrived in England, drifting across the Atlantic with my mother, away from conscription to the new war in Vietnam. Twenty years after the end of the war, he said, there were still holes in all the cities, and he recalled that my mother had believed as a child, growing up with her parents' stories of The War and her grandparents' stories of The Great War,

160

that every generation had to flatten the cities of its forefathers. It occurs to me now, reading about the dilemma of post-war building, that some of my father's 'holes' may have been ruins deliberately left as memorials, as the ghosts of what was no longer there. Argument rumbled for years: as ever in this country, it seems that most people wanted a sentimental bodge of old and new architecture, being too conservative to tolerate innovation but not conservative enough to live with the inconveniences of the past. It is tradition that the English embrace, not history.

In 1950 the Reconstruction Committee issued the conditions of the competition to design and build a new Coventry Cathedral. The building had to accommodate an altar at the liturgical East; a bishop's throne; twenty-four stalls for clergy; the usual pulpit, lectern and font; a Lady Chapel, a Guild Chapel, a Children's Chapel and a chapel for private prayer. There had to be a Chapel of Christian Unity, to be shared with other denominations and not part of the central building but somehow, umbilically, attached. There had to be space for a congregation of 1,250, and the surviving tower and two medieval crypts had to be retained. Apart from that, anything could happen.

Two hundred and nineteen designs appeared, two hundred and nineteen imagined cathedrals. Most of those entries are now lost, and almost all of the minds that conjured them are now also gone. There should be a book, many books, of buildings not built. One was entirely underground, intended to work as a shelter in the event of nuclear war. Several tented the ruins in curving glass. Most used concrete. My favourite is Alison and Peter Smithson's, a concrete square with a white marble roof rising from west to east, the whole building floating above ground-level on a podium. Critics accused them of wanting to sweep away all the ruins, to obliterate both the

object constancy

Miriam was still there in the morning, still breathing, her bedroom again smelling of shampoo and sleep as well as clean sheets and dirty tights. No need to wake her. We will need, her headteacher had said, an Individual School Health Plan. We will need a photo of her, for the board in the staff-room, so that everyone knows who she is. We will need a meeting with the School Health Team. We will need staff training. None of that sounded like the kind of thing that happens quickly, and for now, for just a few days, I wanted to let it ride, let it float. I wanted my daughter at home, her presence our benediction. As if I could no longer distinguish between an absent child and a lost one, as if I had lost what in babies is called object constancy, meaning the knowledge that something absent continues to exist out of sight and hearing. The acquisition of object constancy is said to be an important developmental stage: Mummy is not *gone* but *elsewhere*. Teddy is under the cot. The problem, it seemed to me in those days, is that object constancy is one of those lies we tell ourselves to make it possible to live. Important things may cease to exist when you look away. I rested my hand on her hair a moment and then went to wake Rose, the antidote to sentiment.

Rose used to wake at five every morning, regardless of how late we kept her up at night, and Miriam taught her how to tell the time at the age of four so she could be bribed not to demand attention at unconscionable hours. We shouldn't have worried, we should have just enjoyed her company while we had it. Now I have to wake her every morning. She had rolled herself up in her duvet and her face and pillow were damp with sweat.

'Good morning, Rose. Time to get up now. I'll make a special breakfast if you're quick.'

She sat up, still cocooned in the duvet, and eyed me as if she'd never seen me before. She pushed her hair out of her eyes. 'Can we have a cat?'

'No. Would you like French toast for breakfast? There's time.'

'Joey says his mum says the cat's no trouble.'

'French toast? You could have it with honey, Grandpa brought some from his neighbour.'

'Everyone else in my class has a cat. Well, some of them have dogs but nearly everyone has a cat.'

'It's PE today, right? I can't find your plimsolls, might you have left them at school?'

'It's not fair. Mum had loads of animals when she was little. Mum even had a horse.'

'Mum also had a field in which to put a horse. If you had a horse in our back garden, you wouldn't be able to get the back door open. Which would be particularly difficult because the only way of getting the horse there in the first place would be through the house.'

'That's why it would be better if we got a cat.'

'Time to get up, Rose. Get through the bathroom before Mimi needs it, OK?'

She emerged from her cocoon. 'Oh yeah, I'd forgotten that she's back. Can I have chocolate spread on the French toast?'

'No,' I said.

Downstairs, Emma had the radio on. Another new disease, or a new mutation of an old disease, had been identified in central Africa. A few hundred people had died. What, the radio asked, was the risk of it coming to Europe? How soon should we expect British deaths? How long would it take to develop a vaccine? For heaven's sake, said Emma, it's transmitted in body fluids as long as they stay warm, it's December and when people get that sick here they go to hospitals where there is an apparently unlimited supply of gloves, gel, soap and water. If they want to worry about British healthcare, I can give them a list and if they want to worry about mortality rates in central Africa I know other people who can give them a list but let's stop it with the racist scaremongering, no? I'm not here for the racist scaremongering, I said, I just wanted a cup of tea and I'm making French toast for the girls, do you want some?

I emptied the dishwasher while the bread sat in its egg-and-milk, gave the teapot a proper wash before I made the tea, kept my hands busy so I didn't go up to check on Miriam again, and before I'd flipped the French toast I was rewarded by footsteps on the stairs. She'd reverted to her old blue cotton pyjama bottoms worn with a T-shirt in which she's not allowed to leave the house because it says across her bosom 'Because the patriarchy's not going to fuck itself.' No, Mim, Emma says, we're not censoring your feminist views and if you're worried about your freedom of speech, look higher than your parents, but you may not walk around town with the word 'fuck' on your front. Yes, we do say it occasionally, given due provocation, yes, it is just an old word for sex, no, we don't think sex is obscene or unspeakable and no, you are not leaving the house wearing that T-shirt. It is a battle to which Miriam still occasionally reverts when her mood or developmental instincts dictate a fight and there is no more immediate conflict to hand and to that extent at least, the T-shirt is useful.

'Morning, Mim. Did you sleep well?'

She leant in the doorway. 'Yeah. Think so. I kept waking up wondering why I couldn't hear the monitors but I went back to sleep. Am I going back to school today?'

I put down the mug I'd just lifted. Emma's spoon hovered over her muesli.

'No,' I said. 'Did you forget? We talked about it.'

Cognitive impairment. Brain damage.

'Did we? Oh yeah, they need to fill in forms.'

'Yes. So it'll be a few more days.' I glanced at Emma. 'Gives you time to get back into the right timezone and remember where everything is.'

'I know where everything is. Unless you've been moving my stuff around.'

'No-one's touched your stuff, sweetie. Have some breakfast. Grandpa's coming over soon.'

'Oh good. He's still here.'

I looked at Emma again. Leave it, her eyes said, don't panic, don't frighten her.

'We might go for a walk,' I said. 'You and me and my dad. Mum's going into work for a bit, while Rose is at school.'

Miriam sat down. 'I'm going to text Charlotte and Sophie. See if they want to come round after school.'

They might bring allergens, I thought. We never really got to the bottom of that cereal bar. They might have been touching animals or eating peanuts, although I had myself watched the soft skin on Miriam's forearm resolutely oblivious

166

to the application of peanuts, and there was no suggestion that there had been animals present at her collapse. It is not fair, I cannot lose my daughter as well as my mother, I thought, although God knows, the radio was as I thought this reminding me, thousands do, and they live on somehow. And anyway I had not lost my daughter.

'OK,' I said. 'Good idea.'

another half-millennium

I was working sitting on our bed with the laptop balanced on my crossed legs, because my father was downstairs with Miriam and despite his encouragement I hadn't felt like going out to a café. We'll be fine, he said, she'll be fine, I don't think you've been anywhere on your own for weeks. Adam, he'd said privately, when Miriam went to the loo, she'll be back at school soon, you need to practise letting go, this is understandable but it won't help either of you in the long run. It's not the long run, I said, it's three days since she left hospital, and I'd gone off to my room as if I were the teenager.

Basil Spence lived and worked in Edinburgh then, in the canyons of Victorian tenements under the shadow of Arthur's Seat. Since the war, he had been deep in the architecture of the big exhibitions, Britain Can Make It, Sea and Ships at the South Bank, the Festival of Britain, building the narratives of national resurrection. Glass skins on metal buildings. A form of architectural journalism, he said, ephemeral. The first Coventry Cathedral had been built around 1043 by Lady Godiva and Earl Leofric and demolished by order of Henry

VIII in 1539; bits of it can still be seen as the cornerstones and lintels of shops and restaurants in the one surviving sixteenth-century street. What became the second cathedral was originally a parish church built beside the first cathedral in 1433. The new cathedral, the third chance, should be designed to stand for another half-millennium (hubris, in 1950, or optimism?). The conditions for the competition began with a prayer: 'The Cathedral is to speak to us and to generations to come of the Majesty, the Eternity and the Glory of God. God, therefore, direct you.'

Architecture as a form of prayer. Worship in glass and stone. God direct you.

He went to find his wife and they got into their car and drove from Edinburgh to Coventry, three hundred miles and no motorways in those days, to hear what the ruins might say to him.

The ruins said that they were still a church. They said that they were still holy. They said that there are places that cannot be destroyed.

He stood at the north end, where once there had been effigies and tombs, where the light from stained glass windows would once have fallen around his feet, where the echoes of boys' voices had flown for five hundred years under the fallen roof. He looked out over the rubble-strewn land where the new cathedral had not yet risen. There were the shells of bombed houses, as across all British cities. There were trees, some dead and some still dropping brown and yellow leaves, the open hands of horse-chestnuts, probably, and since Dutch elm disease was still thirty years in the future let us allow ourselves an elm tree or two. He saw a great high altar there, with a huge image of Christ behind it, and he saw them darkly, through the bodies of saints etched into the air.

The Cathedral appeared to him.

a note just too high to hear

I put the laptop down and went to lean over the banisters. My father's voice, deeper than mine. I don't hear his accent but other people say he still sounds American. Nothing from Miriam, who was probably knitting again, as if the alleged scarf had become her work for these days. I opened my browser and tried again to find research on genetics and anaphylactic shock, tried to find someone telling me that what had happened to Miriam and probably to my mother was not also waiting to befall Rose. To repeat itself. Below me, Dad was still talking.

Spring came slowly on Bear Mountain Ridge. Snow fell throughout February. The world was white and grey and blue as far as the eye could see, and Eli began to hunger for green. Further west, he knew, in Oregon and California, there would be trees budding in sunshine and the smell of flowers on a warm wind. He had never meant to settle here.

Rainbow rummaged in the attic, where she was storing apples picked from the old orchard back in September, and came down with dust in her hair and two pairs of old snow-shoes, made of ash and leather, in her hands. Antiques, Eagle said, and they speculated about the people who had lived on the farm fifty years ago and put them away one spring. Indigo was lying on one of the cushions, red-cheeked, eyes glittering; he'd been sick for a few days. Maybe they got too old, he said. Maybe they got proper skis, Scott said. Maybe she was pregnant, and then couldn't go out snow-shoeing with the baby, Joan said. Do you think it would be wrong to try them, asked Rainbow. Do you think they should be in a museum? Honey, said Eagle, I bet the museums round here have more snow-shoes than they know what to do with. I bet they have cellars stacked with the things. Go ahead, if you want to. Try them. Eli, ever been snow-shoeing? Of course not, a Jewish boy from Brooklyn.

The clothes he carried weren't really adequate for more than half an hour or so outside, but Rainbow had knitted him a hat and a big scarf, using more of the itchy brown yarn that Joan had found for almost nothing last summer, and he borrowed Eagle's sweater, tried not to notice the smell of Eagle's sweat. The sun was blinding white in the blue sky and the tree-shadows fell blue on snow too bright for his eyes. He'd never even seen anyone snow-shoe. Rainbow had done it once, she said, as a child staying with cousins, and that time she'd more or less picked it up by the end of the morning. He staggered and lurched against a tree. One of those things like ice-skating or riding a bicycle, he said, easier to learn when you're small and used to falling over. No, she said, look, I've got it, but of course she hadn't. Get up, he said, the snow will melt into your clothes, and he pulled her to her feet and into his arms.

When they returned to the house, hungry and sore-eyed but laughing, there was a silence, a tension inside the door as if a note just too high to hear rang in the air. Joan was sitting beside Indigo now, stroking his head. He appeared to be asleep and you could hear his breathing from the hall.

171

Eli went over to Joan. She didn't look up. 'Joan? You think he's really sick?'

Her hand kept moving over Indigo's hair and her face stayed bent over his. 'He's not answering. I tried to wake him.'

Eli knelt beside them and rocked Indigo's shoulder. 'Hey, Indy. I just tried snow-shoeing. I'm even worse at it than Rainbow. You should have a go. Indy?'

The child turned his head, muttered.

Joan looked up. 'OK. We need a doctor.'

Eagle leant in the doorway. 'We can't pay a doctor, honey. Plus, they'd fill him with drugs. Kids do get sick, always have. They wouldn't have had doctors and pharmaceuticals out here in the old days.'

'Yes, and a lot of kids died out here in the old days. Have you seen the churchyard? Go down to town and call a doctor, Eli. He's not responding. He's had a fever for days.'

Rainbow came over and touched Indigo's face. He turned away from her cold fingers. 'He's kind of responding, Joanie. But she's right, Eagle, he needs to see someone. We could carry him down to the car, drive him to the hospital.'

'No,' said Joan. 'He'd get too cold. Get a doctor.' She put her lips to his cheek. 'He's even hotter. Jesus, have we not even got a thermometer here?'

Rainbow went over and tugged at the window, which hadn't been opened since Eli arrived and was part-blocked by snow anyway.

'Open the door,' said Eli. 'Joan, a thermometer wouldn't make him any better. We can cool him down a little. I'll bring a damp cloth.'

The child was limp when they tried to take off his sweater, and his breathing seemed to fill the house.

Eagle came over and touched Indigo's cheek. 'Sponge him

172

down,' he said. 'Give it a little time. Maybe this is the crisis and he'll be better in an hour or so.'

Joan looked up. 'Call the fucking doctor or I'll leave him here with – with' she looked around '– with Eli and do it myself.'

Indigo coughed, a sound too loud and deep for his ribcage. Eagle stood back. 'We've got nothing to pay a doctor.'

Eli looked at Rainbow. 'I'll go,' he said. 'Eagle, I'm borrowing your sweater again.'

In the hallway, he borrowed Scott's boots and gloves. Rainbow came as he was winding the scarf. 'Here,' she said. 'Car keys. You might need them. Eli, do you want me to come too?'

He shook his head. 'Stay with Joan. You know I don't know how this is going to go, right? I don't have a doctor's number. We probably do need to get him to the hospital.'

He had read, of course, about kids who got fevers and died. Dickens. Steinbeck. It usually took a while. The breathing noise seemed to press against the door. A spirit wanting to get out. How could the kid have been sitting up and talking this morning and like this now? There were voices from the room and then Joan appeared just as he was opening the door. She held a piece of paper.

'Eli. This is my dad's number. Call him, OK? Right after you call the doctor. Tell him Indigo's really sick. Tell him I need him to come.'

Eli looked at Joan, at Rainbow. Joan's parents were not among those who wrote and sent money and gifts. Only, he remembered, a parcel of books for Indigo at Christmas, and a new winter coat for him.

'You sure, Joan? You're sure you want me to do that?'

She held the door for him. 'Do it. And thank you.'

There was a doctor in the town, and when he heard Eli's story he said a few things about irresponsible hippies but he got out his truck and coaxed it a good way up the mountain road before tramping the rest of the way at Eli's side. None of his business, he said, what Eli and his friends were doing up here, but it was plain stupid not to think about emergencies, plain stupid to have a child up here and no phone.

Eagle wasn't there when they arrived. Indigo still seemed to be asleep, although maybe his breathing was a little quieter. He muttered again when the doctor shook him. Joan sat back, her face closed, and they all watched the doctor listen to Eli's chest.

'Sit him up,' the doctor said. He pushed his hand under Indigo's shoulders and lifted him. Indigo's head flopped forward. Joan held him while the doctor held the stethoscope to his back.

'Pneumonia,' the doctor said. He looked around at the cushions and the piles of clothes and blankets along the wall. 'How long has he been like this?'

The doctor and Eli took turns carrying Indigo back to the car. Joan followed, silent. As they were putting him onto the back seat, he opened his eyes.

'Mommy?'

'I'm here, sweetie. I'm here. I'm coming with you.'

He nodded and closed his eyes again.

Eli left two days later, walked down to the town with his haversack and thumbed a lift to the next town, making his way towards the city where Indigo was making good progress in the hospital and Joan was staying in a hotel with her parents. Bear Mountain Ridge had turned out, he thought, to be just another family, another angry dad and another anxious mother. It was not for this that he'd left home.

He was going to miss Rainbow, in the next place.

still

Miriam went on knitting. She'd borrowed Emma's iPad and found, of course, a website that showed her how to do it a better way than Emma had remembered. The website had a large American woman wearing a regrettably girlish home-made jumper and speaking very slowly while smiling into her webcam. So, you put your right needle – that's the one in your right hand, I mean, not the one on the right-hand side of your screen – into the front loop, here, like this, and then you take your yarn in your left hand – I know it's a little awkward here at the beginning but you'll soon get into the way of it— Mim, I said, how many times have you watched that?

She touched the screen and looked up from the sofa. She'd put on weight in hospital, all those treats and no exercise, and it wasn't going to come off with knitting. 'A few. You learn by repetition. Muscle memory.'

She waited a moment, the way, I thought, she wouldn't have waited, wouldn't have paused, before, and then when I said nothing more took up her needles and wool and focused again on the screen. Muscle memory. Maybe she was finding her own occupational therapy. Maybe she'd just found a wholesome new hobby. I would call school again, remind them that she was still here and still waiting for her Individual School Health Plan, still needing an education so she could still have a future.

'What about seeing some of your friends?' I said. 'You said you were going to text Charlotte.'

She was frowning at her wool and didn't reply. I overcame the desire to snatch the web from her hands and throw it across the room. Speak to me. Come back. Come out, wherever you are.

'Mim?'

'Yeah. She's coming over. After school.' She stopped again, wound the wool around the needle, frowned and wound it back again.

'Oh,' I said. 'Good.' I watched her for another moment. 'Do you want to come for a walk? To the park?'

She shook her head. We like the park, Miriam and I. We like the way a group of elderly Sikh gentlemen meet on the benches by the glasshouse every fine afternoon, to share tea from thermos flasks and pass around Punjabi newspapers, and the way one day last summer we could have taken a photo of the local folk dancing club doing the Gay Gordons on the grass, watched by a group of women in burqas picnicking under the trees with an assortment of small children, like a promotional film for a version of Englishness that is now not going to happen. We share snide remarks about the people using their phones to film squirrels.

'Come on. I haven't been, either, since you – for weeks. I'll buy you a coffee in the café. Grandpa's collecting Rose, we've got time.'

She didn't look up. 'I'm happy here, thanks.'

I watched her hands. Come on, Mim, do something, get

176

up off that sofa and march against austerity or ban the bomb or fuck the patriarchy or something.

'I'll make a cake,' I said. 'Charlotte likes cake, right?'

'Uh-huh.' She glanced up. 'Everyone likes cake, Dad. It's probably a thought crime not to like cake in this country. It probably means you're a terrorist. Baking: we're all in it together.'

Ah ha. A reaction.

'You mean it's not still counter-cultural for a man to make a Victoria sponge?'

She was moving the wool again. 'Barely. You're going to have to join a book group or take up Pilates to stay ahead. Do some dusting.'

'I do do some dusting. Weekly. You'd notice if I didn't.'

'OK, Dad. Whatever you say.'

I started to cream together the butter, which was still hard from the fridge, with less sugar than the recipe suggests, because there are some risks we can mitigate and Type 2 diabetes is one of them. My dad, who was still getting used to texting, sent a message to say that he was 'talking Rose to the pork'. I knew what he meant. He was trying to compensate a little for Rose's indoor life, for the intensive farming of modern urban childhood. Since he couldn't give her a tideline, a wood and a vegetable patch, he would take her to the river and the swings, show her face to the sky and the last of the winter daylight before bringing her back to our heated hutch, where the windows frame the neighbours' television through their garden doors at the back and the car park of the flats across the road at the front. I squashed lumps of butter against the bowl with a wooden spoon. It's not my fault, I thought, I didn't plan this, didn't intend our cramped prosperity, but the truth was that I hadn't planned anything. I had done a PhD because I was interested in Ashbee and was offered funding, without feeling particularly driven towards an academic career. I had met Emma and coasted along cooking for her and writing my thesis without attending the conferences or publishing the articles that would have helped me to get a job afterwards because it didn't really occur to me to do so. I had bumbled through six cheerful months in Hamburg where she was doing a medical rotation and I thought about Ashbee, learnt German and went running every day around the lake, and soon after that Miriam came and saved me from planning much beyond puréeing sweet potatoes before lunch and making sure we didn't run out of babywipes. (God knows how parents coped and of course in much of the world cope now without babywipes; they are one of the minor miracles of the twentieth century.) I didn't mean it, Dad, didn't mean to end up in a brick box in the Midlands where some of the rooms are smaller than the car on the drive and we're still always, endlessly, grateful that we've been able to buy a house at all and especially grateful that we've been able to buy a house close to pleasant parks and paths across the fields and also fast trains to London, grateful that, as Emma says, our house earns more some years than she does, simply by sitting here and being bricks on soil, being cramped and messy and having a third of the floor area devoted to bathrooms, more square metres of bathroom than garden. I know it doesn't look like it to you, Dad, raised in America and spending your adult life in intentional communities where money is a dirty word and space unlimited, but we're lucky here, lucky and privileged, and I didn't mean it. I took the eggs from the fridge. Shut up, Adam, you're not in court. He probably just meant that he's taking her to the park.

'Mimi?' I said. 'Mimi, do you ever want to move to the country?'

Her gaze moved slowly, as if she was drugged. 'What?'

I cracked an egg. 'Do you ever want to move to the country?'

Her eyes returned to her knitting. 'What, so I can't leave the house unless you drive me and there's nothing to do? Nope.'

I beat the egg. It doesn't actually make any difference when the mixture curdles.

'Dad? You know it would be a total cliché to move to the country because I nearly died?'

She did die. Her heart stopped, and then it started again. I cracked the other egg. 'I was actually thinking more about what might make us all happy than about what might look like a cliché. There's no audience, you know, life isn't a performance. Maybe clichés do make people happy, maybe that's why they're clichés.'

'Or maybe they're clichés because they further the interests of global capitalism, like convincing people that buying and selling property is the key to happiness and that better people own more land.'

I bit my lip to hold my smile, as if smiling at her were for some reason unsafe. I weighed the flour. Not damaged, then, not in any essential way. And, of course, right.

'OK,' I said. 'You win.'

But she didn't get up to answer the door when Charlotte arrived. You go, she said, I'm in the middle of a row. She's your friend, I said, you haven't seen her for weeks, surely you can put down the knitting, but Charlotte knocked again and I didn't want her to go away so I opened the door. (The doorbell, I think, may be another casualty of rising house-prices: who now can afford a house in which you can be far enough from the front door not to hear someone knock? Shut up,

Adam, says Emma's voice in my head, can you not stop with the political analysis of everything for long enough to answer the bloody door?)

Charlotte looked just as she had done a month earlier, which shouldn't have been surprising. I've known her for ten years, since she was an elfin four-year-old in a neat uniform who watched pityingly as her classmates, swamped in shirts bought for growth and with ties down to their knees, clung to their mothers and in some cases wept on the first day of school. There were, as usual, only mothers and they were, as usual, not talking to me, until Charlotte's mother said, I sometimes think my daughter doesn't actually like me very much, I sometimes think I've spent so much time at work that she no longer cares if I'm there or not. I had never seen either of them before. I'm sure she cares, I said, you're raising an independent young woman, you probably wouldn't worry about it if she were a boy. Yeah, she said, sorry, I'm Kate, I don't usually spill my guilt all over strangers, it's an odd day. It was an odd day for me too, the six hours to come my longest separation from Miriam since her birth, but I had enough sense not to say that to Kate, who had seen in my masculinity a fellow in employment, to whom it had not occurred that a man might be on the other side of the great divide between gainfully employed and stay-at-home mothers.

Charlotte is still elfin, although now she accessorises her fine blond hair and bird-like legs with layers of makeup and an attitude you wouldn't want to meet down a dark alley.

'Hiya, Adam. How are you?'

'Come in,' I said. 'Fine. Mim's on the sofa, she's taken up knitting, of all things. See if you can make her stop.'

Charlotte came in, slipped off her shoes, left them at the bottom of the stairs where people would fall over them, and

180

went to hug Miriam, who held the knitting out of the way in one hand.

'Hiya, girl. It's been so long! You OK now?'

'Totally fine. It was only that day, and then they kept me in for another two weeks for no reason.'

I peered into the oven. It was not only that day.

'Poor baby. Hey, what's with the Madame Defarge?'

The cake wasn't ready yet. I straightened up. 'Have you read *A Tale of Two Cities*, Charlotte?'

'Yeah. Last year. 'Cause Miss Smith said it was unreadable so I kind of had to go and read it. Was all right once it got going.'

Mimi looked up from her knitting. 'Unreadable to Miss Smith. She'd be fine as a TA.'

I gave thanks that I am not a secondary school teacher.

'I usually find that Dickens is hard work at the beginning and then I get sucked in,' I said. 'Do you want a cup of tea?'

Mimi frowned at me. I was embarrassing her again, being too matey or too paternal, talking like a teacher. I was failing to forget that I'd taught Charlotte to ride a bike when I looked after her every day of the summer holidays between Reception and Year 1, and also carried her past the dogs in the park and cleaned up after she was sick from too much ice-cream at a party. I was not being mindful of my own imminent redundancy.

'If you two can keep an eye on the cake, I'll go get on with some work. Take it out when it's done, OK?'

Mimi picked up her knitting again. 'How do we know when it's done?'

Charlotte sighed. 'Because it looks like a cake you eat rather than like cake mixture and when you press on the top, it's firm like cake not wet like cake mixture, yeah?'

'She's got it,' I said. 'Call me if you need anything.'

181

I sat on the bed with my laptop again. I hoped Dad and Rose were taking so long because they were having a good time rather than because he was too busy doing CPR and dialling 999 to send a text. I hoped the silence was not because the emergency services had called Emma, had called Mum, instead of me.

transmuted

The architect had a vision in mathematics. He saw the algebra of his unbuilt form, an interlocking and repeating pattern of pillars and tracery. He saw a geometry that never needed to be explicit, but once he had seen it he knew what to do.

We all live in patterns we do not see. We are all following magic ravens, even when we are lost. Otherwise, there would be no story.

He saw an ark of British arts and crafts, a treasure chest holding the best and most beautiful things of its age, sending into the future the work of hands that had known war and were now building for justice and for peace. He saw a tradition not ruptured but forged by Auschwitz and Hiroshima. He, who had first seen the stripped bones of churches in French villages in the war, still saw sunlight transmuted by bright glass, saw a robed bishop on a canopied throne, heard boys' voices rising from carved choir stalls to a vaulted roof. But his pillars were steel, tapering to such a fine point as they neared the marble floor that they seemed more like anchors than supports for a ceiling faceted like a precious stone. His windows, not needing the support of stone, were interventions

183

in the air. His walls rose like cliffs, like bulwarks. His tapestry, Christ in Glory, stood the full height of the building, its solid colours and softness a counterpoint to the brilliance of stained glass, gazing down the length of the nave at the ruins behind.

He fainted, and in a dream saw the windows of the nave not as he had planned them, as bays in curved niches, but set into zigzag walls, invisible until you are half-way towards the altar and then overwhelming. He saw their jewelled light reaching across the floor towards Christ in Glory, colours subdued by cloud and lapping at your feet by sunlight.

When the first design was finished, he did not want to send it in to the competition. It was too much his own, too much part of his mind, to expose it to judgement and perhaps for profit. Don't be an ass, his wife said. He wrote the report required to accompany each submission and, having left it too late to rely on the post, travelled to London to hand it in himself. He was not entirely surprised to find many of his competitors doing the same thing.

every time you ice a fairy cake

Charlotte's dad came to collect her on his way home from work. He'd never done the school runs, despite his wife's work had stayed firmly in the role of the breadwinner orbiting the world of cake sales, sports days and dinosaur/Ancient Egyptian costumes demanded at short notice, and he doesn't know what to say to a stay-at-home dad. He would of course appear just as I was turning out the cake. Come in, I said, would you like a cup of tea, you know she's welcome to stay to dinner if she wants, I can drop her back later. No, he said, not to worry, don't want to put you out, not at a time like this. It would be no trouble, I said, we're getting back to normal now, but I'll call the girls, they're upstairs.

He came to lean on the kitchen counter, watched me run a spatula round the springform cake tin and then open its hinge. His suit gave off an air of car air-freshener and meetings in carpeted rooms, almost visible in our room full of books and old furniture.

'Looks as if you really know what you're doing. I don't get much beyond a ready meal myself. Well, apart from the barbecue in the summer.'

I slid the palette knife between the cake and its metal base and then eased it onto one of the plates from the Chipping Campden pottery.

He shifted his feet, as if his balls were too big for him to stand straight. I never know what I'm supposed to say to remarks like his. Ooh, look, someone who has mastered both peeing standing up and cleaning a sink. Don't you find, mate, that your dick shrinks every time you ice a fairy cake?

'They're not keeping you too busy up at the University, then?'

But you haven't actually chopped it off, have you?

'Oh, I'm very part-time there. Just teaching once a week.' Just to get me out of the house, I didn't say, to make a change from Pilates and getting my hair done; look, mate, it's a job, the making of cakes and the washing of sheets, the co-ordination of laundry with PE lessons, the handling of the Christmas shopping and the girls' dental appointments, and the fact that your wife does it on top of her paid work without you noticing does not make you clever.

I heard the girls on the stairs and at the same time, at last, it having been dark for some time, my father and Rose came back. He'd been showing her the stars, she said, but there was a lot of light pollution and when could we go to Cornwall so she could see them properly; sorry, he said, I should have thought you might be worried, I'm sorry, Adam; bye, said Charlotte, come back soon, yeah, we miss you, and she and Miriam hugged again while Dave tried to exchange a comradely and misogynist glance with me: girls! Wash your hands, I said to Rose, do you have homework, it's nearly dinner time.

At nine o'clock, Emma still wasn't home. Rose was reading in bed, having asked politely to keep her light on until Mummy came back, Miriam was knitting again and my father and I were watching her while I did the ironing and he, for no particular reason beyond a need to be useful, polished a pile of shoes. Look after them properly and they last longer, he said in response to Mimi's incredulity, it's better for the environment and shows more respect to the people who made them and the cows who died for them. Yeah, she said, but Grandpa, Rose and I outgrow them way before they wear out anyway, well, mostly. Then they'll be more use to someone else, he said, when you pass them on, and I frowned at her not to say that we recycle them, that children need properly fitted shoes for their own feet and not cast-offs moulded by someone else's walks and games. I smoothed the iron over Emma's white shirt, easing out the tension in the shoulders and across the back, bothering also with the tail which is always tucked in.

My father turned the left one of Rose's favourite green shoes in his hand, smiling a little as he worked polish into its scuffed toe. 'Emma's late. She'll be very tired.'

'She's on her way. She sent a text.'

Mimi didn't look up. 'She always sends a text. But she's always late.'

'Mim, you know what it's like. They're down two doctors and the patient list just gets longer—'

'And the government thinks GPs should be able to see patients all day and all night at the same time as doing more administration and taking more responsibilities for more complex conditions and the whole system is now running on the last dregs of the goodwill of burnt-out doctors. I know. But do you honestly believe they're all working the same hours as Mum?'

'That's not fair, Mim. She's doing her best for her patients and her best for us.'

No. Honestly, I don't. Honestly, I think she's proving

187

something, probably to her father but partly to me, about hard work. Honestly, I think she finds it easier to be at work than at home. Easier to do the next thing and then the next thing from an endlessly regenerating pile than to sit in a room and talk with her husband and her daughters.

'I didn't say she wasn't doing her best. I just suggested that other people might be doing their best in less time.'

I shook my head.

Dad picked up the other green shoe. 'What's your current career plan, Mimi?'

She held up her knitting. The scarf, if that's what it was, was a record of her progress, uneven and lumpy at the beginning and then smooth and now developing some kind of lace pattern. 'Human rights lawyer.'

'I'm going to put the ironing away,' I said.

'Have fun,' said Mimi, but as I gathered the clothes we heard Emma's key in the door.

She dropped her briefcase as she came through the door and sat on the bottom step with her head in her hands.

'I'm so tired. I didn't stop once.'

She'd been out of the house fourteen hours. By 'stop', she means 'pee' and 'eat half a sandwich'.

'Poor love. There's the baked chicken thing with potatoes and salad.'

She lay back on the stairs, her hair spreading across the carpet. 'Maybe later. I ought to have some water. Is Rose still awake?'

We heard Rose's bed creak and then her footsteps. 'Mummy, I got a star for my spellings.'

Emma lay another moment and then I saw her pull herself together, haul herself up by the banisters and push her work shoes off her feet. 'Well done, sweetie. I'll come up and you can tell me about it.'

In the kitchen, I tried to arrange an overcooked chicken breast and some slightly wilted salad to look appetising. I would not want the girls treated by a doctor as tired and hungry as Emma.

My father looked up from his shoes. 'You're a good husband, Adam. A good husband and a good dad.'

'There's room for improvement,' said Mimi. 'He's not, for example, as good at cooking as he thinks he is, it's mostly the same things every ten days and they're perfectly all right but they're not amazing or anything. And he talks too much. But he does all right. Considering.'

an effect realised

He worried, of course, after he'd sent in his design. He thought maybe the Non-Conformists who were meant to share the Chapel of Unity wouldn't want to be able to see all the bells and smells of an Anglican altar. He thought maybe the font was in the wrong place. He knew exactly the effect he wanted from his stained glass, hidden at first and revealing itself only as you progress towards the altar, the pools of jewelled light seen on the floor before the windows are visible, but he'd never seen such an effect realised, didn't know if it would work or if the judges would be able to imagine it working. Anyway, every serious architect in England and many from beyond had sent in plans. He was competing with his entire profession. Of course he wouldn't win. Maybe he might come third. It would be crazy to think of winning.

He thought of winning. He knew everyone else was also thinking of winning. He knew that what a person thinks about between submitting an application and learning the result has no effect whatsoever on the outcome, that he might as well settle down and imagine himself triumphant and his cathedral drawing visitors from across the world in five hundred years' time, when probably people would travel using technology no-one had yet imagined and eat foods presently undiscovered.

Of course he wouldn't win.

He went to London for a meeting. The phone on his client's desk rang. It was for him.

He had won.

He left the meeting and went and sat alone under the dome in St Paul's for an hour.

Then there were press conferences, drinks receptions – there was champagne again, by 1950, although rationing was still in force – hate mail. Strangers sent death threats, obscene suggestions, proposals of marriage, and some of them, he reported in horror, did not even use a stamp. His design, poorly reprinted in newspapers, was too revolutionary. It was hideously modern. It was an insult to the Church, to the nation, to the fallen, to God. It was a concrete monstrosity. Letters to the Editor boiled across the national press.

He and his wife packed their car and drove across England and France and Spain to the Costa Brava.

Albi Cathedral, a fourteenth-century brick cliff whose great porch gave him ideas.

Gaudí in Barcelona, uninhibited stone.

The steps at the west front of the cathedral in Girona.

He almost telegraphed the committee to say he wanted a raised porch, a sweeping flight of stairs, a figure of St Michael raised high on the right of the approach.

Wait. Wait and think.

everyone to be buried

I woke in the night. The small hours. There were long pauses between the cars on the main road towards the motorway, irregular as the gaps between the last few breaths of a quiet death. On the far side of the bed, Emma lay so still that I reached to make sure her back was warm. A mattress creaked on the floor above – Rose – and something slid to the floor. A book, probably, but there was something wrong, some gap in the silence, something out of place. I remembered an internet story about a mother who had woken in the night, followed her instinct and hurried to the bedside of a child whose heart was in the act – or in the surrender – of arrest, a mother who had been able to start CPR and get an ambulance on the way before it was too late because of this sleeping intuition. Careful to leave the duvet wrapped around Emma's shoulders, I slid out of bed and trod quietly up the stairs.

I could hear Rose's breathing from the landing, saw her turn over and pull her toy owl close to her chest. Her room exhaled the chamomile air of small children at bedtime, a smell I was going to miss. Miriam's door was closed but I slowly lowered the handle and pushed, hearing the sigh of wood on carpet. Shh. She was crying.

'Dad? What are you doing?'

Creeping into your room at night to listen to your breathing, that's what I'm doing.

'Sweetie. What's wrong?'

A long, jerky breath ended in a sniff. I sat on her bed and passed her the box of tissues from the desk under the window, where a pile of books had cascaded into an array of papers, mostly the photocopied sheets issued by schools that no longer aspire to buy books.

'What do you fucking think is wrong?'

OK, fine. 'Don't speak to me like that. Death?'

She wept. I stroked her shoulder. I can't help, I thought, I can't solve it, I can't call your teacher and have a little chat or advise you to be calm but assertive with your classmates or even make a doctor's appointment for you.

'Dad. If I'd died what would you have done with all my stuff?'

I heard my own intake of breath. 'Yeah. I thought about that. I suppose after a while we'd have gone through it and decided what to keep and what to pass on. It would have been painful.'

We would, I did not say, probably have moved house, to get away from the emptiness of your bedroom, or maybe been unable ever to move away from the place where you had lived. We would have had to go away, to take a year or six months and run away from all the places where you had been, and at the same time would have needed to stay where your feet had walked and your hands had touched, where your skin was only gradually departing from the dust and the marks of your grubby fingers were still imprinted on the paint under the light switch.

She was controlling her crying. 'Would you have buried or burnt me?'

'Jesus, Mim.' Not that I hadn't thought about it. Not that part of my mind was not always going down the other road, the one we nearly took. Not that I didn't find myself, in the middle of filling the washing machine or putting tinned tomatoes in the supermarket trolley, planning a funeral, finding the words to tell Rose that her sister was dead. 'Buried, I think. To have a place to go. Because—' I swallowed. 'Because I can't bear the idea. Of burning.'

Her hair, her skin, her eyes, flame and ash. The body I had known in baby creases, the feet I had tickled before they were flattened by walking.

'If it happens again and I don't survive, burn me, OK? It's better for the environment, there isn't room for everyone to be buried.'

Wait a minute. 'It can't be better for the environment. Burning requires energy and generates smoke. Burial's just entropy. Decomposition.'

Rolled round in earth's diurnal course, with rocks and stones and trees. My mother was buried in the grounds of the village church, under a headstone paid for by her parents.

'OK, but then I want a green burial. I've seen them, you can have a cardboard coffin that biodegrades fast and a tree instead of a stone. There's no excuse for ripping up mountains to quarry stones for graves.'

The sky was still brown and starless. A heavier vehicle passed on the road outside.

'Mimi, you're not going to die. You survived. We don't have to plan your funeral.'

She pushed back her hair in the darkness. 'I am going to die. We all are.'

'Yes. But not yet.'

194

'You don't know that. People keep saying everything's OK and it's not OK. No-one knows when they're going to die.'

'Not usually, no. Things can still be OK.'

'Until you die.'

'Yes, until you die. And maybe thereafter, who knows. But meanwhile you're alive.'

She grunted. 'That's totally banal. People keep saying things like that. Live every day as if it were your last – no-one would ever revise for their GCSEs or do their homework.'

I was getting cold. 'I didn't say live every day as if it were your last, terrible advice, everyone would spend all their time drunk and scared.' And having sex, which I hadn't, not for weeks. 'I said that mortality and things being OK were compatible. Mim, most people in most times and most places knew death much more intimately than we do. Infant mortality rates are in some places and were here until very recently fifteen times ours. Whole generations lost to war. It's our normality that's odd, not theirs. People still took exams and went to work and wrote books.'

She pulled her knees up to her chest under the duvet. 'Does that make you feel better, thinking about dead people's bereavements?'

'I don't know. Not better. More accepting. More grateful to live now. And here.' And not somewhere where children die violently every day, as they still do all over the world, and that doesn't stop people taking exams and going to work or even starting wars. 'We should both get back to sleep. Mum's going to be getting up in a couple of hours.'

I stood up and she lay down again.

'Are you going to be OK now?' I asked.

'No,' she said. 'We're all going to die. Good night, Dad. Sleep well.'

In our bedroom, Emma's face was blue-lit by her phone. She looked up. 'Are the girls OK?'

I got back into bed and stretched my feet into the warmth on her side. 'Yes. Mimi's awake. Thinking about death. She was a bit upset.'

'She OK now?'

OK, all right, phrases to which we cling, the comfort blankets or blindfolds of our time and place. There is no pre-twentieth-century version of 'OK', which may or may not tell us that it is a modern delusion that normality is not frightening, that it is normal not to be frightened. I personally don't like depressing subjects, people say, as if mortality is a lifestyle choice, disease and violence and sorrow a matter of taste.

'She's still scared of dying. But I think that probably is OK.'

Emma scrolled something on her phone. Put that bloody thing down.

'Probably inevitable, anyway. We should maybe look at some psych support for her, there's probably a bit of PTSD going on there.'

I moved back to my side of the bed. 'I wish you could stop medicalising everything. It doesn't have to be PTSD, she might just be scared because death is scary and she nearly died and now has to live with the idea that it might happen again.'

Emma put down her phone, though its glow continued to pollute the darkness of our bedroom. 'Yes, and if she's still too scared to sleep in a couple of weeks, a few counselling sessions might help her manage the symptoms.'

I turned over. Don't say it. It won't help. 'Em, it's not about sessions and symptoms. She nearly died. She's scared of death. She's actually being pretty bloody brave and clever about being scared of death.'

She sighed. 'I didn't say she wasn't brave and clever. You can be brave and clever and have PTSD, in which case a brave and clever response might be to seek professional help.'

'Yeah,' I said. 'OK. Let's talk about it another time.'

'Sure. Fine. I'll get back to sleep.'

And to all appearances, she did, but after a while I went downstairs, made a cup of tea and opened my laptop.

azure and purple and gold

He had won, but he was an architect; he knew that no-one possesses a building, especially one that has not been built. He had to present his design to the Royal Fine Art Commission, where he had enemies as well as friends. The Commission interviewed him, and postponed its decision. He had to appear before the Central Council for the Care of Churches, which convened in the Jerusalem Chamber of Westminster Abbey. He spoke there for two hours, of sacrifice and resurrection, and the next day they told him to proceed. He presented his designs to the Reconstruction Committee, and they allowed him to approach his chosen engineer, Ove Arup, and his chosen weaver, Graham Sutherland. Arup accepted immediately, perhaps with the mathematics of the pendant pillars already sparkling in his mind. Sutherland wasn't sure, wanted to talk about it, was living in Villefranche-sur-Mer and thought Spence ought to come out for a week or two.

It was January in the West Midlands, rationing still in force. He went.

*

Boats painted red and yellow and green nosing the edges of the Mediterranean, white houses under a blue sky, terraced vineyards climbing the hills above the sea. Bouillabaisse, aoïli, sharp-crusted bread, papery ham. Wine rough from the salt air and sun-bleached soil. They read the Book of Revelation together, he and Sutherland. *Behold, a throne was set in heaven, and one sat on the throne.* They, between the deep sky and the faded hillside, under the sun, spoke of colour. *And he that sat was to look upon like a jasper and a sardine stone; and there was a rainbow round about the throne in sight like unto an emerald.*

They went to Matisse's chapel at Vence: white marble, such thin glass stained azure and purple and gold that it was like being inside a lantern.

They went to the Musée d'Antibes, a white shell for Picasso's tapestries. Like that, they said, yes, like that.

whatever he was looking for

My father left.

Don't take me to the station, he said, I can walk, it's not far, I'm going to be sitting for the next seven hours on the train. We'll walk with you, I said, Mimi and I, we need the exercise and we can pick up some bread from the good bakery on the way back. You do your work, he said, and Mimi said, you stay here and write, Dad, and I'll walk with Grandpa, if you give me some money I'll get the bread too. But— I said. But you haven't been out alone since it happened, I did not say. But what if despite our knowledge that you have often eaten toast and butter and Marmite for breakfast and then climbed a mountain or played netball or swum fifty lengths, in fact walking to the station after this meal once again combines the fatal ingredients? But what if you drop your epipen somewhere, or you carry it but anaphylaxis strikes too fast for you to use it? Thank you, Miriam, my father said, that would be very kind, and when she went to put her shoes on he said to me, it's the first time I've heard her volunteer to leave the house, she's going to be all right, Adam, you've mitigated the risks as far as you can and now you have to let her be fifteen again. I can't, I thought, I need to check with Emma, we can't just let her walk the streets alone. OK, I said, all right. Take your phone, Mimi, and for goodness' sake keep the damn thing turned on, you're not in hiding, no-one's after you, the whole point is that we can contact you when we need to. Keep your hair on, Dad, she said, and what kind of bread do you want?

Come visit, my father said, OK? Come and see me. You need to see the sea. The children need the beach. Promise me you'll come, at Christmas or in the spring, and he hugged me in his easy, American way, a thing I never quite learnt from him.

The house sat cold and tight around me, as if the walls had inched inwards when everybody left, as if the cold water evaporating from the clothes drying in the bathroom were a chill fog drifting down the stairs. Traffic passed outside like waves breaking on a shore, an implacable rhythm of people going places, and from the hall I could hear the woman next door emptying her dishwasher. My father and Miriam would be crossing the main road now, under bare trees with the drifts of dead leaves damp under their feet; I remembered gathering the fallen leaves in the orchard at Bryher Farm with Petroc and James, raking up piles of amber and yellow and red and scooping them into a wheelbarrow, the brandy smell of windfall plums in the long grass and James, who was the smallest, riding with the leaves in the barrow until we tried to tip him onto the compost heap. They would be walking along the avenue, where people our age who bought their first houses twenty years ago instead of ten tend to their vegetable gardens and buy new gravel for the drive. They would be all right, probably.

I began to put away the shoes dropped at the bottom of the

put your bloody shoes on

I had an email from Simon Godnestone-pronounced-Gunston, saying that he was glad to hear that my daughter was out of hospital and wondered if he might now ask me if I could join a project meeting next Wednesday? Everyone would understand of course if I was still needed at home, but if I could spare a couple of hours it would be good for the team to share their work and progress since the last meeting.

I'd stopped between taking the laundry out of the washing machine and hanging it on the airers in the bathroom to check my phone, to see if there were any messages from the world beyond the kitchen and other people's dirty pants. Dampness from the load in my arms began to press through my jumper and T-shirt. A meeting. I used to believe that friends who'd stayed in academia, Anna Bennett and Tom who's now at Cambridge, exaggerated about their colleagues' behaviour, until I attended the first of these meetings. I understand now why the derangement of senior professors forms a significant proportion of my friends' conversation, but for a visitor with little at stake it is all highly entertaining, and makes me feel better about not having a proper job in which such behaviour would be normal. I needed distraction. And the meetings take place in a meeting-room with coffee urns and pairs of biscuits in tartan wrappers, where people who do not think about death all the time become exercised about the politics of procedures. There are some adults, interested in ideas. I understand that the novelty of these things wears off, but the thought that someone considered my presence worth coffee and biscuits and carpet and central heating was exotic. But Mimi, I thought. There seemed to be no progress with her Individual Health Plan and she was still spending her days at home, lying on her bed reading or communing with her laptop except when I compelled her to run errands or walk in the park and along the canal with me. I could perhaps leave her in the university library, where she could read peacefully about man's inhumanity to man while I ate the free biscuits and, if anyone cared which they wouldn't, defended my use of long words in a geolocative media app.

I hung the clothes and then went to find her. Her bedroom door was shut and inside the air was thick with the smell of nail varnish. She was lying on her stomach on the floor, doing something on her laptop which she closed as I opened the door. Come on, Mimi, I said, I told you we need to go into the town this morning, we're out of fruit and there won't be any dinner if we don't get some ingredients. You can choose if you like, the spinach and feta thing or the green pancakes you liked last time, the ones with the lime yogurt? Yeah, she said, in a minute, I'm just doing this. But you're always just doing something, I said, please just stop now and come and put your shoes on, you've already closed the window, whatever it was. No, she said, I told you, in a minute, I need to finish something, please stop annoying me, I don't actually care what we have for dinner and you wouldn't like it if— OK, I said, but please really just a minute, I'm going to go to the loo and then I want you to come downstairs and get ready without any more nagging. You're too old for this, I didn't say, it was faster when you were a toddler and I had to take a spare set of clothes in case you wet yourself and a sippy cup of water and a couple of healthy snacks and get you into a puddle suit and wellies or cover you in sunscreen and argue about a hat, it was faster when your sister was a baby and I had to replenish the nappy bag and make sure that I had enough of Emma's expressed milk stored and carried at the correct temperature but not so much that it would be wasted, and all those years I thought it would only get easier. And in truth, I thought, going down the stairs, into the bathroom, many things are easier, I must remember that, it is only leaving the house that seems to remain inexplicably harder than arranging the invasion of a small country. I went down to the hall and put on my own shoes and coat, remembered to take two from the flock of cotton shopping bags whose advance through our cupboards has no effect at all on the number of plastic bags we require, and of course she still did not come down. Miriam, I called, Miriam, come here, come down now, you've had nearly ten minutes, we're only going to the greengrocer, please come down. I could have written enough articles to get a job in the time I spend waiting for the girls to put on their shoes and coats; multiply by most of the parents in Britain and the time spent waiting for children who are not putting on their shoes and coats probably constitutes a significant economic loss to the nation. Miriam, for – for the love of little green apples, *put your bloody shoes on* when you're asked.

No, I had meant to stop doing this, to live in a state of grace bequeathed by the state of emergency. She is alive, she is clever and brave still, undiminished by her probable four minutes of hypoxia, and we are vanishingly lucky, other families whose children stopped breathing would give anything at all to

wherever you want singers

He wanted to get the music right. He wanted the building to sing. The Reconstruction Committee told him to talk to a famous organist and professor of music, but the famous organist didn't like his building. The volume of the nave was too great, the professor said. There was nowhere for dust to accumulate and so the acoustics would never work. The congregation wouldn't be able to hear the priest, he said, much less the organ or the choir. Hopeless, the whole thing, what's the point of a cathedral if you can't hear the words? Drop the roof by ten feet, he said, and while you're about it do you really think that roof will keep out rain?

A friend passed him along to a man who'd worked on the Royal Festival Hall. That was better. They found a firm of organ-builders and appointed a panel to write an organ specification. But meanwhile the new expert thought the two choir stalls were too far apart. Bring them closer together, he said, or the music won't sing, but bringing them closer together would have blocked the congregation's view of the altar and there had already been years of argument about the congregation's view of the altar. He thought maybe the Bishop and the Expert could sort it out between them, but they didn't. The Bishop thought the music was secondary to ecclesiastical ritual and the Expert thought you couldn't have ecclesiastical ritual without music. In a 1950s episcopal and professional way, they turned red-faced and shouted at each other.

He made the choir stalls movable. Far apart, close together, rearranged so you can get a brass band or an entire orchestra between the altar and the congregation, or indeed right up under the West Screen. Push them around like chairs, sing wherever you want singers.

before it was too late

Emma had worked the last two Saturdays and so had a Thursday off; it is the men in her practice who take Mondays and Fridays as time off in lieu and she is unable or unwilling to challenge this convention. Emma's days off are rarely successful, for while by Sunday she is usually able to sit over a second cup of coffee for up to half an hour after breakfast, midweek she is too much in the habit of producing a quantifiable outcome and a new patient every ten minutes. The night before a day off, she makes a list of objectives: essential, desirable, ideal, and I have never known her not reach at least the middle of the desirables. We could go out to lunch together, we used to agree, but on the rare occasions when we did Emma kept her phone on the table and wanted to leave as soon as we'd finished the main course. We could have had afternoon sex of the kind unknown since Miriam's birth and rare before that, but when I came to find her, on the phone or computer switching our utilities providers or booking a cottage for half-term or arranging her annual quota of Continuing Professional Development, sorting through the girls' outgrown clothes or steam-cleaning the oven, she patted my hands and pushed them away. I know I always say later, but I really have to finish this, it's been bothering me for weeks. A reproach, a ball-withering reproach: I work sixty hours a week and then have to spend my day off doing your jobs.

I'd been up in the early hours talking to Miriam again and then been unable to go back to sleep again and so done some more work on the Coventry project, thinking that at least for once I'd be up before Emma, would be the one able to score points with a passive-aggressive cup of tea brought to the bedside, although usually when I attempt this she's in the shower before the kettle's boiled and I find the tea cold on her dressing table hours later. Mugs, tea-bags, the small arms of marital war. Had you already bought Christmas presents for me, Mimi had asked. What would you have done with them if I'd died? What do you think about life after death, honestly, deep down, because I didn't see even the light they say is the last flicker of a dying brain, there was nothing at all, which is what I always thought, the mind is produced by the body, just electricity in the blood, same as the beating of the heart, and when it stops there is nothing.

And we were left darkling, I thought, nothing will come of nothing, and later, when Miriam, unburdened, slept, I had crept down in the cold to my laptop, set the electricity in my head in communion with the electricity behind the screen, and made a story about music silent these fifty years, and after that I had after all returned to my bed and slid into wordless oblivion, and now it was nearly eight o'clock and Emma must have been up for two hours, would have already packed up the clothes from the bottom of the laundry basket to take to the dry-cleaner, washed the pan I'd left to soak the night before and probably cleared the gutters and weeded the gaps between the paving slabs as well. I sat up, my mouth sour. I could hear Rose talking over the *Today* programme downstairs, a descant to John Humphrys' catalogue of the morning's new injustices and terrors. Emma was emptying the dishwasher, which she didn't need to do, which I would have done without noticing if she'd left it.

I stood up and went to check on Mimi, whose door I'd deliberately left open four hours earlier. Breathing, warm. All right.

Downstairs, Rose was sitting at the table eating porridge with apple compote.

'Is that nice?' I asked Rose.

'It's all right. Not as nice as Coco Pops.'

'High praise.'

Emma passed me a cup of tea. 'Did you have another bad night?'

'Mimi was awake. Then I did a bit of work.'

She put the cutlery basket on the counter and started to empty it. 'You know they made the psych referral in hospital. We can follow up any time.'

'I know. You keep reminding me.'

Rose looked up. 'More hospital?'

'No,' I said. 'Not more hospital.'

'So can we get a cat?'

'No.' A rare moment of unison.

'Maddie's mum says pets can help people when something bad has happened to them.'

'Rose's mum says that cat food stinks, she deals with enough body fluids at work and parasites make it worse when something bad has happened. Rose's mum adds that Maddie lives in a house about twice as big as ours where you could have a dozen cats and not see them from one day to the next.'

'Is a dozen ten?'

211

'Rose,' I said. 'We're not getting a cat, or ten cats, or a dozen cats, which is twelve. No cats. Em, I made her packed lunch yesterday, it's in the fridge.'

'Have I got crisps?'

'No. Just like all the other days, you don't have crisps. Pitta, hummus, cucumber, a cut-up apple and a flapjack.'

'Everyone else has crisps.'

'Well then everyone else is breaking the rules about healthy lunches.'

'Everyone else in my class has a cat.'

Emma put her own breakfast bowl in the dishwasher. 'Rose, go up and brush your teeth, please, we need to go in five minutes.'

Rose looked me up and down. 'Are you taking me to school in your pyjamas?'

'I'm taking you to school,' said Emma. 'And I don't like being late. Teeth!'

'My tummy hurts.'

'Try going to the loo. But be quick.'

Emma turned to me. 'What's your plan for the day?'

Exactly what I would have done if you hadn't been watching, I thought. 'I'll try to get Mimi to come for a walk this morning. I thought I'd bribe her with coffee and cake in a café. Clean sheets all round, load of laundry, do the bathrooms, maybe try to get her out again to the library before we collect Rose. And you?'

'I'm going to chase the Schools Health Service until they do their job. It's the only Essential for today.'

The toilet flushed upstairs.

'Jolly good,' I said. 'Good luck. If that's Rose out of the bathroom, I'm going to have a shower.'

I had chased the Schools Health Service and they had receded, slipped away from one bush to the next. I'm afraid we'll have to ask someone to call you back, Mr – sorry – Goldsmith, was it? She's not at her desk just now, could I take a message at all? Right, and what was it you were hoping we might be able to do for you? Oh, you know. Just arrange it so that my daughter, my brave and clever daughter, doesn't lose her education along with her health and the end of her childhood. Just maybe do your job, which is, as I understand it, to make sure that the council is fulfilling this country's legal obligation to educate children. I had also chased the Allergy Clinic and the ward where Miriam was supposed to be having one last test for a rare condition that she almost certainly didn't have but would be very bad news if she did, and each time I had shortened our waiting time by making a fuss, by offering to drive to other hospitals in the region, by asking about short-notice cancellations. Unfair. Abuse of middle-class pushiness, of learning the system, of not being afraid of doctors and their customs. Yes, I do worry about what happens to kids whose parents don't argue and nag and yes, I do feel responsible for pushing them even further down the list and no, I'm not going to stop doing it for my daughter, leave her in frightened uncertainty one day longer than I have to. Middle-class socialists, we won't pay for private schools or private healthcare but we will storm anyone's office and insist on our rights. Bring on the revolution. Meanwhile, my daughter had missed too much school and my posh bossy wife was onto it.

I felt better when I'd showered and shaved, the tiredness subdued somewhere under my ribs. The washing machine was running. The boiler grumbled. I dressed. I combed my hair and looked at myself in the mirror: I do not think I am physically changed by this. By Miriam's event. Emma is thinner, Mimi older and still chubbier than she was. There should be something behind my eyes that is different but I couldn't see it in the mirror, only my hair receding no faster

suddenly the scent of citrus

I made her go to the park. I expended more energy, more force, than the occasion could conceivably have justified. I took away her pocket money for one week, two, three, and then opened my laptop and logged into online banking then and there when she said that I was always threatening her allowance but never actually got round to stopping it. I unplugged the router and locked it in the car to get her off the internet, and it was only when I not only threatened to take away her laptop but actually picked it up and began to walk away that she relented. OK, fine, I'll put my fucking shoes on and walk with you to the fucking park, but you're fucking nuts if you think this is any way of having a nice time. Don't speak to me like that, I said, it's not OK. Now come downstairs, please. Emma looked up as I went past: have fun, she said, I hope you know what you're doing. I'm getting her out of the house, I thought. I'm making her look at trees.

It was one of those winter days when a low grey sky brightens all the colours, as if the rain held in the air saturates the last few peach-coloured leaves and the slate-grey bark of old trees and the red of Victorian bricks, their clay dug a hundred and fifty years ago from a pit where now herons fish between the floating leaves. Look at that sky, I said to Mimi, it's almost purple, almost as if there might be thunder later. Can you imagine, I said, how this park must have seemed to the people coming from south of the river, where the houses are crammed up against the old factory yards with the railway running past at eye-level, shaking the beds and panting coal smoke into rattling windows? And then to walk a few streets and be here, under the beech trees, looking for the first snowdrops, it's the horticultural incarnation of Victorian benevolence, a pleasure garden then as now for people who would never own their own backyard. And now it belongs to all of us, socialist gardening, the people's horticulture, the antithesis of the garden fence. Dad, she said, will you for God's sake shut up, the way you witter on is so fucking annoying I'm actually like embarrassed for you even when there's no-one listening. The people's horticulture for fuck's sake, has no-one ever told you you're not Che Guevara? Don't speak to me like that, I said, but I could feel myself reddening. Shut up, Adam. Let people be angry when they're angry, stop trying to propitiate with talk.

She pulled her hood forward over her face and pushed her hands deeper into her pockets. Oh hell, the epipen, I'd been so intent on getting her out of the house that I'd forgotten the fucking epipen.

'Mim, your pen, we have to go back. Now, come on, hurry. I mean, don't hurry, don't run—'

'It's in my pocket.'

I looked at her. Well, at the shell of her coat and the hair over her face. 'Oh. Sorry.'

'Yeah.'

I took a breath. 'Sorry, Mim.'

216

'Uh-huh.'

'I just – I just don't want you to turn away from everything. You can't stay in your room day and night, it's not healthy, I just want you to go out and see the world.'

She didn't reply. We kept walking. We came to the park. There was new planting in the flowerbed by the gate, and three gardeners at work around the clock-tower. Isn't it great, I said, isn't it remarkable, that the council has gone on investing in the parks even now the library's open less and they ended the music in primary schools. Look at the shapes of those trees against the sky, look how they've thought to plant those white star-flowers, what are they called, against the dark tree trunk. Look at the buds on that magnolia, not even yet Christmas and you can see that the year's about to turn. Let's go along the river, shall we. I'm cold, she said, my hands are cold.

Cold, you may recall, can be one of the triggers for exercise-induced anaphylaxis, although only in combination with at least one of exertion and whatever the problematic food may be. Let's go into the glasshouse, I said, let's see what's flowered since we last looked. The glasshouse is a small – OK, very small – version of the Palm House at Kew, by the same architect but allowed to disintegrate in the 1960s to the point where it became justifiable to restore it to use modern glass and solar power. We stepped through the doors from pale and leafless December into a rainforest of greens and damp warmth. Something with red flowers the size of table napkins cascaded over the entrance and the air was spiced. There is a curvy bench and I sometimes wonder if I could bring my laptop and write here, but I suspect the humidity would be bad for it and usually I need too many books to work away from home. I led Miriam under the banana tree to the bridge over the fishpond. There, I said, do you remember we used to bring Rose here to watch the fish, that winter she learnt

217

to walk? Do you remember how much you loved the swings, and we used to come in here to warm up? I leant on the rail and watched the fish flickering through their plants, disappearing under the reflections of the bridge and the glass roof and reappearing.

'I still like the black ones best,' I said. 'I don't like the way you can almost see the pink ones' innards, they're not quite decent.'

Miriam pushed her hood back. 'You don't like the pink ones because they remind you of your own skin.'

No, I thought, I don't dislike my own skin. Do I?

'I like the way the black ones are hard to see,' I said. 'And the gold ones are just vulgar. Overblown.'

'And in fact orange.'

'I suppose "gold" sounds better. Or maybe they used to be more yellow or, actually, maybe they were introduced here before the word "orange". Do you know that English didn't have a word for "orange" until the appearance of oranges? That's why we say people with orange hair are red-heads.'

'And carrots used to be purple, and several European languages don't have a word for "purple". Yes, Dad. You tell us about once a month.'

I remembered telling them once before, when Rose, reading historical fiction, asked what the House of Orange had to do with oranges. For centuries we were a country in green and grey and brown, and then suddenly the scent of citrus, the flicker of gold through water. If I had dared, I would have reached out to put my arm around my cold, sad daughter.

represent our generation

He had been thinking about the glass from the beginning. He had been an architect for long enough, and had worked with public institutions for long enough, to know that sooner or later there would be a problem with the budget, and he was determined to commission the glass first. No-one would suggest that he should leave off the roof if it was unfinished when the money ran out, but someone, some committee, might well require an interim solution in place of the stained glass. Just for a few years, just while we raise some more funds.

During the war, he'd been part of a British unit supporting the American liberation of Chartres, and as soon as de Gaulle's speech was over, he'd marched his superiors off to see the cathedral. 'Although they were none too keen,' he writes, 'I insisted it was a matter of duty ... especially as we had helped to save it for posterity.' He'd seen too many burnt-out churches, their wooden beams bared and upturned like ribcages under the sun, and now he was going to see a living one and they were going to come too. But when he got there, it wasn't living. The glass, like the glass of York Minster, which spent the war in sea-caves outside Whitby, had been removed and stored for safe keeping; in fact General Patton had ordered the destruction of the whole cathedral in case the Nazis were using it as a base, and had reluctantly rescinded the order only after one Welborn Barton Griffith, may he rest in peace, volunteered to go behind enemy lines to see what was happening in the cathedral before they started shelling it. (Nothing.) So Chartres Cathedral was a shell, muffled and empty, 'like a head without eyes', he recalled, and he learnt that the alchemy of colour and light is necessary for a holy place, that without it, a church is only wood and stone.

He'd already had his vision of the West Screen – I'm saving that for later – which left the baptistry window and the windows hidden in the angles of the nave, the ones you don't see until you've walked past them but which light the entire east end.

The artists whose work excited him most were two students at the Royal College of Art, untried and untested. He wanted the Reconstruction Committee to commit thirty thousand pounds to them for the nave windows, approximately eight hundred and fifty thousand pounds in today's terms. You don't get great art without taking risks, he said. If this project is to represent our generation for the next five centuries, we need artists without inhibitions, not people already gagged by gold medals and letters after their names. The head of the Committee had to go to the Minister of Education to authorise a contract with the RCA nominating two students and a lecturer as employees, but they got there in the end. Make it modern, he said. Make it rich and strong.

a work of natural history

Of course Emma got Miriam back to school, but even she couldn't do it by the end of the week. You're going to have to come with me, I said, I'm sorry but you know what it's like trying to get to campus and back, I have no idea how long I'm going to be and I'm just not willing to leave you home alone for what might be four or five hours, I'm sorry and I'll get less anxious as time goes by but not now, we'll start gently, I'll go running again or something, leave you for a shorter time that's more under my control, but you have to come with me today, sorry. She looked up from her bed, peered from under her hair like some shaggy dark-eyed animal, a Highland cow.

''S'all right. I like campus. As long as you give me your card so I can go to the library.'

'Deal.'

It is not possible to go to the University. In strictly physical terms, I mean: in some departments anyone possessed of a bank account and a basic grasp of English grammar is warmly welcome to come and take an MA, and for those paying international fees the grammar is negotiable. Like all universities, it is always building. The percentage of the

221

earth's surface occupied by universities increases year by year, an arms race of new facilities and more accommodation that will end when they start to have to define borders. The university instead of the nation state: it probably wouldn't make much difference. In this case, they built over all the green spaces a while ago and are now building over car parks and indeed about to demolish existing buildings in order to build taller ones in their place. The problem with building over car parks is that the car parks were always full before they started to build on them, and now a swarm of angry drivers is permanently circling campus, late and later for teaching and meetings and unable to stop because someone else has already parked on every flat surface, including the middle of the roundabout and the library delivery bay. The size of the swarm varies through the day, as people give up and go away or run out of petrol and are rescued from their insanity by the AA, but it is always there. There are buses, but they are all as full as the trains leaving Pakistan in the hours before Partition long before they get to our end of town.

So mostly I cycle, an act of another kind of faith because there's no alternative to a five-mile stretch of fast, narrow A-road heavily used by lorries as well as distracted and impatient commuters. One or two students die each year cycling that route. It was night-time, I tell myself, maybe she was drunk, he probably didn't have good lights, he was undertaking a bus. Not like me. I'll live to die from the diesel particulates I inhale, but since our car is also diesel there's some justice in that.

'We'll have to drive and then walk across the fields,' I said. 'It's been raining, you'll need your hiking boots.'

The Authorities, by which I mean, I think, the senior administration of the University and the local council, have not yet realised that it is still possible for ordinary people to park their cars at ordinary times of day in a village less than two miles, as the public right of way goes, from the edges of campus. Then you just follow a nature trail through a wood and pick up the footpath across the fields, where admittedly ploughed earth alternates, in season, with some rather vivacious cows, and you'll need a torch on winter afternoons and stout footwear in all seasons, but it works. You can get to work.

'Are the cows there?' Mimi asked.

I had no idea. Probably not, in December. 'No.'

'Good. Because I'm not going through if they are. Have you read *Animal Farm*?'

'Yes,' I said. 'But not as a work of natural history.'

Four years ago, when I first started coming regularly to this campus for my pin-money teaching, there were stretches of grass and mature trees between the low-budget Brutalist buildings, and the construction work was around the edges of campus as the Business School and shiny apartment blocks for international students shyly established themselves barely over the boundary of the green belt. This has never been a beautiful university, not by the fashions of our era although perhaps in fifty years the 1960s concrete buildings will be venerated and the teaching block generally known as the Pigpens will have become the subject of a geolocative media app, but even four years ago you could discern in the shape of central campus the coherent design of a sane mind fifty years before. Students played ballgames in the open spaces and sat under the trees in the summer term. Many of the trees predated the University and one of my colleagues liked to say that there was a left-over acre of the Forest of Arden between car park 29 and the Engineering Department. We were encouraged on Open Days to draw parents' attention to the bike and running trails along the river, and the institution won awards

223

for putting a bike track half-way across the fields to the city. We were a Sustainable Campus.

And then fees went up, the government's cap on student numbers was removed and universities, unable for now to compete on price although that day is surely at hand, began to jostle each other for the 'top students', or at least those best trained to complete the formulae of A-level exam questions. More buildings. More 'facilities'. I imagine there is some market research behind universities' manifest view that what every bright eighteen-year-old craves is more overpriced coffee brought to them as they sit on more red leather sofas under more sepia images of Paris and New York. It's not even really coffee, just warm sweet frothy milk, caramel lattes and mochaccinos with so much cream and syrup that they now come under C-cup domes. You'd think that what The Youth of Today wants most of all is to recline in a soft red place and suck on the breasts of franchised multinational corporations, but only until you met the students. It is plain that the high-ups do not meet the students.

Mimi and I left the car outside a row of oversized new houses apparently designed by Tesco in collaboration with Prince Charles, showcasing bin sheds and parking spaces because the double garages and paved driveways aren't enough to accommodate the vehicles of families who require five bathrooms and an eruption of uselessly undersized balconies. We set off through the wood, following the track of the old railway line. Dead leaves clogged the puddles underfoot and the bare trees closed over our heads; the sky was a meek English grey, threatening nothing. She pulled the sleeves of her jumper out from under her coat and balled her hands inside them.

'Don't you have your gloves?' I asked.

'The epipen's in my pocket.'

'That wasn't what I meant. I don't want you to be cold.'

'You don't want me to show symptoms of that cold allergy thing and it was what you meant.'

'Sorry. But I will leave you in the library while I go to the meeting.'

In the library where it's warm, there are plenty of people to witness a collapse and the opportunities for exertion are limited.

'Can't I go to a café?'

Full of potential allergens. 'They're all owned by evil multinational corporations, fuelling sugar addiction and profiting from the declining health of your generation.'

'Yeah, but I like hanging out there. What if I go to the Union bar?'

'Maybe. We'll see. I don't think the meeting's going to go on that long anyway.'

We came out into the fields, where there were no cows and the hedgerows were festooned with old-man's-beard, still in places beaded with dew. Too late for even the last, north-facing blackberries, even the rosehips wrinkled and dry. A pair of kites circled high over the bare trees, as if in a holding pattern, as if passing the time until something changed.

'How are you feeling about going back to school?' I asked.

She went ahead of me through a gate, handing me the chain to loop back over the post, metal-on-metal loud under the grey silence of the day.

'OK.'

'It'll be good to be back?'

She shrugged. 'It's school, Dad. I have to go.'

Is it better, I wanted to ask, than my school, is it worth your limited time on this earth, is it good enough for the hours of your life that we make you give it? If you die, should I forgive myself for sending you there?

'We're switching back to packed lunches,' I said. 'So at least you'll know what you're eating.'

If it happens again, we'll have a list of ingredients, names for what's out to get you.

'Whatever.'

From the top of the rise, we could see campus spread out like the roadworks-and-diggers set at playgroup. Three red cranes dwarfed everything, dizzying to look at their cabs and surely the University couldn't be building anything so tall. Six or seven skeleton buildings were being articulated, and between them the ground crawled with large yellow vehicles, each one spraying a cloud of mud.

'Are people taking exams in the middle of all that?' Mimi asked.

Which term is it, I thought, what is the date, where is the rest of the world, where time didn't begin anew with the crack of the defibrillator?

'Not yet. There aren't many at the end of this term anyway. But people are trying to give lectures. And, presumably, read.'

We reached the edge of the works, where they surge beyond the confines of the university buildings, swallow a stream and embark on the fallow field.

'Oh look,' she said. 'The Imagining's spread.'

'I fear it was always meant to become endemic.'

The first signs of Imagining were observed a few weeks after the latest, wholesale sack of campus began almost two years ago, signalling the death throes of the retiring Vice-Chancellor's literally earth-shaking vanity. First they filled in the Wetland Corridor, unfortunately before taking down the signs explaining to visitors and prospective students that it represented the University's commitment to biodiversity and sustainability with particular reference to the wading birds who have found on campus a safe refuge from the surrounding cities and traffic. Then diggers crashed through the Nature Reserve, leaving trees killed in the act of blossoming lying brittle and trembling in the side-wind of passing cars. The obliteration of what had seemed permanent was surprisingly fast, and then for weeks we all walked past the decaying bodies of wild plum trees and oaks under which Cromwell's troops had allegedly massed until one morning they had put up palings, as if concealing the excavation of a mass grave, some indecency more categorical than the one they had in fact committed, and the next morning the first set of slogans had appeared on the palings under inflated pictures of smiling students looking serious but pretty in laboratories and happy but responsible in gowns and mortar boards: Imagine You Are Walking Past the Future. Imagine You Make Every Day Count. It's part of the new University Brand, which is all about Possibilities.

Mimi pointed. 'The students must have got hold of the stuff to make one themselves.'

I looked. Imagine the Fridge Said No.

I looked more closely. 'They've done a very good job. But the slogan's too silly, it's like the Chomsky meaningless sentence. You know, colourless green ideas. I suppose it shows that the PR machine's gone beyond parody now, quite an achievement.'

'Dad? I think it might be real.'

'They're not that stupid.'

She sighed. 'It's one of the problems of you not being on social media, you persistently underestimate the stupidity of everyone else.'

'Sounds like quite a good reason for staying off it to me.'

'Makes you naïve. I bet they mean it.'

'I bet they don't.'

if I could stop light

It's only, it had turned out, meetings involving people from outside the University – I don't count – that take place in the carpeted room with free coffee and biscuits. Today's was in the department, in a teaching room still in use as the hour approached. I leant against the wall, reading the notices on people's doors; they have a famous bearded trouble-maker whose fame derives from his public assaults on the universities for which he has worked, demagoguery carried out under the name of 'research', and his office door was pasted with newspaper clippings recounting his latest declamations. 'Prof says universities "run like prisons"'. 'Universities "deny freedom of speech"', and a picture of him addressing a multitude, fist raised. It is rumoured that the Troublemaker takes a salary second only to the Vice-Chancellor's from the institution he has publicly compared to the Stasi; all the Marxist freedom fighters around here are men in jobs for life earning four times the national average wage and owning more than one house.

I saw Jenny coming down the corridor and waved. Jenny is a Teaching Fellow, which is to say someone who does five times the teaching of a tenured professor for about a fifth of the pay. She finished a Cambridge PhD three years ago and is now on her third temporary, hourly-paid contract. If she's not careful she'll turn into me when she grows up. She was carrying a pile of brown paper packages, which is usual because she lives in Oslo and gets all her online shopping delivered to the department to avoid Norwegian import taxes.

'Hello. That looks like a good haul.'

She nodded. 'Not sure they'll all fit in my case. It's Matthias' birthday next week.'

'Weren't you being a toy mule last week as well?'

Matthias is her four-year-old. Her partner is a Norwegian artist. It's cheaper for them all to live in Oslo, pay her weekly return airfare and send Matthias to the free forest nursery, staffed by people who hold post-graduate qualifications in child development, than it was for them to live in England, commute by train and pay hundreds of pounds a week for a nursery staffed by people who failed their GCSEs and had to settle for the minimum wage. Every English family with preschool children should move to the civilised world and put the breadwinner on a plane once a week.

'Yes. But these are more creative presents. Anyway, I'm here over the weekend for the Open Day and feeling guilty.'

I caught a package that was sliding off her pile. 'If you posted those to yourself from work, would you still have to pay import tax?'

'Probably. Anyway, Hannah would never let me and quite right too. I can manage on the plane. Did I tell you about the light sabre?'

Hannah is the departmental secretary, up to all our tricks.

'Tell me,' I said, 'about the light sabre.'

She leant against the wall and hugged her parcels. 'So, we had this long discussion about whether it was OK for Matthias to have a light sabre, whether it counted as a weapon—'

'Yes.'

'And decided that he really, really wanted it, and it's not a gun, and we don't try to stop him making toy swords out of sticks. Stop looking at me like that. Anyway, so it came last week and I couldn't get it in my case so I just carried it.'

'Through the airport?'

'And when I got to check-in, I answered all the questions and the woman said, what's that? and I said it's a light sabre and she said well, you can't take that on the plane and I said well, can you check, because it's my son's birthday present and I really don't want to disappoint him and she said yes, but it's not safe, is it? and I said it's perfectly safe, it's meant for young children and she said I suppose if you say it's a toy. It looks like a real one, that's all. I'll have to ask.'

'A real light sabre? Handy.'

'And I started to say look, if I could stop light I probably wouldn't need your aeroplane in the first place, would I, but then I thought no, Jenny, just shut up and board your damn plane. With your damn light sabre. So I did. And then I sat on the train with it all the way home.'

'Shame,' I said. 'We could have used it in the meeting.'

'We could always order some more. For meetings.'

Talking broke out behind the door, chairs scraped, and a lecturer emerged, closely followed by three or four students getting under his feet like ducklings. Do you have just a minute, please? I'm really worried about my essay. I think I might need an extension. I'm lecturing now, he said, office hours at five. The less anxious ones were taking their time, chatting, checking phones.

'Let's go in,' said Jenny.

We stepped into a warm miasma of coffee, sweat and the pear-drop breath of people with colds. There were used tissues on the floor around the bin and paper coffee-cups on the tables. Jenny began to shove the desks around to make a central meeting table, which made the remaining students leave; I dragged chairs across the scarred lino floor. The windows, single-glazed, had misted over, and I tugged on the wobbly steel handles to let some of the airborne viruses out into the winter afternoon.

'Careful,' said Jenny. 'We had a window fall off when someone tried to open it the other day.'

I peered down five storeys onto the courtyard below, where the usual huddle of smokers gathered under umbrellas beside the sign saying No Smoking within 15 metres of this Building. 'Did it fall onto anyone?'

'No, but the glass went a long way.'

'Adam?'

Simon Godnestone-pronounced-Gunston and some other people, the kind of people who don't get to meetings until someone else has arranged the furniture, had come into the room to see my rear end sticking out of the window. I turned round. My fingers had picked up something sticky from the window handles but it was too late not to shake hands. The head of department, who is a man in a tweed jacket with a face like a startled horse and the air of being liable to bolt at any moment; a nice woman from the Architecture Department whose life's work is the history and politics of English planned towns; a secretary to take the minutes, and James McClary, otherwise James Contrary, a sidekick of the Troublemaker.

We sat down. James McClary objected that the minutes of the previous meeting misrepresented the view of someone who wasn't present today and implied that the misrepresentation was more conspiracy than cock-up. James McClary objected that a decision taken by the previous meeting with regard to the provision of tea and coffee during a proposed half-day workshop was unconstitutional and risked the misuse of departmental funds. James McClary further ventured to suggest that the students would not be at all happy when they learnt that, despite their petition, the department was continuing to accept catering provision using paper cups whose lids, while biodegradable, may include material sourced by the displacement of food crops in Central America; he ventured to suggest that, were students to learn of the scorn with which their views on the lids of paper cups were received by certain members of staff, they would be understandably angry and that this anger might be manifest in the annual Student Survey, which is used to compile national rankings of departments. He ventured to suggest that the presence of such lids at a workshop bearing the name of our project would merely confirm to interested observers the head of department's failure to oppose the University's interest in profit before education and the student experience. Jenny nudged me. Under the table, she had opened her package and was offering me a Playmobil knight in armour, with a sword in his hand, a bow slung over his shoulder and a quiver of arrows on his back.

The head of department replied that, while he wholeheartedly deplored the use of Central American farmland to grow corn for the lids of coffee cups rather than sustenance crops for Central American farmers and had in fact signed the students' petition, he felt it important to offer tea and coffee at the workshop to colleagues who, having travelled from other institutions, would already be alarmed and dismayed by the experience of attempting to reach campus. He believed that presenting the University and the project in a welcoming and professional manner, especially given some of the recent and damaging publicity generated by certain members of the department, on this occasion might reasonably take priority over concerns about the students' opinions of the lids on coffee

233

time passed

Miriam went back to school.

I should have been pleased, as I used to be pleased at the end of the summer holidays, to have six hours a day at my own disposal again, to order my time as I saw fit without witnesses. I should have finished the Coventry project and then revised my CV and sent it out again, because there are other universities within commuting distance of our town and even without contemplating the realms of 'proper jobs', I could have been earning more money than I did, taking more pressure off Emma.

The house was too quiet.

The girls were too far away.

Every time I heard a siren, I stopped what I was doing and strained to work out which way it was going, towards Miriam's school or Rose's. I kept my phone beside me or in my pocket and after a siren had passed, I took it out and held it in my hand, waiting for the call. There's been an incident.

I would return from the school run, clear the breakfast dishes off the table and tidy the kitchen, make a cup of tea and set out my laptop and notes and then decide to go upstairs to check the girls' bedrooms. I had never used to make their beds, but now I found myself plumping pillows and smoothing sheets like a

Victorian housemaid, obliterating the shapes of their sleeping heads and growing bodies with the promise of their return. I straightened the piles of books at Miriam's bedside the way I had once built towers of wooden blocks for her to knock down, and sat Rose's menagerie of stuffed animals primly against her headboard as if for some strangely formal picnic. I put away the girls' clean clothes instead of leaving piles on their beds, dusted their bookcases, made sure the blinds on their skylights were fully open and the windows ajar for fresh air; I had seen several suggestions that the rise of asthma in the younger generation is associated with poor ventilation and volatile chemical compounds in new buildings. Where before, I had often been frustrated by the disappearance of my afternoons, by the way 3.15 followed so fast on lunch that I could hardly begin again to write, now I found that the minutes of two o'clock seemed as long as the plateau of late morning.

I knew that it would have helped me to start running again, but I didn't. If I wasn't going to work, I could have repainted the hall, obliterated the small grey finger-marks made by smaller girls who would not come back. I could have printed and framed some of the photos we'd been meaning for years to print and frame, in salutation of time past. I could have planted spring bulbs in blue-glazed pots and begun to try to find travel insurance so that we would be able to go on holiday next year; there is no reason, Dr Chalcott had said, why not. I could have engaged in the kind of pre-Christmas hyperactivity urged upon home-makers in every magazine and shop-window and website, made a wreath for the front door and put up jars of mincemeat.

I did very little.

Time passed.

idiosyncratic economies of guilt, absolution and cultural pressure frankly reminiscent of the medieval church

A week before the end of term, Rose had a birthday party invitation. You don't have to go, I said, I know it's been a long term, I know you're tired, it's OK if you'd rather have a quiet weekend at home, I'll even get the waffle-iron out and make those blueberry waffles for breakfast, we could do some potato-print Christmas cards like last year. Dad, said Mimi, she's too old for potato-printing and no-one sends Christmas cards any more, haven't you noticed, they're an exercise in pointless consumerism anyway, I'll take her to Bella's party if you can't face it. Of course I can face it, I said, do you have any idea how many children's parties I've faced in the last fifteen years, I just don't want her to feel she has to go if she's going to have a miserable time. It's a party, said Rose, of course I won't have a miserable time, they've rented the whole pool and it's going to have a bouncy castle in it and the wave machine and everyone has to choose if they want chicken nuggets or pizza and chips for tea and Bella doesn't like reading so please don't make me give her a book the way you always do because it's totally embarrassing. OK, I said, fine, I'll have a look in the present box, although I knew that most of the things in the present box had been in circulation around Rose's classmates for a couple of years and were really now too young as well as totally embarrassing. There is a kit for making puppets out of socks, which requires the sacrifice of perfectly good socks in order to add to the number of crap toys in the house, and a box of something called 'science putty' whose fame precedes it; science toys for girls are of course invariably laudable but the relevance of science to a substance with all the qualities of tar when applied to domestic interiors is unclear.

I bought a copy of *Little House on the Prairie*, some more glitter to encourage Rose to make a birthday card and a roll of not-Christmassy wrapping paper, because I could see that having a birthday ten days before Christmas meant that special effort should be made. Emma had come home from work and gone straight to bed the previous night, no dinner thank you, sorry, it was nice of me to cook it for her but she was just too tired, she couldn't face it, no, not even hot chocolate made from the real thing, not even a cup of tea, sorry.

On Saturday I had woken early as usual, no birds and little traffic, the house cold but the girls warm and breathing in their beds. I shut the kitchen door and turned the radio on low while I emptied the dishwasher, waiting for the good bakery to open so I could buy croissants for Emma and the girls. The radio said the NHS was at breaking point and, as predicted by its staff, unable to cope with the midwinter surge in acute illnesses; an angry woman described her elderly mother's last hours on a trolley in a hospital corridor. We had no beds, a manager said, we did the best we could to care for her but we had no beds, we are understaffed and underfunded. The Americans and the Russians had been bombing the people they wanted to bomb and may or may not have hit other people as well. A right-wing British politician had been recorded airing racist views from which his party wished to distance itself. Ten thousand people were dying of hunger and cold on top of a mountain where they had fled enemies intent on genocide; other people dropping aid parcels from helicopters had had cold, sick babies pushed into their arms and had had to hand them back and fly away. And now over to Gary for the sport.

I finished the dishwasher and then noticed that the sink needed cleaning, and by the time I'd done that and crept upstairs for a load of laundry it was time to go for the croissants. The damp cold and the weight of the winter night on the sky reminded me of running. This time last year I had been going out at the same time, my breath my ghost companion as I ran through the sleeping streets and out across fields glazed with frost.

As I came back down the road, I saw that the kitchen light was on, ours the only house on the close showing signs of wakefulness, although at the bakery there had been two hollow-eyed dads pushing cheerful toddlers in buggies. It gets better, I wanted to tell them. One day you will not spend the first few hours of every Saturday waiting for the sun to rise so you can go to the playground. You will not be wanting your lunch before most people have had breakfast and indulging in wild fantasies involving four hours of uninterrupted sleep.

Emma had got up and dressed and was at the table with a cup of tea and her iPad. I kissed her, my lips cold on her mouth.

'I bought croissants. And I got you a pain au chocolat. Should still be warm, you should eat it before the girls come down.' I put down the bag and began to take plates from the

239

cupboard. 'We can have a romantic French breakfast to get the weekend off to a good start.'

She pulled her gaze from the screen. 'You're sweet. Thank you. Have you seen what they're saying about nurses? They have no idea, do they, none at all. They think—'

'Em?' I said. 'Could we maybe not talk about the health service? Just while we eat our croissants? I agree with you, you know that, but just for half an hour could you not be a doctor?'

I saw her face change. She is a doctor, the way priests are priests. It's not a suit that you put on to go to work and take off when you come home.

'I don't mean don't be a doctor. I mean don't be an employee. Let's not talk about institutions. Sorry, Em, I'm being daft. Here, more tea? We should talk about Christmas.'

As if talking about Christmas were ever a soothing bonding experience for a couple with parents and children. We had already agreed that we were not going to Emma's sister, not this year. Emma said it wasn't fair on Clare, having to do the whole thing year after year, their parents after twenty-five years of divorce still sniping over mealtimes and walks. I rather felt that Clare might have to continue to face the disadvantages of owning a six-bedroom house in a Cheshire commuter town, but Emma was looking thinner and more tired with every passing week and I couldn't bear the idea of her spending two of her four days off packing and travelling. And then the girls said no, not Aunt Clare's house, please not Aunt Clare's house, it's so boring and George is horrible and Uncle Rob watches sport all the time. So we were staying at home. Miriam's still fragile, we said, and Emma's working Christmas Eve, next year we'll all get together, maybe even rent a big cottage on the coast, take the pressure off Clare. (Next year, I thought, we will bugger off to Cornwall and see my dad, celebrate Hanukkah or the solstice in some ideologically and environmentally defensible manner, but I saw no reason to mention that plan while next year was twelve months away.)

Emma sipped her tea. 'I thought we could tell the girls we can do whatever they want as long it doesn't cost much and means we can start and end the day at home. We don't have to have turkey or Christmas pudding and you don't have to spend the day cooking.'

I opened the jam. Last year's, home-made with damsons from the side of the golf course. 'I really don't want to cook a turkey. Especially not for four of us. It'd be occupying the freezer for months.'

'I like the bits,' Emma said. 'Bread sauce and the little sausages and things.'

'They can all be made in advance. It could be a holiday activity. We could just have those.'

'Take them somewhere. A Christmas picnic.'

'Nowhere's open. Well, except on campus for the poor befuddled international students. And you know it will probably rain.' I imagined the four of us huddling on a bench beside the crater that is to be the Major Donor Business School, passing cold chipolatas under a driving rain and trying to convince each other that we were being radical. 'Let's just stay at home,' I said. 'We can go for a canal walk or something in the afternoon if Rose is bouncing off the walls.'

It's not a figure of speech, in Rose's case.

'Be nice to have a day off making them put their shoes and coats on, wouldn't it?' Emma broke her pain au chocolat in half. 'I'll save some for the girls, I shouldn't be having cake for breakfast anyway. By the way, I can do the party today, if you like.'

I looked at her. She, like most sane adults, loathes the carnival of mass greed and hyperactivity with which the first ten birthdays are celebrated, but she is also sensitive about her habitual absence from the school gates, and is occasionally moved to attempt to compensate by making ridiculous commitments to the PTA and dragging herself to Mums' Nights Out where the conversation is all about the inadequacy of husbands and she gets told repeatedly how lucky she is that I help her with the children and allow her to work full-time.

'Do you actually want to?' I asked. 'I mean, setting aside any – ah – idiosyncratic economies of guilt, absolution and cultural pressure frankly reminiscent of the medieval church that might be running in your head?'

She was eating her pastry! 'Do shut up about the medieval church. No. Really I want to take Mimi into the city for Christmas shopping and an edgy Bohemian lunch. I hate swimming. But you don't have to do all the boring things.'

I shrugged. 'I had loads of time with Mimi. And I don't think I'd recognise an edgy Bohemian lunch if I met it on the streets of Prague.'

'Yeah. Well, it was that and the changing room thing.'

'Oh.'

The changing room thing is that the father of daughters too young to be sent alone into the women's changing room with any serious expectation that they will emerge at the other end appropriately washed and attired and having left their clothes somewhere dry must take them with him into the men's room. Even stay-at-home dads who know how to use the delicates cycle on the washing machine and clean a toilet before it needs doing can't go into the women's changing room. The power dynamic between small girls and a room full of naked men is not, under these circumstances, the obvious way round, and the men don't like it, and can't get angry with the girls. Look here, mate, I'm not being funny, I've got my own little girl, but do you see her in here? I am fairly sure that the mothers of small boys have an easier time in the other room, although I know that is partly because the difference in social and political power between adult women and little boys is much smaller than the difference between adult men and little girls. I am not suggesting that it is generally, taking any view wider than that of a provincial leisure centre, better to be a woman.

'There'll be plenty of mums there,' I said. 'And if not, she'll just have to cope. It's not a reason for you and Mim to miss your lunch. Though good luck with the shopping.'

She shook her head. She'd stopped eating after less than half a pain au chocolat. 'Sherratt & Hughes. Credit card. Anyone who thinks they don't want books just hasn't found the right one yet. I'm not going anywhere else, it's two Saturdays before Christmas and I'll have a Marxist eco-warrior with me, I'm not stupid.'

'I never imagined that you were. Have a croissant.'

'I'm fine, thanks. I'm going to wake the girls or they'll stay up all night and we'll never get to talk.'

We could talk now, I thought, if you would stay at the table with me, if you would eat the breakfast I went out to buy for you, if you were capable, these days, of rest and food.

watching the kiddies like that

The pool was probably no worse than usual. You can smell the chlorine from the car park, which is quite reassuring once you get through the lobby with its vending machines – quick, replace any calories you might have used before you leave the building – past the desk where the angry women keep guard, down the barely lit stairs, through the paste of mud and hair on the changing room floors and out into the brutal lighting and echoing screams of the pool itself, where old plasters bob like driftwood against the handrails and toddlers pause furtively at the shallow end. It is odd that the aural effect of excited children at play is roughly what one might expect in one of the outer circles of hell. Adam, you don't have to get wet if you don't want to, Bella's mum had said, though if you don't mind staying that would be great, just in case any of the boys need taking to the loo or anything. It is my life's calling, I did not say, to escort other people's sons to the loo. It is my service to society.

I sent Rose into the women's changing room with her bag and clear instructions to find Bella's mum and follow Bella's mum's instructions to the letter, and then I waited in the lobby by the windows overlooking the pool, as if gazing into an enclosure at the zoo. Swimming pools, I thought, may be the only place in England where you can look at a person for several minutes without recognising his or her social class. I remembered a professor of English in Berlin telling me about an experiment in socio-linguistics which suggested that a Dane needs to speak Danish for four minutes before another Dane can guess his social background, level of education and regional identity. It is two minutes in France and about five seconds in England, and in fact I don't think we wait five seconds, I think we know before a word comes out and I dare say that someone more knowledgeable than I am would be able to make such a judgement by seeing a person in a pair of swimming trunks. But it is harder than when people are clothed. I saw Bella's mum appear in a pale blue swimming costume spattered like a curtain with pink roses and ruched across the breasts, looking as if she'd been getting dressed when fire broke out in a country cottage owned by the National Trust and had wrapped herself in the nearest vintage tablecloth on the way out. All right, harder than when men are clothed.

'Excuse me.' One of the angry women from behind the desk. Rose – an incident—

'Only we've had comments.'

I looked at her. Late middle age, older than me, wearing a green tracksuit with the leisure centre's logo embroidered over the left breast. Worn plastic shoes.

'Some of the mums don't think it's right, a man standing there watching the kiddies like that.' She glanced towards two young women standing with pushchairs at the door, one speaking on her phone and the other gazing at the screen of hers. 'Mentioned the police and all.'

I looked at them, at her, back at them. The one on the phone turned her back and the other looked away.

'I was waiting for my daughter,' I said. 'Waiting to see that my daughter had come through the changing room and was in the water with her friends. Then I was going to go sit in the gallery and do some work, because the birthday girl's mum wanted me to stick around in case any of the boys needed help with anything.' In case there are bad people there. Well, bad men, men like me who look at children, menace them with our gaze behind which anything at all could be going on in our heads, acts of depravity, thoughts about swimwear and the class system or an anxiety about running out of milk (which we would do if I didn't buy some on the way home).

'Well, I wouldn't hang about here if I was you. Giving the wrong impression, see.'

I looked at the women, who were probably calling on the body-building fathers of the children in the pushchairs to come and deal with the paedo hanging around the kiddies, who had perhaps already taken pictures of me to post on social networking sites.

'I'm looking for my daughter,' I said again.

'You said that. Where's her mum?'

Oh for— 'Having an edgy Bohemian lunch with my other daughter, last time I checked.'

Do you want me to phone her, I wanted to say, but after all nothing in this depressing encounter was the woman's fault. I saw Rose come out of the changing room, talking to Phoebe, whom she likes mostly for her long red hair, as if she might acquire it by association. Rose waved to me and I waved back.

'There she is,' I said. 'And now, if it won't upset anyone, I'm going to go sit in the gallery and read until I'm needed. Though I can't promise not to look up every so often.'

'I'd just be careful, if I was you. 'Cause most people would say you can't be too careful around kids. Not these days.'

Not her fault, not her fault, badly paid and tired and badly educated, only doing her job. It's men, I thought, men who can't be too careful around kids. If you get lost, I've told the girls, find a mum with children and ask her to help.

I went up to the gallery, took one of the red plastic seats on the top row, from which I could see the chewing gum and graffiti on the seats below. Kim loves Mikey. Meena gives head. Ben 4 Kayla 4 evah. I opened a book about the new towns of post-war England, the dreams of a new country to be built in concrete on the ashes of élitism and hereditary privilege, and despite the screams and splashes below me I was, more or less, concentrating on it by the time Molly's mum came running up the stairs, a towel wrapped around her like a strapless gown, wet footprints in her wake, to tell me that there had been an incident, that it was Rose.

the sense of doom

She had started to wheeze. She wasn't turning blue. You
could maybe see the dip in her throat sucking air the way Dr
Chalcott had told us to look for in Miriam, and you could see
her ribs rising and falling under the damp pink swimming
costume. Call an ambulance, I wanted to say, call a fucking
ambulance right now, get her some oxygen and charge the
defibrillator, because you can't be too careful with kids, not
when they're yours and they stop breathing. Call a fucking
geneticist, because the doctors told me this wasn't going to
happen and they were wrong, weren't they, they were wrong
and I was right. She was sitting on the side of the pool and
there were three mums around her, three mums and a first
aider and me, and a whistle in her chest that I could hear
from standing. She looked up at me with wide eyes and I
thought she's panicking, she's hyperventilating, and then I
remembered the sense of doom that is an early symptom of
anaphylaxis, or, as Mimi would say, a normal and indeed
desirable response to losing your airway—

'Find someone with a blue inhaler,' I said to the mums.

'Rosie-pose, you're OK, it's just a bit of wheeze, people often get them when they go swimming.'

Get her to say a sentence, if she can't finish a sentence we need an ambulance, although as Mimi says this rule does not allow for the length of some people's—

'It looked as if you were having a good time. Who were you playing with?'

She took a breath. 'Phoebe.'

The out-breath whistled.

'What were you playing at?'

'Otters.' Whistle.

'Tell me about the game.'

'I'm scared.' Wheeze on the in-breath. 'I can't breathe.' Whistle.

'You are breathing, sweetie. We're getting you some help. You're OK. Tell me about the game.'

I put my arm around her and over her head mouthed 'Ambulance' to Bella's mum.

It wasn't much of an incident, not really, not by Miriam's standards. Not once your definition of *serious* involves the use of a defibrillator and the deployment of the air ambulance to bring a doctor. Two of the other party guests had blue inhalers in their mums' handbags, and by the time I heard the siren in the car park and the men in green jumpsuits came purpose-fully to the poolside, outdoor shoes leaving grimy footprints on the tiles, there was still a descant to Rose's breathing but her sentences had more than one clause and she had expressed a desire not to miss the birthday tea. We'll just monitor her for a bit, they said, won't take her in unless we need to, we've got nebs in the back, but get her round to the GP first thing Monday, OK, Dad? Pop some clothes on for me now, love, and we'll just go sit in the ambulance for a while, I bet you've never been in an ambulance before, have you?

She stood up in her damp towel. You could see that her muscles and bones weren't working so hard, that breathing was coming almost naturally to her body. My sister has, she said, my sister stopped breathing and then her heart started fibrillating and— That's not what's happening to you, I said, you just had a little wheeze, now go with Phoebe's mum and get your clothes on and with any luck you'll be eating your chips with everyone else in half an hour. And then I went to wait in the lobby outside the women's changing room again, careful this time not to look at the kiddies or indeed at anyone else, careful to keep my gaze on my phone like a normal person.

a fire alarm in your head

I didn't call Emma. We were still afraid of our phones, still began every conversation with everything's OK. Everything's OK, I just forgot to put toothpaste on the list; everything's OK, only Rose is going to play with Molly so could you collect her on the way home. What would I say, while Rose ate pizza and chips with her friends, balloons drifting under their feet and a plastic banner reading Happy Birthday Bella blu-tacked to the breeze-block wall above their heads? Everything's OK but. But double jeopardy, we could lose them both. But whatever the research says, I was right, it's genetic, sorry. But don't leave your lunch, don't turn pale and sick and walk out of the bookshop leaving your arcane Christmas selections on the bestseller table, don't walk dazed through the crowded streets, Christmas music jangling like a fire alarm in your head, to the station where you will then have to await the next train home. Don't – this isn't it. One day, I would have to make that call, or receive it. But not now. I sat on a plastic chair in the corner of the room and watched the children. They were all breathing. Bella's mum put a paper cup full of sweet milky tea in my hand.

Try not to worry, Adam, they'd have taken her in if there was any concern, you do know that, you do know that lots of children wheeze a bit sometimes, she's maybe coming down with a cold, they're all exhausted, aren't they, by this time of year, such a long term, nearly twice as long as the summer term sometimes, when Easter's late, no wonder they get all these bugs, just in time for Christmas. Do try not to worry.

outlive

Rose seemed to have forgotten about it when Emma and Mimi got home. The party was fine, she said, did you buy all my Christmas presents, did you get everything on my list, what's in that big bag? Look, there was another of those bouncy balls in the party bag and mine's purple and glittery, look. Not in here, please, Emma said, we keep telling you, something will get broken, take it into the hall if you have to throw it around inside. Well obviously I have to throw it around inside, Rose said, because we don't have any outside space, do we, it would just bounce straight over the garden wall, and you won't ever let me play in the street although the cars move about as slowly as a slug and I'm not stupid, I can hear them coming, everyone else in my class is allowed to play out on their own. Enough, Rose, I said, put the cake in the fridge and take the rest of the party bag up to your room, give Mum and Mimi a chance to unpack their shopping, OK? And put your swimming things in the laundry, please. Hi, Mimi, good lunch? Yeah, she said, I'm going to put some things away.

I put the kettle on. Em, I said, Em, as you can see

everything's fine but Rose got a bit wheezy in the pool. No swelling or anything, no sense of doom, not that I could see, and it all settled with two puffs of Fatima's inhaler, but it did happen and Em, I'm sorry but she couldn't finish a sentence so I'm sorry but we called an ambulance but it was fine, everything's OK. Everything's OK, I did not say, because she already knew it, everything's OK except that it seems that neither of your children can be trusted to keep on breathing.

I saw her pause. Saw her body stop.

I saw her begin again. She reached into one of the book bags and pulled out a paperback promising to explain the previously unappreciated centrality of candles to the development of Western civilisation.

'For your dad.' She put the book on the kitchen counter, as if bargaining or beginning a game of chess. 'She was wheezing. Rose was wheezing.'

I rinsed the teapot. 'It started in the water, apparently. I wasn't there. I mean, I was there but I was watching from the gallery, Jo said no need for me to go in the water with them so I thought I'd do some reading, try to get back into— Anyway, Lucy came to find me. Ella's mum. It sounded quite—' Quite bad. As bad as Mimi's breathing has ever been. 'She was a bit scared. So we borrowed an inhaler but because she couldn't really finish a sentence and I thought I could see that chest thing, the tugging thing with the throat, I said call an ambulance. I mean, I could probably just have put her in the car and they weren't sure she really needed the nebs anyway, it seemed to be settling just with the inhaler but – well, they didn't seem to mind, anyway, they said I was right to call. But she's fine, Em. Ate lots of tea and did some running around, she's OK.'

Emma fiddled with Dad's book. 'Yes, she's OK now. Oh Christ, Adam.'

The kettle boiled and I filled the teapot. 'Yeah. I know. The paramedic said take her to the GP on Monday.'

Emma shook her head. 'They won't refer her anyway, they'll just give her an inhaler, it's not even enough for a diagnosis, one episode.'

I found the biscuit tin. However much lunch Emma had eaten, she needed more food. 'Em, how likely is it that she'll have anaphylaxis too? I mean, Mimi and my mother – I know they keep saying it's not that simple but it bloody looks it from here.'

She sighed. 'It's really not. The tendency to allergies is obviously hereditary but expression varies enormously. I mean, you've never had a reaction to anything, have you? And not everyone with asthma has obvious allergies and not everyone with allergies gets asthma, and fatal or near-fatal anaphylaxis is rare, and fatal or near-fatal exercise-induced anaphylaxis is pretty much unheard of so—'

I poured her a cup of tea. 'Yeah. I know. But I'm not really interested in the national mortality rate for exercise-induced anaphylaxis, I just want to know if Rose – I just want—'

She knows what I want. What we want. And being a doctor, she also knows that we can't have it. Your daughters are always going to be all right. They are going to have long and happy lives in safe places and enjoy good health far into old age; they are going to see your grandchildren and your grandchildren's grandchildren grow and live in wholeness and prosperity, and everyone will live happily ever after. That's what we want. Although try this: if you could know what is going to happen, if you could know the lives and deaths of your partner and your kids and yourself, if you could know their loves and losses, triumphs and failures, sicknesses and last moments, would you? No. You think you want a story, you think you want an ending, but you don't. You want life. You want disorder and ignorance and uncertainty.

'I'm going to put these presents away,' she said.

Mimi came down and sat on the sofa knitting while I cooked dinner. A hat for grandpa, she said, and look, she'd worked out how to do cables. He'll like that, I said, something hand-made. I chopped onions. Rose sat on the floor with my laptop and watched cats on the internet; don't worry, Dad, said Mimi, I'm keeping an eye on her. After a while, too long for her to have been on the loo or putting away presents, Emma came down and started to tidy up, rounding up Rose's floorplans for her dream home (an entire floor for the cats, just under the rooftop swimming pool) and letters from schools. Dear Parents and Carers, as part of our Curriculum Enrichment Programme we are taking Year 3 on a trip to the Canal Museum – volunteers and helpers welcome please! I stirred the onions, chopped garlic. Emma was moving around the room but there was a stiffness in her shoulders, something closed in her face, that reminded me of the early days in hospital.

We ate. Even less than usual, in Emma's case, and Rose already full of chips. Eat some salad, Rose, Emma said, never mind more carbs. Have an apple. Miriam talked about the new city library, and was amusing about their quest for the right place to have lunch. I passed on the gossip from the party: Holly's mum is starting a business up-cycling vintage clothes (yeah, said Mim, put a bird on it, or maybe a yappy dog in gingham), apparently Jack's dad's given up his job, sick of commuting to London and never seeing the kids, but Jo's going spare because he hasn't got anything to go to and you know they just moved house. Emma doesn't care, she never sees any of these people. Rose is sick too, she did not say, no-one is safe, breathe for me now both of you. Behind Miriam's and my inconsequential talk, I heard the wash of fear against the walls.

Emma washed up and tidied the kitchen to her own standards, which are different from mine, while I persuaded Rose to get into the shower, helped her to wash her hair and, with some difficulty, persuaded her to come out and dry herself: it's too cold, she said, you should turn the heating up, and for a moment I wondered if it was my fault she had asthma, if greater generosity in the matter of fossil fuels and the gas bill would have saved her lungs. No, if anything, less use of fossil fuels, less air pollution, would have saved her lungs. We suffocate our children with our cars. Although not as fast as our parents and grandparents and great-grandparents were suffocated with smog and coal fires and steam trains, it's worth bearing in mind. We are capable of improvement.

I dried Rose's hair and required her to stop capering about naked and complaining of the cold, put on her pyjamas and get into bed. I read her the next chapter of *The Railway Children*, about which she is lukewarm and I enthusiastic, more because I know the bedtime-reading alternatives are worse than because I whole-heartedly endorse its oddly bourgeois socialism: it is instructive to experience poverty and wrong to despise porters, but even so the happy ending consists of the reinscription of the middle-class norm with Daddy's return. I left her reading her preferred works about little girls and their ponies and went down to divide the Saturday newspaper and a box of mint chocolates with Mimi while Emma communed with her iPad, and then in the middle of reading about rising sea levels and melting ice, I found my mind composing a eulogy for Mimi, standing at the front of a crematorium's chapel trying to find words for her wit that were neither maudlin nor mocking, trying to find the sentences that would let her go. No. There she was, licking mint fondant from her fingers while she read the travel section. I swallowed, blinked and tried to finish the article, but after a few more sentences I went up to see how Rose was doing.

I woke in the night because Emma was crying. Trying to cry quietly, not to wake the girls, but her hair and pillow were wet from it. She was curled away from me so I curled around her, offered water, tissues, listening, but her back shook against me and she had nothing to say. I gave her all I had, which was my presence, and after a long time she turned into my arms and let me hold her while she sobbed. Shh, I said. Shh, it's all right.

No, she said, no, I don't want to lose them both, I don't want – I don't want – to outlive—

premonition

No ambushes with cups of tea and croissants in the morning. She was still asleep when I woke so I stroked her hair, propped myself up so I could see her hollow sleeping face. She was too thin, too tired. It was as if I had been given a premonition of her deathbed. I touched her forehead. No, I thought, this has to stop, the double secrecy of our terror. We say that we are learning from Miriam and not living in fear but it is not true; if we are protecting the girls we are not protecting ourselves, or each other. This is not how to live.

She woke up. Her eyes in mine, my eyes in hers, and without thinking about it, without reference to the story of our abstinence these past months, without telling myself that I should be full of ardour but not pushy, desirous but not demanding, I reached for her and she for me.

Afterwards, lying with my pyjamas wedged between her legs because it was so long since we'd had sex that I'd moved the bedside loo roll up to the girls' bathroom when they ran out, Emma rubbed her cheek on my chest. That was nice, she said, we should do that more often, and Adam, I have this ridiculous idea, this very persistent desire, I know it's quite mad but I keep wanting another baby, every time I see one at work—

I pulled the duvet up around her shoulders. It's not mad, I said, it's perfectly understandable, but you know it's not the right thing to do, it's the last thing the girls need, poor Mimi really doesn't have to know that her parents have sex and we've only got three more years of having her at home, we don't want to be distracted by a new baby, and anyway where would we put it, we'd have to move house and buy a bigger car, you'd have to take maternity leave again and it made you miserable both times—

And anyway, Em, you're forty-two and you just discovered that your children are mortal, how could you not want another baby, a back-up baby, an insurance against childlessness. You want a third chance, the magic occasion to get it all right. But you can't get it right, darling. With every birth, a new death comes into being. With every love, a loss. There is no back up, no alternative, no chance to change whatever plot we are living.

I know, she said, I told you it was mad, I'm not saying we should do it, I'm probably too old anyway, I don't think it would make me miserable now but we can't afford the maternity leave, I'd be sixty with a teenager, you're quite right that Mim and Rose need everything we can give them and more. I know perfectly well that babies don't solve problems. I'm just telling you I want one.

I kissed her. Thank you, I said, for telling me. Hey, do you think a cat would make a good substitute?

Not you as well, she said, don't you start. I'm going to get up now, shall I bring you a cup of tea?

If we had another child, it might be a son.

It might be healthy.

a Christmas scene

I had made Wienerschnitzel and sauté potatoes for dinner on Christmas Eve. It was a treat in my mostly-vegetarian childhood, a dish my mother would make once in a blue moon in homage to my father's occasional hankering for the food of his childhood. Mitteleuropa, blood attenuated by two Atlantic crossings and then the betrayal of my parents' marriage. Meat fried in breadcrumbs, of course the girls like it.

I upended the jar of sauerkraut from the Polish deli into a colander in the sink and rinsed it with cold water; Emma has passed her love of pickles to the girls.

'Dinner!' I called.

At Bryher Farm we had an old brass bell, and in the closing stages of cooking a child would be sent outside to swing it back and forth, a satisfying task particularly in the winter dusk when the sound seemed to shatter the chill under the bare trees and the fading sky.

'So,' I said. 'Are we doing anything differently this year? Mimi, will you come with me to the Cathedral? Midnight Mass?'

I wanted to see the angels, Hutton's angry angels, by night, their shadows ominous on the walls. I wanted to hear the voices rise past the concrete columns and sing under Spence's roof.

'Nope. It'll take more than coloured glass and old music to make me sign up to homophobia, misogyny and the grandfather of all patriarchal institutions.'

I took a mouthful of sauerkraut. Should have rinsed it again, or maybe soaked it in fresh water. 'I wasn't trying to sign you up to anything. I just want to see what it's like. For the project.'

She eyed me. 'Yeah, right. You're in no way willing to go along with an offensive ideology because you find the art and music pretty and because the whole caboodle fills you with nostalgia for the good old days of post-war socialism.'

'Fine, don't come. I was only offering.'

'Caboodle,' said Rose. 'Can I come? I'd like to see the angels.'

I looked at Emma. 'Maybe next year, sweetie. I won't be back till after midnight. Father Christmas might not come if you're not here in the middle of night.'

Rose and Miriam exchanged glances.

'Dad,' said Rose. 'I'm sorry to tell you this, but the thing is, I don't actually believe in Father Christmas. I know it's you and Mum.'

'She knew last year as well,' said Miriam. 'But she thought you'd be upset if she told you.'

I ate a potato. Good but maybe not worth the washing up. We never tried very hard with Santa. The logical flaws seemed overwhelming and Miriam at an early age decided that she objected strongly to the alleged presence of a strange man in her bedroom at night. For a while, Santa brought presents to the door once she was asleep, knocking like a normal person and asking the adult who answered kindly to put them in one of my red hiking socks left on the fake mantelpiece over the fake fireplace unconvincingly situated on an internal wall. Rose had not yet started school when Mimi told us not to bother any more. Fine, we said, but don't tell your sister; it was more surprising that she had waited four years than that she had, in the end, told.

'Why did you think we'd be upset, Rose?' Emma asked.

Rose ate some meat. 'Because Molly in my class told her parents she knew it was a lie and she said her mum actually cried. And Lily's mum told her not to tell her dad she didn't believe it any more because he'd be really sad.'

'We're not sad,' I said. 'It's just part of growing up. And we want you to grow up.'

Emma pushed her potatoes around. 'Do you mean that all the kids are pretending to believe in Santa to protect their parents?'

'To protect their parents' weird ideas about childhood,' Mimi said. 'Because even the eight-year-olds have worked out that they're supposed to be performing some—'

'Kind of,' Rose said. 'I mean, some of my class probably still thought it might be real until the rest of us said it wasn't. School made us write letters to Santa, see, and Jack said it was silly to write to someone who didn't exist and then Mrs Wasley tried to shut him up but you know what it's like trying to shut Jack up and anyway they can't stop us talking at playtime. Ellie woke up and saw her mum putting things in her stocking and Bella's big brother told her two years ago it wasn't true.'

'—some creepy, profit-driven adult fantasy. It's completely toxic, the attitude to children in this country, it's no wonder we're all mentally—'

'Why "we"?' asked Rose. 'You keep saying you're not a child. And you never believed in Santa, you said so.'

'I'm legally a child. It's really stupid, I'm a child if I want control of my own body, like for example consenting to medical treatment or having sex but I'm an adult if I commit—'

'You're not,' I said. 'Even in this country, the criminal justice system doesn't treat a fifteen-year-old as adult. Not in theory, anyway.'

'Why would you want to have sex?' asked Rose. 'You're too young to make a baby.'

Pause.

'It's not just about babies,' said Emma. 'When people are grown-up and ready and in a secure relationship and *over sixteen*, Mimi, it feels good. Grown-ups sometimes do it for fun. Anyway, no Santa. Does that mean no stockings and we'll do all the presents after lunch?'

I drank a glass of water and did not look at Miriam.

'Let's have stockings,' said Rose. 'So I can eat the chocolate coins before breakfast. But don't give me a tangerine, I can always get one from the bowl if I want it, and you don't have to put out a mince pie or any of that. Actually, don't bother with the hiking sock, I just want the chocolate when I wake up.'

'Mim?'

'To be honest, I'd rather have a lie-in.'

'OK,' I said. 'That's easy.'

So there was no Father Christmas, no last-minute search for wrapping paper different from the one in which we'd wrapped the other presents, no arrangement of crumbs on the plate from which Santa was said to have eaten, no carrot for the reindeer. I saw Rose into bed, read to her, looked in on Mimi who was lying on her bedroom floor because the bed was covered with books and clothes, reading a probably ill-advised text from the university library about Islamic feminism and listening to music reminiscent of hyenas enraged by a demented percussionist.

Downstairs, Emma was taping up the last few presents and arranging them under the tree, which although barely shoulder-high on Rose seemed to take up half the floorspace. I held down paper points while she taped them: books, knitting wool and some expensive-looking makeup for Miriam, books, craft supplies and a reprinted early-twentieth-century book of paper dolls and paper villages to cut out and assemble for Rose.

'Will she play with those?' I asked. I could see the appeal – rose-wreathed cottages and frilled pinafores, even a paper kitten on a patchwork cushion – but not necessarily the appeal to Rose.

'I think she'll enjoy the cutting out and assemblage.'

Yeah, I thought, and then they'll sit in her room not being played with but being hand-made and pretty and therefore too precious to throw away. It doesn't matter. They bring pleasure. One of the cottages opened to display a Christmas scene, a tree decorated with candy sticks and candles, cards over a mantelpiece where a log fire grew flames in autumn shades.

'I thought I'd make that fig and poppy-seed challah,' I said. 'For tomorrow's breakfast. And we can take the rest of it on our walk for when Rose needs a snack.'

Which is usually about fifteen minutes after leaving the car.

'How perfectly appropriate. You can leave it to rise while you go to Midnight Mass.'

The challah dough did indeed prove while I stood in the Cathedral contemplating the dark shadows of Hutton's angels huge on the walls, while I rose to my feet and sang with the congregation and the organ. Yea, Lord, we greet thee, born this happy morning. Before I went to bed I plaited the loaf, following the photos in the book because I had never seen my mother do it, because I had never seen the Shabbat candles lit on a Friday night or heard the blessing said. Did you ever think of converting, I would have asked my mother, did you ever think that raising me Jewish could have mollified Dad's ancestral voices? Did you – perhaps as the sense of doom became a wall rushing towards you and the waters closed over your head – understand that without you, the rest of Dad's life would be passed in exile from the diaspora, in double alienation? I covered the loaf with a clean tea towel and left it to rise again; you cannot mend history by cooking.

I did not then steal into the girls' rooms to fill their stockings as parents all over Britain were doing at that moment, and I did not wake early to butter a turkey and put it in the oven. We slept late, breakfasted slowly, and Rose, it turned out, knew enough of the art of deferred gratification to tolerate at least the first three-quarters of a walk along the canal before we returned to presents, to a modest lunch and later a dinner requiring no outrageous labours of anyone. We lit the pudding three times because the blue flames, really, were the point; no-one wanted to eat more than a token spoonful, a secular communion with everyone else in these isles gathered around their tables with the curtains drawn and wrapping paper littering the floor.

who would voluntarily relinquish hours in the company of our children, of a girl who in the best case would be leaving us in three years' time. It crossed my mind now sometimes to wonder how Emma told herself the story of the girls' pre-school years, whether she ever wished she had not hurried back to work before either of them sat up, ate solid food, pronounced their first words. (Not, in either case, a flattering 'dada' but, in both cases, 'no' which is all a baby really needs, and the basis of every useful utterance for weeks to come. *No* coat, *no* pushchair, *no* bath, *no* seatbelt, *no*.) I wondered whether she ever wished she had understood then what I believe she saw now: the clichés that turn out, in the face of death, to be the truth.

Rose and I made another chocolate cake and tried to ice it before it had fully cooled so that some of the icing ran off the edge, like a mudslide, and some soaked into the cake, and then Mimi tried to redeem it with hundreds-and-thousands and then Emma tried to redeem that with buttercream until Sophie observed that the overall effect resembled a cow-pat from a cow that had been eating polystyrene balls. A cow wouldn't eat polystyrene balls, Rose said, and if it did they wouldn't make it through four stomachs with the pretty colours intact, not that she'd ever seen polystyrene in pretty colours, and Sophie said she didn't mean it literally and Rose said they'd done similes at school and a simile should still make sense. I suggested fudge ice-cream to go with the cake and caught Mimi's eye while she was still putting together a bovine and/or digestive simile for fudge ice-cream. Rose fell asleep on the sofa before eleven and couldn't be fully woken an hour later, Sophie said something that made Charlotte cry while they were all up in Mimi's room and since Charlotte's parents didn't want her to have even a very weak Buck's Fizz, we left the champagne in the fridge rather than upset her again. Ordinariness. Ordinary children having ordinary feelings about ordinary things. Normal life very nearly indistinguishable from the version of normality in which people keep breathing as a matter of course.

But not quite.

clinical observation

Some days later, Emma returned to work and I took the girls to the Respiratory Medicine Clinic, where they had appointments two months earlier than originally offered because Emma had told me to phone every Monday and Thursday to ask about cancellations. Familiar now with hospital canteens, I packed lunches. Familiar now with outpatient clinics, where they order several patients to arrive at the same time and then see them in an order that cannot be as arbitrary as it appears, I packed books and paper and pens for the girls, assembling a small bag for each of them so that they could feel ownership and control of some discrete thing, and all this reminded me of plane journeys. We would fly again, I thought, maybe even, with my income this year, this summer.

They started with Miriam, two nurses taking her weight and height and shouting the numbers across the corridor, past the chairs where people waited. Don't you think, Mimi said, that for some girls actually having your weight announced like that might be quite upsetting? Especially if you're weighing people with their coats and shoes on so the numbers are going to be high? Well, said the nurse, now someone's not backward about coming forward, no lack of confidence there. Mimi looked to me. No, I should have said, we're lucky, she's assertive and straightforward and not, by the way, rude; we're blessed with a girl who will speak on behalf of those who don't share her confidence and she's also, on this occasion, right. Oh, I said, hey, you've grown, you'll be overtaking me before long. A manifestation of the miraculous resurrection of the cells in her body that had stopped and begun to die a few weeks earlier. Me too, said Rose, I've grown, I know because I need new school shoes for tomorrow. Right, I said, OK, I suppose we'd better go to the shoe shop on the way home, would have been helpful if you'd mentioned that earlier.

We waited. I watched the other families, mostly of course mothers and children because mostly of course the dads were at work. Or had never been around, or had stopped being around, would never know the daytime world of children and women. The waiting, the passing of the time, the knowledge that children and women can always wait, have nothing better to do, not until the school run. Most of the mums were in rapt communion with their phones, either immersed in the lives of people more active than themselves or reporting on their own passivity. Still waiting, over an hour, kids fretful. Who would care for second-hand boredom? The children fiddled with their bodies, as pent-up children will, picked their noses, fingered their ears, bit their nails. *Sit still, will you. Can you not just sit there, just for a minute. Just let me do this and then I'll—* The smaller children pressed the buttons on plastic toys that made strange exclamations in American accents and sang in synthesised voices that became more sinister with repetition. There were no windows, not even a view of brick walls and sky. It was too hot, and there was a heaviness in the air, a smell of bleach and putrefaction, that made it seem a different gas from the one outside, as if hospitals had their own elements.

Boredom, for example, and fear. Come on, I wanted to say to the girls as I grabbed their hands, let's run for the airport, let's go see some big skies in Wyoming and Montana, let's hop on a train to London and hang out under the great dome at the British Museum, let's get in the car and follow signs for The North. I'll buy you lobster and chips, knickerbocker glories, candyfloss in purple and green. I'll buy you rainbow-striped jumpers and T-shirts with swearing on the front, patent boots and blue hair dye.

I got up, suddenly sickened by the dirt ingrained in the plastic chair under my thighs. There were the usual posters about cutting down on sweets and fizzy drinks, not smoking around babies and phoning the number below if you were worried about your drinking. There were the usual racks of leaflets about conditions that aren't the one you thought you had, reasons why your occasional headaches or digestive troubles might be symptoms of fatal disease. Rose was reading *The Worst Witch*, as if for the first time, and Miriam, although holding a novel that called itself an 'eco-thriller' in one hand and an apple in the other, was watching the scrolling text on the screen over my head. Ten reasons to get a flu jab, five ways to lose weight, call this number for help giving up smoking. Preferable, Emma would say, to a healthcare system invested in profit from your sickness, and I would, almost always, resist the desire to point out that a wide range of alternative systems are associated with better results and indeed fewer smokers, drinkers and fat people.

'Miriam Gold – Goldsmid?'

Goldschmidt. My father changed it back from Goldsmith, which his parents had considered safer for a would-be American family in the late 1940s, and I, for once, used my cultural capital, my inherited double exile, to insist that my children should bear my name. There are, after all, plenty of

Wilsons. Somewhere in my ancestry, I like to think, running through my veins, is a real goldsmith, a man in a long coat and a yarmulke hunched over small confections of gold and bright stone in the back streets of Vienna.

Dr Ruthven. Shorter than me, dapper, pink cheeks and thick grey hair, suit and tie, though they're not supposed to wear ties, or sleeves below the elbow. He stayed behind his desk, holding a file of notes and continuing to read them when we had occupied the row of plastic chairs against the wall. Rose resumed *The Worst Witch*. There was no window in this room either.

'Right,' he said. 'So. Chalcott wanted you to see me. Seems to think Miriam had an anaphylactic episode.'

Mimi's eyes widened.

'She was in cardiac arrest,' I said. 'Secondary to respiratory arrest. She needed CPR and an AED.'

'Well, some kind of funny turn, I gather. Not unusual in girls of that age, I must say.'

Mimi looked at me again. Say something, Dad, stand up for me.

'Dr Ruthven,' I said. 'I don't think there's any question – I mean, surely the notes—'

He lifted his hand. 'And then Rose had a transient wheeze. I'm a little surprised at your GP for making the referral. Still. Any more trouble from Miriam?'

'Not since she was discharged. But she was in for two weeks and most of that—'

'Right. And just the one episode for Rose.'

'Yes, but it was sudden and seemed quite—'

'So what did you think I would be able to do for you?'

'I'm worried it might be genetic,' I said. I glanced at the girls: Grandma drowned when she went swimming alone in big waves, long ago when Dad was only a couple of years older

273

than you are now, Rose, and it was very sad but after a while you can remember people quite happily.

He sighed. 'Asthma is very common and yes, it does seem to run in families. Do you ever have trouble with your breathing, Mr Goldschmidt?'

'No.'

'No allergies or hayfever?'

'Hayfever. But nothing like Miriam's—'

'There we go. Asthma's not dangerous when it's properly controlled, and it's not hard to control. But we certainly wouldn't diagnose it in – Rose, is it? – on the basis of one event. Carry an inhaler, that's my advice. Anything else?'

Last chance.

'Mim, would you mind taking Rose out? Just for a minute?'

Dr Ruthven sighed.

Mimi raised her eyebrows but ushered Rose out and closed the door.

Dr Ruthven looked at his watch.

'I'm sorry. I'll be quick. My mother drowned while swimming in the sea in her mid-thirties. She was sober and a strong swimmer, also a known asthmatic. One daughter, also a known asthmatic, very nearly died of exercise-induced anaphylaxis. The other one had an asthma attack while swimming. Do you see, Dr Ruthven, why I'm worried?'

He leant back. 'Your GP is the person to see about anxiety, Mr Goldsmith. I'm sure she'll be able to help you. Not my bag, I'm afraid.'

I should have gathered the tatters of my dignity and left. I should have thrown a chair at his head.

'I was just wondering if there's a connection. If Rose is also at risk.'

He turned his chair back to his computer screen, called up the details of the next patient.

'Clearly there's a connection, but we can only go on clinical observation, and my clinical observations are that your daughters are well. And now if you don't mind—'

'Yes,' I said. 'Sorry.'

Stop fucking apologising, you wimp.

Everything felt fragile again on the train home, all the work on the new normality jeopardised. Hospital visits would become normal, I thought. It is simply not possible to live in a state of acute fear and shock for more than a couple of weeks, and so the mind finds a path, a story, a way onwards. Shock is by definition transient, even when the shocking thing is here to stay. I remembered the other families in the waiting room, their narratives also broken. I used to think that there were ordinary families, like us, and then there were the families on the news to whom terrible things happened, an ordinary enough reading of the world, well designed to protect from fear, the same distinction made by the people who say they can't imagine what we must be going through. Oh yes you can, exactly what you would be going through under the same circumstances, but it's quite understandable that you don't want to imagine it. I looked around the carriage at the late commuters with their phones and newspapers, one or two sleeping open-mouthed with their heads against the dirty windows. Fifty people in this carriage, sixty, and some of them would be carrying horrors no-one wants to imagine. Missing children, suicides, incurable degenerative diseases of the mind and body. Violence, addiction, road accidents and house fires. Many of us, in fact, have learnt to sicken at the sound of sirens, for one reason or another. There is a large overlap between ordinary families and those to whom terrible things have happened. It is possible, necessary, to be both.

start again

The girls went back to school, and on the first day I went running again. It had been too long, of course; by my age, you can't stop running for three months and expect to return immediately to your usual routes, north out of town past the Victorian villas and then the inter-war semis with their Tudorbethan beams and front gardens paved over for parking, out across the fields and up the hill from which you can see sunlight on the corduroy contours of ploughed fields and the spires of village churches rising from stands of beech and yew as in the fantasies of Tory politicians and junior aristocrats in the trenches of Flanders. Down the lane – 50 mph and no pavement, to be attempted only between rush hours and by daylight on days when death feels unlikely – towards Old Millerton, where the fruit trees spreading their skirts across old stone walls are perfectly groomed and the very drainpipes kept freshly coated in shades of business attire, as if the Queen were daily expected. There is a fourteen-year-old boy buried in the graveyard there, three years dead and fresh flowers changed twice a week because what else can you do, what other service can replace the washing of socks and the cooking of dinners, the nagging about untidiness and the need to pack schoolbags the night before? On, anyway, over fields now raw as a fresh cut but in summer high with wheat rippling like water troubled by wind, fields bounded now by the kind of red-brick houses that manifest plastic conservatories in which nothing is conserved but sofas and pink toys, round the back way to the canal, along which you can run as far as you like, mile after mile, the city one way and Oxford the other, until thought falls under the rhythm of feet and lungs, until there is only the pacing of the mind.

Not today. I'd been cold on the school run, had worried about Mimi's refusal to wear a coat and the disappearance of one of Rose's mittens. My running jacket was still on its peg, under an accumulation of winter coats. The last time I'd worn it was the morning Miriam stopped breathing, barely an hour before the phone call, and it still smelt of the sweat of that innocent body. I put it on, laced my shoes, took the earbuds out of the pocket. So sweat some new sweat. Start again.

algorithms for seeing

He had sketched a vaulted roof, its geometry dictated by his mathematical grid and its presence somehow natural, mandated by the fact of an English cathedral. When he and the engineer, Ove Arup, came to discuss the roof, he realised that he hadn't thought about it properly. It was decorative and structural and that wasn't enough, not for something that was going to last five hundred years. He played with his ideas and nothing sang to him, not until he separated the structural roof from the decorative vaults, like the inner and outer walls of a tent. Then he began to see the vaults taking the geodetic form of the fuselage of Wellington bombers – he must, I thought, surely have known that a new consignment of Wellingtons remained grounded at a nearby air base on the night of Coventry's blitz because the Air Force didn't want to risk exposing their base or losing their new kit? Too expensive, Arup said, and how are you planning to integrate the columns?

Then he saw a photograph of a fly's eye in the *National Geographic* magazine, magnified in a way that would have been impossible before the war, part of the new vision of the world enabled by the technologies of war. Yes. Organic facets, the mathematical juggling of light and shade. Algorithms for seeing.

Now the concrete columns had to change, had to say something that would connect the marble floor with the flies' eyes above. They ran the sums again, and found that now each column carried surprisingly little weight. They could taper towards the floor, like table-legs. (I am not worthy so much as to gather up the crumbs under thy table, murmurs the liturgy in my ear, but only say the word and I shall be healed.) They could be star-shaped. But he didn't want concrete landing on marble. Some punctuation at the meeting point. Glass spheres. Light made solid, sand and heat made liquid, and the astonishment of seeing a cathedral apparently standing on glass, on light, on nothing at all.

But no glass manufacturer could guarantee a lifetime of five centuries. Bronze, then, after all.

all just fantasy and self-congratulation

Emma came home early, while I was cooking and also test-
ing Rose on her eleven times table and also trying to make
sure that Mimi was doing her homework without making it
obvious that I was trying to make sure that Mimi was doing
her homework, because then she would have diverted her
energies from homework into arguing about whether she or
I had more invested in her future and therefore more responsibility for decisions about doing or not doing homework, and
whether homework was in fact principally a technique of
social control for the unruly energies of teenagers, intended
to keep them from taking to the streets in protest against the
manifest injustices of modern Britain with busy-work backed
up by the threat of detention, which is probably a violation of
habeas corpus anyway, not that teenagers in this country have
even the eroded and partial human rights still just about
accorded to adults of the right colour and in possession of the
right passport. She was lying on her front on the floor with
her neck at a horrible angle, propped up on her elbows and
still somehow able to type on the laptop staring her in the
face. Sit at the table, I wanted to say, you'll ruin your back,

you've got a perfectly good desk upstairs, but I knew that at the same age I too had scorned furniture as the manifestation of middle age.

'Nine elevens, Rose.' I had sharpened the knives that afternoon and was able to chop the garlic fast, like a chef.

'How's it going, Mimi?'

'Fine. Geography.'

'Ninety-nine. Why do elevens do that?' asked Rose, who was fiddling with Mimi's knitting needles in a way that was going to cause trouble.

'Dunno,' I said. 'Eleven twelves.'

Mimi rolled her neck. 'Ow. Because we work in base ten.'

'Tell her later,' I said. 'Get your homework done. Rose, do you have anything else?'

'History. We're doing the Mayflower.'

I sliced open the peppers and pulled out their hearts. 'Are you now. Not the Blitz or the Victorians?'

The Victorians were primarily concerned with fashion, writing on slates and wholesome toys like hoops and spinning tops. Don't mention the Empire, child labour, working conditions or the rise of socialism and the trades unions.

Mimi looked up. 'Let me guess, the Mayflower was a lovely old wooden ship chartered by brave men in funny hats and their wives in pretty dresses who had heard about a beautiful country across the sea, a place where red apples glowed on the trees in the day-long sunshine and corn sprang from rich ground. They sailed across a bright blue sea whose waves were only high enough to please the children with the ship's movement, and soon came to a wooded coastline where they built sweet little log cabins. After a while some interesting Noble Savages with feathers on their heads—'

I added the chopped peppers to the pot. 'Don't tell me you've been reading Rousseau.'

'Who? No, Edward Said. You told me to, remember?'

'Go on,' said Rose.

'Oh God, can't you even recognise a parody? I was joking, Rose. It was more like, a bunch of religious fundamentalist nutjobs whose ideas threatened the equally fundamentalist nutjobs running England and most of Europe at the time pissed people off to the point at which—'

'Mim, don't use that language in front of Rose, please.'

'Fine, you tell her.'

I stirred the vegetables. I was making a kind of pasta sauce.

'OK. So in the sixteenth century, England was ruled by the King or Queen, and the King or Queen had a lot more power than the Queen does now. One of the ways for the monarch to stay in power was by working with the Church, because in those days everyone had to go to church every week and everyone who wanted to be allowed to live in peace either believed what the Church told them or pretended to believe it. So the Church supported the monarchy and the monarchy supported the Church, and between the two of them, almost everyone was under control, partly because the Church and the King also owned a lot of the land.'

'Still do,' said Mimi.

'Do your Geography, Mim.'

Rose fiddled with Mimi's knitting again. 'I liked Mimi's story better.'

Mimi looked up. 'Yes, of course you did, because I was telling you a fairy tale and everything was pretty. That's how it works. It's like liking sweets although they're really bad for you. It's like all the fucking baking—'

'Mimi—'

'It's the idea, Rosie-pose, that if you give people pleasure they won't go looking for truth. You'd rather have a story about shiny apples and long dresses than listen to Dad talking

282

about monarchy and power. Most people'd rather watch posh girls twiddling around with pastry than learn about what the food industry's doing to our generation. There's no point in history if it's all just fantasy and self-congratulation.'

So she does listen to me. Even if she then appropriates what I say.

'It's like – sorry, Dad, but it's true – it's like Dad and his Arts and Crafts stuff and now the Festival of Britain Cathedral gubbins, it's just ways of not thinking about how crap things are now.'

Jesus.

'No, Mimi, it's ways of thinking about how things could have been different. Understanding why they're crap now. If they are.'

'Yeah, *could have been* different. Not *could be*.'

'How's the Geography?'

'Nearly done. Only I can't find flights from Turkey.'

'Flights from Turkey?'

'She asked us to plan and budget for a round-the-world trip. We have to say why we want to go where we want to go and then research the countries.'

I could feel a stone in my belly. 'Imaginative assignment. Go on.'

'So I'm doing post-conflict zones, and then I thought by the time I'm old enough to do this Syria will be post-conflict, probably, I mean if only because the Russians—'

'Tell me you've not been working out how to get to Syria. Not on the same computer on which you were looking at nuclear whatevers whenever it was.'

She looked up. 'Yeah.'

'Fuck it, Mim—'

'Da-ad! You said it!'

'Sh, Rose. Mimi, have you any idea – Christ almighty.'

There was someone at the door. No, they can't be that fast. Surely. It's not as if she'd bought a fucking ticket.

Emma. Home early. Again?

I went into the hall. 'Em? Everything OK?'

Three years ago, a patient made a personal complaint against her and she came home early and sat at the bottom of the stairs weeping in front of the girls.

'Yes, fine, why wouldn't it be?'

Let me count the ways.

'No reason. You're early.'

She took off her shoes. 'No, just not late.'

'For the second night in a row. I haven't even finished cooking.'

She kissed me. A proper kiss.

I responded, put my oniony hands up her top.

'Mm. Later.'

'Yeah. Em, Mimi's been looking up flights to Syria.'

'What?'

'For her Geography project. Try telling that to the police.'

Mimi came to the door. 'Dad's totally freaked out. I can show the police my homework, can't I? If they come knocking, which they won't.'

'Just like those poor bloody MA students showed the police their homework. Yeah, great.'

'So Dad's turning himself into an arm of MI5, which is exactly how it's meant to work, isn't it? Make everyone so scared of the police that they start acting like the bloody police. Might as well close down the universities now.'

'Excellent,' said Emma. 'Just an ordinary evening in homes up and down the land. I'm going to change my clothes.'

I stood in the hall for a moment, breathing.

In the kitchen, Mimi had opened tins of tomatoes and chickpeas and added them to the pan.

'Dad, if I finish cooking this will you make another of those soufflés?'

I had made two soufflés the week she came out of hospital, when I was bending all the magic I could raise to her enchantment. Look, is not life worth living when four eggs in their brown shells can rise to such a substance?

'They don't always work,' I said. 'It was a bit of a fluke to pull it off twice.'

'Try again.'

'OK. If there are enough eggs. Have a look in the fridge for me?'

'Imagine the fridge says no.'

Rose looked up from her drawing of a lovely old wooden ship chartered by brave men in funny hats. 'Yuck. Squishy eggs out of hens' bottoms.'

'Vaginas,' said Mimi. 'Actually I think they might be cloaca, in hens. You came all squishy out of Mum's vagina.'

'So did you.'

We did have enough eggs, and a lemon that needed using. 'Stop it, both of you. That's a feeble insult, we all came out of our mums' vaginas, you could say it of any mammal.'

'Including cats,' said Rose. 'Why can't we—'

'Mimi, I'll make the soufflé if you'll help with the washing up.'

'I'm cooking,' she said. 'I've got homework. You don't make Rose help with the washing up.'

'That's because I'm younger than you and I get very tired after dinner and need to go in my bed. Also, I can't reach the tap.'

I started to crack eggs. Emma came and put her arms around me from behind and Rose said ewww and Mimi said awww.

285

waters of the River Creuse

They had trouble with the tapestry. As William Morris could have told them, an artist who doesn't do his own weaving is giving hostages to fortune, but William Morris never made a tapestry twelve metres wide. Graham Sutherland had worked with the Edinburgh Tapestry Company before, for the famous Wading Birds tapestry, and he wanted the same people for Christ in Glory. Spence asked them to weave the Calf, one of the Four Beasts of Revelation, as a test piece, and they failed. The colours were wrong, he said, the drawing bad, and when Sutherland came from London he agreed. 'Disappointment and friction all around,' Spence says.

They went to France, first to Paris, to consult Madame Cuttoli, who had commissioned all the tapestries they'd seen in Antibes years earlier. Her apartment was full of Picassos, bought for a few francs to help the artist before the war, and also commissioned work from Braque, Matisse and Léger. She sent her visitors to a company called Pinton Frères, near Aubusson, where they set their dyes in the alkaline-free waters of the River Creuse as the Aubusson weavers had been doing for centuries. The Pinton family had a loom large enough for the whole work, five hundred years old, made of the trunks of two trees that were already full grown when the band of brothers fought upon St Crispin's Day.

Christ in Glory took as long to weave as the Cathedral to build. Sutherland kept going to ground, not responding to Monsieur Pinton's letters, and when Spence and his wife stopped at Aubusson on their way to Lake Maggiore in 1958, Spence had to tell Pinton to go ahead and do his best on a trial without Sutherland's supervision. Sutherland appeared in Paris, expressed himself satisfied, and the weaving of the whole piece began in June 1959. Only the future, Spence writes, holds the results of this great adventure.

the massed ghosts of England

Emma took a week off work and we rented the same cottage as the previous year and went to Cornwall for half-term. Dad does invite us to stay with him, and I'm sure would make every effort to contain his need for solitude and quiet, but his idea of a simple life is Emma's idea of a primitive one, and she's right that washing clothes and dishes by hand is an easier proposition for a single adult than for a family. It is my holiday, she says, and I want the arrangements to be at least as comfortable and convenient as they are at home. She loves grand hotels, and before the girls came would save for months for a few days in the kind of place where they leave chocolates on the pillow while you're having dinner and change the flowers on the dressing table daily. I do not point out that the washing of clothes and dishes invariably falls to me.

I enjoy the fact that the road the Romans built to connect Lincoln and Exeter is still the fastest route from our house to Dad's. It's not safe for running or cycling, but I never drive it without thinking of the hands that built it and the feet that walked it two thousand years ago. Roman legions, I say, imagine them shivering and swearing here in their sandals, although in reality it seems unlikely that with four hundred years to get used to the weather, they were still wearing sandals in February. Yes, Dad, say the girls, we know, you told us last time. And the time before. But the Romans never made it into Cornwall, I say, mostly to myself. Too wild. We'll overtake them at Exeter.

I drive on the way to Cornwall. That's just how it is. I settled into the swoops of the road, which tackles any gradient rather than bend, felt my spirits rise as we crossed the border between the red-brick Midlands and the honey stone Cotswolds. Most of these towns – Moreton-in-Marsh, Stow-on-the-Wold – stink of money and smugness now, full of shops selling bits of wrought iron and old cake tins painted matt grey by women called Persephone, or cheese made from the unpasteurised milk of endangered goats belonging to retired pop stars. But a hundred years ago, the little double-barrelled villages were dying on their feet, the young fleeing childhoods of hunger and barely paid field-labour for something nearer a living wage in the cities, and there were alternative communities of artists and makers taking over the once-glorious houses of wool merchants, spinners and dyers. William Morris at Kelmscott, the Ashbees at Chipping Campden, Charles Wade at Snowshill, all remaking Englishness in bearable form. They are still there, somewhere, behind the Range Rovers and the Agas and the silly cheese. Still bathing naked in the lakes and walking the fields in hand-dyed smocks, undermining the local clergy and upsetting the ladies of the manor, paying living wages and treating their craftsmen as human beings.

I flicked a glance over my shoulder at Miriam. Reading. She reads until she is about to be sick and we have to stop, and as soon as we set off again she opens the book again. She prefers, she says, nausea to boredom, and no, our conversation does not constitute a third way, not for six hours. I couldn't see or hear Rose, directly behind me.

'Rose? You OK?'

'Yes.' She sounded surprised, although it wasn't the first time I'd asked her. Are you breathing well, do you feel at all wheezy, do you want an inhaler? Do you have a sense of impending doom? Stop it. Contain the fear in your own head, don't let it seep like fumes through the car. Miriam would have noticed, wouldn't she, if her sister had collapsed back there? (No, not if she liked what she was reading, in which case a cloud of purple-frosted cupcakes could flit around the car on sparkling silver wings and she wouldn't look up.)

Yes, I thought, we had inhalers for both girls, Mimi had her epipen, she was wearing her medical ID bracelet, and if she lost the pen Emma could always write a private prescription for another. (No, Em would say, no, I can't, we get into trouble for that kind of thing, there are other ways, but she could and would rather than leave Mim in jeopardy.) There isn't a chemist in the village, not any more, but the big supermarket on the main road probably has one and if not there's Helston. Chalcott had, after all, not only allowed but encouraged us to go on holiday. Just carry the pen, he'd said, and don't let her exercise alone, not until we have some idea what the trigger food might be. Though we might never know. At the cottage and along the coast, all the places I wanted to go, the ambulance response time would be more than ten minutes, more than enough time for a person in respiratory arrest to die, but that was why we had the pen and they'd send the helicopter if we needed a blue-light transfer. We were in the jurisdiction of the John Radcliffe in Oxford now, I thought, though there's a community hospital at Moreton where they could probably stabilise her, and the next tertiary ones would be Bristol, probably, and then Exeter? The layers of geography: Romans, wool merchants, intentional communities, paediatric respiratory medicine wards. In each new place, I could make a new emergency plan and then push it out of sight, but the problem with travelling was that the plan was unstable. It will be better, I thought, when we get there. Our future holidays will have to consist of going and staying somewhere. No Orient Express. No Great American Road Trips. Not that we will ever now be able to get travel insurance for a Great American Road Trip. We were coming down the hill into Bourton-on-the-Water, known to the Oxfordshire Tourist Board as the 'Venice of the Cotswolds' and to us as Bring-on-the-Revolution.

There is a traffic light controlling the flow of cars over a fifteenth-century stone bridge with gargoyles and carved foliage; I stopped with a shiny burgundy Range Rover behind me and a shiny scarlet sports car in front. At least, I thought, if she can't go to America she won't get shot. Not that they usually shoot white women. At least she won't be on a transatlantic flight when someone blows it up.

Emma was biting off the skin around her fingernails. Sometimes she makes them bleed.

'This would have been normal,' I said. 'This fear.'

'What?'

I glanced back. Miriam was still reading. Rose doesn't listen much. 'Everyone would have been used to it. You know. Adverse outcomes in paediatric medicine.'

Miriam looked up, meeting my eyes in the mirror. 'Dead children.'

'Where?' asked Rose, as if they might be at the roadside.

'What the parents are talking about. Adverse outcomes. It means dead people.'

We fell silent. The Range Rover and the sports car and we made our cautious way between the parked cars, past shops

291

selling objects of neither use nor beauty. Miriam returned to her book.

I glanced at Emma, who was intent on the road ahead. 'I don't mean it would have been any easier to bear, that theory was exploded pretty soon after it was advanced and anyway you can tell from reading almost any literary text before antibiotics and modern plumbing that every time it was devastating, however often it happened. But the idea wasn't shocking. The principle of – of an adverse outcome in paediatric medicine wasn't a surprise. John Donne. Wordsworth. All those Brontë siblings. Pearl.'

'Pearl?'

'There's a new girl in Year Two called Pearl,' Rose said.

I stopped at the lights at the top of the hill. Even in February, the pavements were solid with breathless old people who didn't like the slope. 'It's also the title of a medieval poem. A father writing about his daughter.'

His dead daughter.

'All I mean,' I said quietly, to Emma. 'All I mean is that the way things are for us now is the normal one, globally and historically. It's everyone else who's anomalous. Everyone who doesn't think it could happen to them.'

She put her hands in her lap. 'And this comforts you? All this – this academic *stuff*?'

'Yes,' said Mim. 'He tried to tell me about it too.'

It comforts me to think that most parents in most of time and most of the world have lived with this fear as a matter of course. It comforts me to think that while I have little fellowship in my fear with the parents at the school gate, the massed ghosts of England and the majority of parents living in the world now are with me. Although it turns out, of course, once people have a reason to tell you, that more of the school-gate parents than you used to imagine live in the overlap between ordinary life and tragedy. You know, they murmur, we had another child, before Matt. My sister's son, they say, he spent a long time in that hospital. Before we moved here, there was a family in that school, completely unexpected.

'Yes,' I said. 'A little. I think it does.'

But I didn't know what might comfort her.

We set off again, down towards the fast road to the motorway.

you don't want to leave

Rose had stopped reading somewhere around Plymouth and taken to kicking my seat and asking if we were nearly there yet.

She kicked again. 'Why does it always rain here?'

'It's not really rain, Rosie-pose. Just mizzle. Because it's a narrow peninsula sticking out into the North Atlantic.'

'Phoebe's grandma lives in France. In a house with a swimming pool.'

'Your grandpa lives in a house with a beach.'

'A cold, wet beach.'

Miriam put down her book. 'All beaches are wet. Otherwise it would be a desert.'

'Wet from the sky, stupid.'

Emma looked back. 'We don't say stupid, Rose. That's not nice.'

'But she was being stupid.'

'You're stupid.'

'No, you are.'

'Stop it. I know it's a long time in the car but fighting won't make it easier for anyone, will it?

'She called me stupid.'

'She said I didn't even know that a beach had sea.'

Emma opened the glove compartment. 'Would anyone like a chocolate biscuit?'

The usual joke places: Indian Queens, London Apprentice, the Chair Museum (if you're all that bored we'll stop and then you'll be sorry), Polyphant. The usual discussion about where to do the shopping, stop at Launceston where there's the good butcher and the bakery or push on to the supermarket right on the road at Helston. Or both. Rose needs to pee again, there's a Little Chef in a couple of miles and no, we're not stopping for tea.

Mizzle, but behind it, even through the car's vents, sea, the air hardly the same element as what we breathe in the West Midlands. Here we are, I thought, all those days on the ward, all that fear, and here we are. Nearly there.

The road from Helston to Porthleven, known the way I know the roads I run. Dad taught me to drive here, in the community's rusty minivan with the sticky second gear. My body leant into the curves before they came and my feet knew when to stay off the brake to get the car up the next hill without changing down. Look, the sea, I said. My, it's a big on-shore wind, look at that!

Porthleven harbour exaggerates the effects of Atlantic gales because harbours aren't usually built facing out to the prevailing winds, so we're not used to seeing waves break over harbour walls and bounce off the church above, but as long as there's no-one standing on the harbour wall at the time, it's a trick. The port was built in the mid-nineteenth century because this coastline was notorious for wrecks and there was nowhere to run for shelter this side of Penzance. They had to remove a sandbar and generally rearrange the geography a bit to build the harbour, and it's still wholly inaccessible during a west wind and the boats in it trapped. But at the harbour entrance there are 'baulks', great slabs of tree that slot into grooves and keep out the Atlantic swell, and 'sluices' that let the tides in and out while excluding the waves. Sanctuary, refuge, as long as you don't want to leave. I looked down at the mizzle crowding the stone houses on the hill, the flashes of green in their terraced gardens, at the well-meant Victorian grandeur of the old workhouse and the church and the school, at the bright boats tranquil in their pen and the roofless stone mine-tower set high on the cliff above the town. I didn't want to leave.

Along the back road behind the town, towards the old miners' cottages at the foot of the cliff path, Rose and Miriam bickering about whose turn it was for the top bunk. It would be harder, I thought, to check for breathing at night in the top bunk. Dad was sitting on the doorstep in the coat he'd had since before Miriam was born, whittling something and waiting for us. Beside him sat the orange casserole I remembered at Bryher Farm thirty years ago, because he had brought dinner for us.

whatever he was looking for

I'd been out at first light, running in the mud along the coast path while Emma got the girls up and made them pancakes, so when Dad arrived I'd just had a shower, was addressing my own pancakes and wasn't particularly keen when he said Emma and I should go out for a walk. He'd brought his new paediatric first aid certificate in a plastic wallet to show Emma, as if she wouldn't believe him without it. I know she would, he said, of course I do, but I thought that if she starts worrying once you're out she might feel better if she's actually seen it. You've got it wrong, Dad, I thought. I'm the one who worries. Or maybe I'm just the one who talks about worrying.

The mizzle was lighter than it had been earlier, and the mine-tower stood clear against the sky. It's pretty muddy on the coast path, I said, I'm not sure a walk would be much fun, my running kit was so mucky I took it off at the door. Do the Penrose walk, he said, Looe Bar, all the lower parts are paved. Emma and I looked at each other. We had not been out together since –, and actually not for some months before, because between Emma's work and the anaphrodisiac effects of paying ten pounds an hour for babysitting to which Mimi objects anyway it was easier to stay at home. If we're trying to live more fully, I thought, if we're trying not to let inertia and mindless economy shape our lives—

'Thank you, Eli,' Emma said. 'You're very kind. We'll be back by lunchtime and we've both got phones. Mimi's epipen is in her pocket and the inhalers are in the bag on the hook in the hall. You've got your phone?'

He waved it at her. 'Switched on, fully charged, four bars of reception. Turns out there's only one service provider in town, good thing I got the right one. Go on. I'm going to teach them to carve. Look in the bag, girls.'

He'd brought two small bright knives, two chisels and some shapely blocks of a dark but loose-grained wood.

He looked up. 'Unless you'd rather I didn't, of course?'

I found that I was not at all concerned about knives and chisels. Cuts can be sutured. We all have to learn. As long as the heart beats.

I took Emma's hand and we set out. The rain had passed out to sea and the sky to the north was blue.

Now, my father said, Rose, did you know I was telling your sister a story? This is about a young man, and his quest for a better way to live. He had just spent the winter in an old farmhouse in the mountains, and now spring was coming and he was on his way west again. West because he started in the east, Rose, and also because in America, the young have been going west for a couple of hundred years.

So, the young man caught a ride out of Bear Mountain Ridge Farm the next day, and travelled south-west with the spring, trees blooming around him as he went. He was going with a tide of young people who didn't want the futures their parents had imagined for them and were still – perhaps would always be – working out the reality of what they did want. Not forty hours a week in an office. Not a tie around their necks. Not suburbia. Not a mortgage and a country club membership, not ballet lessons for their daughters and baseball teams for their sons, not wives with girdles under their wasp-waisted dresses. They were mostly young men, the few women travelling as someone's girlfriend, mostly college-educated, almost all white. He didn't notice that at the time, though he did notice that there were few Jews.

The communes where he stayed were all different, but after a while they were mostly the same. They all had rules, as intentional communities must if only to distinguish themselves from the unintentional wider world. No meat, no sugar, no processed food. Free love, almost invariably – it was young men making the rules – and sometimes exclusive relationships were forbidden. Children, usually tolerated, sometimes unwelcome: to be raised by their parents, or by the community? Manual labour was often glorified, and at least in theory, sometimes required. If he had stayed, perhaps, if he had settled, given allegiance, he would have come to care about these things as others did, but what he learnt from his restless progress was that people legislate for their own desires and it is the desire and not the legislation that makes the difference. Some wish to lead and others to be led, some to dominate and others to submit.

As spring advanced, as he approached the far coast, life in these places became more pleasant. It does not matter so much if there are four people to a bedroom when it is possible to sleep outside, in a hammock under the trees, with only a midnight whisper of anxiety about bears. He lay one night between two apple trees in full, pale plumage, and wakeful watched the slow circling of stars and planets like our own. He woke early one morning and walked into a lake as the sun rose, watched the trees' reflection paint itself in the water holding his body and then swam quietly out past lily flowers taller than

299

his head, his face level with the waterbirds. Bird's eye view, a forest of reeds. He sat until dawn in a circle of people around the fire, singing and drumming and watching the dancers and the smoke rising into the dark sky. He held a newly born baby while the women helped the mother deliver the placenta, felt new life stir wet and sticky in his arms. He stood at the side of an illegal grave and helped to lower the uncoffined body of a man his own age who had died of untreated tuberculosis in the back of a car on the way to the hospital. He tipped a shovel and saw the dirt fill the folds of a tie-dyed blue shroud, turned away as the man's friend dropped dust onto his closed eyes, his hollow face. His right wrist was scarred when the sleeve of a loose smock flamed while he was learning to cook fish over an open fire. When his chisel slipped, a man who'd dropped out of medical school had to stitch a gash clear across his left palm. He caught scabies and ringworm, something that was probably dysentery. He taught a child to read. He learnt to make sourdough bread in one place and taught three people how to do it in the next. He learnt his way around a car's engine. He learnt to weave a hammock. He learnt to mend a roof, to make a cupboard, to build an outhouse and a long-drop toilet. He learnt to milk a cow, to plant a vegetable garden, to harness a horse and cart. He did not learn to fire a gun, but apart from that, he would have made a good pioneer. They were children of the future, given by their parents the Cold War, the atomic bomb, the computer, and they turned their backs, gazed instead on milking-stools, wells dug with spades, bread kneaded by the women's bare hands. The nineteenth century without the massacres and the railways, the eighteenth without smallpox and the slave trade, the Pilgrim Fathers without the patriarchy and the witch-burning, the olden days. He moved on, and moved again. Whatever he was looking for, he hadn't found it yet.

300

a sea star

There are not distinct seasons in Cornwall as in the rest of England. Winter nights are long, with a depth of blackness in the sky and brightness in the stars that I have not seen elsewhere. In summer, light haunts the water and the shore long after the day has gone out west. But it is rarely uncomfortably cold or uncomfortably hot, and usually raining a little. Camellias bud and blossom around Christmas, snowdrops and daffodils come mingled either side of the solstice, fuchsia and gorse foam here and there in the hedgerows at any time. Now, in February, there were violets, cow parsley, buttercups, wild garlic on the air below a south-facing slope. I held Rose's hand as we picked our way through the mud towards the cove. Her boots were too big and twice already she'd put a sock down in the mire; Emma had been right to insist on the washing machine. I turned to see Emma balancing along the edge of the grassy bank above the path, gorse flaming behind her. I strained ahead to see Miriam stride determinedly alone and determinedly competent, her jeans splashed to the thigh with mud.

'Did you use to do this,' Rose asked. 'When you were little?'

'Do what?'

She gripped my hand harder. 'Slither.'

I do not remember many springs. I remember summers, we boys daring and goading each other into the water and then staying there, jumping waves and diving for stones, until we were blue and our teeth chattered. Then we would sit on the rocks until it got boring and we went back in the sea. We used to try to catch crabs, I remembered, and I wore jeans and wellies, but that doesn't mean it wasn't midsummer.

'I think I was always muddy. Or wet. A bit of slithering probably didn't make much difference.'

'You were always on the beach. Every day.'

She's heard the stories. My perfect seaside childhood, my unimaginable freedom, my school where there were two teachers, one of whom still liked to wield one of those springy metal rulers against the upturned palms of naughty boys, and from which we could go home unescorted for lunch.

'We weren't, you know. You get used to having the beach and you don't go all that often. The grown-ups went every day, I think. My mother did. But she'd lived most of her life away from the sea and she never got used to it.'

Rose skidded and grabbed me. 'Not before she died.'

'Not before she died.'

Miriam had stopped on our skyline, where the top of the steps down to the cove began, and I pulled out my phone and took a picture of her there, before she looked round, frowning out to sea with the mist in her hair.

The tide was out, just past the turn, and so the sandy beach stretched south beyond the cliffs that enclose the cove and the rock pools were full. I let Miriam go down the path first, trusting her – showing that I trusted her – to manage the mud-slicked slope and the log steps slippery with winter's rain, the long fall onto the black 'rocks below. The breathing and beat of the waves returned to its place in me. The top of the beach is covered in boulders and I hung back; the girls are agile enough but the shoreline is not Emma's natural habitat. She took my hand to make the last stride. The wind off the sea ruffled her hair.

'Miriam?' I called. 'Mimi? Listen, you can go anywhere you like on the beach, but don't go round the rocks into the next cove, OK? The tide's coming in now and the next one gets cut off in the first hour. And there's no way up the cliff from it.'

She turned but didn't come back. Her voice came faintly on the wind. 'OK, Dad. I won't.'

Emma lifted her face to the breeze, so her hair breathed behind her. 'You really know this bit of coast, hm?'

'The rocks and tide don't change.'

I used to know the turning of the tide the way I knew the rising and setting of the sun, somewhere in my body. It didn't mean I never got caught – I remembered the next cove because there was a beguiling cave there and Petroc and I had had to wade back around the cliffs more than once – but we never got caught out. Miriam had made her way far out over the rocks, ignoring the pools and taking herself out to the water's edge. Weak sunlight played on a patch of sea to the west, but most of the waves were a grey that fitted exactly into my mind.

'Come on, Rose,' I said. 'Let's see what we can find in the rock pools.'

I'd brought the net and the bucket and spade that still live in the back of the car along with bottled water and the spare tyre, as if at any moment as we putter around the Midlands we might need to make a sand sculpture or study a minia-ture green crab. Rose took my hand as we stepped over the rocks, her rainbow-striped wellies bright and sweet on the slate and brown seaweed. Take them off, I wanted to say, let's feel the stone and the slime under our feet, but it was February and I was an idiot. Ahead of us, Miriam sat down, her knees tucked under her chin, and gazed out to sea. The patch of sunlight had spread and the low mist shifted enough to show two ships coming off the Atlantic into the lanes of the English Channel.

Rose squatted down, stirred a pool with her finger. 'Are those sea enemies?'

I squatted beside her. They look like nothing, like leeches or tumours, until they open like flowers. 'Anemones. Yes. You don't need to touch them, but if you swish the water a bit, they might open.'

She gazed into the water.

'We should start on the lower shore,' I said. 'It's a spring tide, a big one, so it goes out further than usual and there are more things to see. We can come up with the tide.'

We gave Miriam a wide berth, her own tidal zone, and came down a stretch of sand between the rocks.

'Listen,' I said. 'Just stand a moment and listen.'

Waves. A gull. The tumble of stones.

She stood obediently, but peered into the nearer pools.

'OK. Now, do you remember that it's like looking for birds, the longer we can stay still and pretend to be part of the rock, the more things we'll see? And some of the things are very tiny, so we need to look really really carefully?'

'I know. I'm good at looking carefully.'

I looked carefully up the beach as we squatted down. Emma had sat on a stone just below the path, not even really coming onto the beach at all, and was intent on something in her gloved hands, which would not be a shapely piece of driftwood or an unusual shell but her phone.

Rose leant forward. 'Is that a plant?'

I peered. 'It's another anemone. A beadlet anemone. There are lots of different sorts. That green one's called a snakelocks. Can you think why?'

I taught her to trail her fingers gently through the weed, as if stroking someone's hair, and to ease away the pebbles on the bottom of the pool as carefully as you might open someone else's post. Disturb no-one, leave no trace, although of course you cannot see a thing without changing it. I showed her the tip of my finger.

'There. Asterina phylactia. A sea star.'

A sea star, a miniature starfish, scarcely bigger than the stone of Emma's engagement ring and patterned with a tiny mosaic in bright terracotta and pale green.

She bent over my finger. I could feel her breath on my cold hand. 'Is it an animal?'

'Not exactly. They're sometimes called cushion stars. Probably a bit more like animals than plants. They lay eggs.'

I turned my finger. 'Can you see, they have a sort of ridge between the top and bottom? And they're not so pretty underneath.'

'I think there might be something under that seaweed.'

She was right. A spider crab, invisible until they move, and in the next pool we found a seven-pointed starfish and then a squat lobster almost too big for the bucket.

'Wait. Put the starfish back first, just where you found it. We don't put two creatures in the bucket at the same time.'

'In case they don't like each other?'

I nodded.

'How would you know?'

'That's the point,' I said. 'You can't know. So you don't do it.'

She cupped her hands around the starfish and lowered

305

it gently. 'Bye bye. You can go home now. What if they like each other?'

'You can't know that either.'

'Dad, is it mean, to go rock-pooling?'

Miriam had stood up and was making her way back towards us. I waved.

'It's probably more benign than a lot of what people do.' The specimens we're admiring, for example, all contain significant levels of flame-retardants, PCBs and heavy metals. 'And the creatures we're looking at – well, you can tell that they can be scared, but I doubt they have much by way of memory. We just treat them very carefully.'

Miriam came nearer. 'What have you found?'

'A shy sea star,' said Rose. 'And a frightened lobster.'

The tide came, nudging our feet, taking the lower shore back into the sea. The girls moved onto the sand, Miriam directing Rose in the irrigation of a complex of sandcastles and fortifications. I went up the beach to Emma, now pacing the sand.

'Are you cold?' I asked.

She swung her arms. 'A bit. Sat still too long.'

'You could have come rock-pooling.'

She glanced at me. 'I know, I could. I just don't have the patience, you know that. Looking at tiny things and putting them back.'

Patience, I wanted to say, like other virtues, is mostly a matter of habit.

She blew into her gloved hands. 'What did you find?'

'Tiny things. We put them back. The girls enjoyed it.'

'Sorry, Adam.'

What did you find, I wanted to ask, anything good on Twitter? Anything more important than a shy sea star and a frightened lobster? I turned to look at the girls. At home,

306

they hardly ever collaborate peacefully, require frequent adult intervention and peace-keeping.

'We could probably have an actual conversation,' I said. 'I'd say we've at least twenty minutes before the tide gets to them.'

She took my arm. 'Do you think if we didn't talk about them or about money we'd have anything to say?'

'There's always the NHS,' I said. 'You could tell me how it's being wilfully destroyed by right-wing bureaucrats and I could wonder whether to point out that not only are people not dying on the streets in France and Germany and Denmark and the Netherlands but actually living longer and healthier lives than we do even though they have contributory health-care systems. And then I could decide not to because you'll only get angry.'

Shut up, I thought, shut the fuck up, a rare chance to talk, to feed our starveling marriage, and I start with the passive aggression. And how far away is Miriam, in the cold? I could cover that distance in less than a minute, if I had to. A beach, in some ways, is easier than a house, because I would see if she collapsed.

Emma touched her head to my shoulder. 'We could talk about the summer. Plan a holiday. We could think about the garden. We were talking about currant bushes, last year. Next door has strawberries and tomatoes, the girls would like that.'

Three plants in a three-storey ceramic pot that cost more than it would to take a taxi to Waitrose and buy an armful of their finest. It's not the point, I know. The girls would see leaves, buds, flowers, small green fruit becoming less small red fruit. Patience. It's too easy to romanticise my own child-hood, remembered afternoons perched in the fork of a plum tree heavy with fruit, the brandy smell of windfalls broken by their fall and rotting, attended by wasps, in the sun. Nostalgia is the enemy of intelligence. I did not have libraries, theatres, museums, trips to London, flights to the Mediterranean. I did not require the frequent attentions of a consultant in allergies or respiratory medicine. How could I wish anything other than what we had, since the slightest variation of the past, the slightest indulgence in fictional time-travel, would tamper with our extraordinary luck? If Miriam's breathing had stopped in the presence of people who did not know what to do (me, for example), if the ambulance had been a minute or two delayed by traffic or a paramedic being on the loo, if the day had not been cold enough for mild hypothermia to protect her brain, if if if. And then I think of all the ifs on which we all depend: all the times we've been caught in the traffic jam behind an accident on the motorway, and if we had left ten minutes earlier, if we hadn't gone back to check that the central heating was off, or on the other hand, if the people ten minutes ahead and now unaware of the fire brigade sawing open their cars as blood drips onto the concrete, if those people had gone back to check the heating, had decided that after all they might want their hiking boots – we cannot live like that. One story at a time. One time at a time. In this one, we are on the beach and Emma wants to talk about whether to plant tomatoes and Miriam and Rose are watching their channels fill with water, their sand buildings blur and slide.

'Adam?'

'Blueberries. They do well in pots. And you can get dwarf plum trees. I've seen them espaliered, we could try that on the back wall. I don't know if we can afford travel insurance for a holiday. We'd have trouble with inhalers and the epipen on a plane.'

She stroked my shoulder. 'We wouldn't. They're used to it. So we stay in the EU, in most of which as you point out the healthcare is at least as good as here. Be good for us all. Show Miriam that she can still travel.'

At last, I put my arm around her. 'Nowhere too hot. Nowhere where she'll want to swim.'

Nowhere, ideally, where either of them will want to swim.

'Mountains,' she said. 'Mountains with big hospitals in between. Do you think we really can still do this?'

'Yes.' No. I don't know.

The clouds began to break up and the sea changed colour, began to flicker a cold light. There was a procession of ships out there, bearing Duplo edifices of containers bringing televisions and bananas and trainers and sofas and paint and oranges and girders and car parts and medicines and ink and fish and rubber ducks, almost everything, along the narrow road, the junction between the North Sea, the Mediterranean and the Atlantic, Britain's moat. A wave came over Rose's wellies and Miriam sat down on the sand and got her jeans wet. Time to go, time for dry clothes and hot water and lunch.

I went last up the steps, hands poised to catch Rose. I turned at the top and looked back. The rock pools were long gone, the girls' earthworks being erased before my eyes. This cove and the next were no longer communicable; it was in the next one that they had found my mother's body.

angels in rage

The West Screen. It had been part of Spence's first vision of the cathedral, during the faint in the dentist's chair when he gazed from the ruins to the yet-unwoven Christ in Glory through the translucent bodies of saints and angels. The West Screen is really what I'm visiting when I return to the Cathedral, because more than anything else, it changes with the seasons, with the angle of the sun and the tilt of the earth. It's not really a screen because it's clear glass, a wall or a cliff of clear glass, rising or falling the full height of the new cathedral and forming a window between the ruins and the new building, so that the engraved saints and angels stand – leap, writhe, float – between the present and the past. I've seen their shadows on a winter's night reach down from the darkened wall of the new building, their long feet and fingers plucking, but on a summer's day they wander the ruins. Haunt the ruins. They're not friendly. Not cherubic. Long dead, wasted, monomaniac as saints must be; an early critic remarked approvingly that he wouldn't like to meet one on a dark night.

I do. I like to meet them on a dark night.

John Hutton and Basil Spence had both worked in

camouflage units during the war – the whole Cathedral is part of the work of that war – and had kept an eye on each other's progress since. Hutton, posted to the Middle East, had become so good at hiding British air bases that RAF pilots couldn't find them from the air, so good at making dummy airstrips that returning Allied pilots tried to land on them. The British Army was so woefully ill-equipped that much of this part of the war appears to have been conducted through the theatre arts: coffee beans from sunk cargo ships scattered to suggest shadows at the bottom of the harbour in Alexandria, scuttled warships hastily repainted with fake shadows so that from the air they appeared unharmed. Painted guns and false shadows. The theatre of war. Hutton had left his wife and infant twin sons living in an intentional community of artists and academics in an Elizabethan manor house in Suffolk.

He kept sketchbooks throughout the war. Refugees arriving at the great London stations from across the Channel. Soldiers in the military hospital in Cairo. Bodies in ditches along the roads in Normandy, the same roads from which Spence was looking at the burnt-out medieval churches of rural France. Bodies on stretchers. An Eritrean soldier pouring a drink into the mouth of a dying comrade. He was never on the front line but often in the aftermath. Before the war, he'd made murals, surrealist, for the first-class cabins and dining rooms of ocean liners and for wealthy private clients. He'd painted clocks. Not now.

He came home. His marriage foundered. He worked alongside Spence on the Festival of Britain, on Britain Can Make It, on the Sea and Ships Pavilion. Murals, not glass, not until Cunard wanted some glass panels for the restaurant on the RMS Caronia. He designed them but the engraving was done by London Sand Blast, and he was intrigued. Wheel engraving, brilliant cutting, sand-blasting, ways of writing on thin air. Willis, the master-craftsman at London Sand Blast, could sling a wall of glass in chains above a grindstone churning in a trough of water and so interpret a design, make a paper drawing manifest in clear glass. Glass is melted sand, sea-shells repeatedly transmuted, solid to powder, powder to liquid, liquid to solid, and still sand writes on glass; one cannot but think also of sea-glass, forged by sand churned through wind and tide. Of the windows of lost ships. Next came the window in the chapel of the Commonwealth Air Forces Memorial at Runnymede; his first glass angels, faces averted already, the trumpets making such raucous music at Coventry already present but soft, symmetrical. Nothing to alarm.

Spence knew from the beginning that he wanted Hutton to make the West Screen. Alternate rows of saints on panels, Spence said, a chequerboard of plain and engraved windows. Hutton started sketching, and didn't like the regularity. A letter came from Ove Arup, who was working out how to suspend so much glass. Reinforced mullions, he said. No choice. Gravity is gravity. Hutton's new design was an answer to that. Flight. Dance. Leaping, leaning, jumping. Rising, writhing. He drew new panels, angels in flight, in resistance. Ghost angels, refugee angels, angels in rage, in protest, in agony. Nobody sees the mullions, only the movement, only the fight, the energy, the dance. Their trumpets sound the music of the ghettos, of the camps; I am reminded of Sebald's account of the troupes of entertainers drifting through the warmer parts of Europe in the late 1940s, concentration camp survivors who danced and made music and had nothing to say to anyone who had not been where they had been. The saints anchor the angels, but there's no comfort here. Hook-nosed Abraham raises his knife, St Cuthbert is cowled like the Grim Reaper, his face sharp and fallen as if after a long dying. Look on St Mary from the new building and you see the young mother, but from the other side the agony of the cross has fallen over her face. It is not all right.

It is not all right, but there is beauty. We have ways of saying that it is not all right, that there is death and suffering and evil, and they are the same ways we have had for hundreds of years. Buildings. Glass. Weaving.

Words.

where we are

There was something wrong and I woke up. Something awry in the darkness, something missing from the silence. I found myself on the stairs, found myself at Miriam's door. I had, to my shame, been oiling the catch so we could open it, check on her, without waking her. I eased the door open, holding my breath, feeling my own blood bang, and there was silence and the shape of her in the bed, too still, no breathing, gone, and I went over and touched her face and it was warm and she murmured and moved her arm. Rose, it must be Rose. I slipped out of Mimi's room, left the door open because every second it takes to reach someone not breathing is another second the brain is without oxygen, and Rose sighed as I entered her room. I went to her bedside anyway, hung over her and stroked her hair, touched her cheek, inhaled her vanilla smell. Missed the little girls my daughters had been. Stop it, leave them be, leave them growing and healing in the company of their dreams. I sat half-way down the stairs for a while, in the moonlight coming through the skylight on the top landing, and thought no, there is nothing wrong, both girls are breathing and so it is all right.

I could tell that Emma was awake from the darkness in the doorway of our room, with its more complex scent of Emma's perfume and hand cream and grown-ups' sheets which are about due to be changed.

'Everything OK?'

'Everything's fine.'

I lay back down and took her in my arms and she lay there, warm and sleepy, and after a while my hand found her face and then her breasts and her thighs and she opened to my fingers and my tongue.

Afterwards, dawn was coming and the traffic and the bird-song outside were beginning. Her head was heavy on my shoulder and my arm beginning to numb but I didn't want her to move. I stroked her back with the other hand, and then the side of her breast where it lay against me.

She shook her head. 'Talk to me. Tell me something. Otherwise I keep thinking. Lying here in the dark.'

So do I, I thought. And so I spin stories, to stop myself thinking.

'I keep thinking about my father. About those huge decisions he made. Leaving Brooklyn. Dropping out. Coming to England. Marrying my mother. It would have been so much easier for him to stay at home and stay safe. And how much his parents must have wanted him to do that, after their own trauma. All they'd seen. It must have seemed crazy to them, for him to turn away from what was comfortable.'

'Maybe they didn't feel like huge decisions at the time. Maybe he was just young and doing what he felt like doing.' She lifted her head. 'Hey, are you wanting to run away? To light out for the territory?'

315

I guided her head back to my shoulder. 'No. I'm wanting to stay here, with you and the girls in a cramped house in a boring bit of England. This is where we are.'

I shifted my arm a bit. Emma's ribs and vertebrae were better covered than they had been a few weeks earlier and her behind was reappearing. I stroked its curve.

'Stop it. Tell me what else.'

myths about which we know nothing

It was high summer now, and across America the children of war were on the move, fleeing comfort and prosperity for free love and a revolution that never made it to the streets. My father found it hard not to resent the newcomers, who had spent the winter in college dorms and expected to be welcomed and fed wherever they presented themselves. He smoked a little dope sometimes, had tried acid, but he was learning that he didn't have the patience for journeys of self-discovery, his own or anyone else's. He liked to get on and do things, and he liked other people who wanted to get on and do things. He believed, in the end, in material acts, in making and doing. He saw people spending hours sitting under the trees while he and a few others harvested gluts of tomatoes and zucchini, picked the bugs off squash and pumpkin plants growing tall and strong in the California sun. In the kitchen, three women kept one cauldron filled with water at a rolling boil to sterilise jars and another stewing the vegetables. On the meadow, a few men were scything the grass for winter's hay. There were children in the school, and often dropped-out college professors teaching them. If you had to take drugs to make things interesting, you probably weren't doing enough in the first place.

He sounded, maybe, like his father. He hadn't written home in months now.

He moved on again. He didn't see why he should work so that others, equally young and strong, could lie in the sun. Wasn't that why people had left Europe for America in the first place, to escape the parasites?

He came in the end, as he must, to the other coast, over the state line and well north of where he'd thought he was going, to a place where the Pacific Ocean ended on a white beach under dark pines and there were mussel shells as big as his hand and driftwood logs taller than buildings, wider than a man's length. Swell that had been rising and running from the coast of Japan, from the other side of the planet, crashed day and night onto the sand below the group's cabins, as if he'd come at last to a place where he could hear the earth breathe. Even now, in August, it was cool here, the green breath of the old forest and the salt sea always on his face.

They weren't farming, the people at Black Rock Cove. Why would we plant, Bill said, when the forest and the inlet are full of food? Mushrooms, berries, and a sea full of fish. The old ways. Hunting and gathering. There was a young anthropologist staying a few weeks, mapping and photographing the last traces of totem poles and wooden houses among the trees. We don't even know, he said, the names of the nations wiped out in the nineteenth century, my thesis is an exercise in hopelessness but it would be worse to give up and forget they were ever there. In the big cabin there was a shelf of books on foraging, and though there were a few fibreglass canoes pulled up above the tideline, the group was working on a wooden one, carved out of a log. They had books about that too.

My father was not stupid to begin with, and was probably considerably more astute than he had been a year earlier. He could see that this was a summer camp, a midsummer night's dream, and also yet another example of the parody of an exterminated culture by its killer. But he liked it here, away from the hippie mainstream. He liked it that Bill and his wife Judy were in their sixties, and that their son and daughter-in-law and baby granddaughter were here too, and he liked the way women and men worked together, washing clothes and sheets in the river as well as taking the boats out to fish. There were no drugs here, and no alcohol except when someone went into town for flour and sugar and brought back a few beers too; they traded fish for milk from their nearest neighbour, a farmer who was well-disposed and entirely willing to pass on what he knew about the land. Bill had been a teacher and had a good pension. His daughter-in-law Annie worked as a nurse a couple of days a week at the medical practice in town. They weren't enclosed, weren't opposed to the rest of the world. They just wanted to do things differently.

He knew from other places how fragile the balance of money and power can be. So he was grateful, cautious. He made sure to rise early, to do at least his share. He learnt to gut and clean fish, to build a frame out of fallen branches for drying what they couldn't eat fresh. He followed Bill around, learning which mushrooms and berries were good to eat. Above his head, the trees rustled and bowed. Birds sang notes he hadn't heard before and sometimes he sensed something watching him, heard it brush through the undergrowth. Bear, probably. The forest floor was dappled under his feet, all the light in movement over the water. As the sun went down, the younger ones drifted to the beach, lit a driftwood fire and sat there, feeling America at their backs and the ocean before them, the day's warmth washing from the sand as the tide rose. He picked up a mussel shell the size of his hand, let it rest in his fingers, stroked the pearled inside and ran his thumb along the sharp edge. His hand was surprised by the shell's lightness. His other hand scooped sand paler than skin and let it run from his fingers into the shell. Sands of time. Hourglasses made of melted sand.

'There's that raven again,' said the anthropologist, whom we'll call Robert.

The raven was larger than Eli thought ravens were, though everything on this coast was larger than he thought things were. It was hopping about on the beach below the group, just above where the waves broke themselves in the last of the sunlight. The raven was pecking at shells like the one Eli held, lifting them, pushing the red seaweed about with its beak in a leisurely way that suggested curiosity more than hunger. The anthropologist, who had been leaning back on his elbows, sat up to watch.

Once upon a time, said the anthropologist whom we're calling Robert, once upon a time when the world was without form and void, there lived in the darkness an old man and his daughter. They had a house by the river, and inside the house the old man had a box, and inside the box was another box and inside that box another one and inside that box another one and so on until there were more boxes than even the old man could count. The raven already existed in the darkness, and he blundered and chuntered around the lightless world, looking as always for food and mischief. One day the raven's wandering brought him to the old man's house, where he leant against the wall and heard the old man talking to himself about the box that no-one had ever seen. In the last box, the man said, is all the light of the world and it is all mine and I am keeping it for ever.

The raven, of course, wanted the light, partly because he'd heard the voice of the old man's daughter as well and he wanted to look at her. So the raven changed himself into a pine needle and floated down the river in the darkness as the girl dipped her basket, and then floated down the girl's belly as she drank. And there the raven slept and grew, in the double darkness of the girl's womb, until its walls straitened around his new body and it was time for him to be born in the new form of a human boy.

The old man came to love his noisy grandson and the boy grew in strength and courage. The raven child began to explore the house, to poke his fingers into cracks and crevices, to pull down the objects his hands found, to mouth and to touch everything he could reach. And at last he found the box. Just the outer one, he said, just let me play a little while with the largest one, just let me lift the lid and touch the corners and fit the lid back on. It is the only thing I want. Please. So the old man gave the child the outermost box, and the child played with it for days before he asked for the next one. No, said the grandfather, and the child screamed and kicked until the old man relented. And then the next one and the next, until the last few boxes glowed and the darkness in the house became dimness and the boy and the woman and the old man began to see each other's forms. Give me the light, the child pleaded, just for a moment let me hold that great golden ball. No, said the old man, certainly not, but as the days went by the child begged and wept and at last his grandfather tossed the light to the raven-child's outstretched hands.

The old man barely saw his beloved grandson before the child's arms became broad black wings, before his nose became a sharp yellow beak, and with the light of the world in his mouth the raven rushed through the smoke-hole in the roof and out into the sleeping sky. For the first time, rivers sparkled in the sunlight. For the first time, the sky was blue, the trees green, and all the creatures of the world began to stir themselves as the first morning began.

But the eagle, also, was astir in all the light of the world, and for the first time the raven's darkness was plain under the bright sky and the eagle could see exactly what he wanted. Almost too late, the raven saw the eagle's shadow scud across the earth below him. Almost too late, he heard the beating of great wings. In terror, he lurched, slipped on the wind, and half the light of the world fell to the ground and smashed like glass into thousands of bright shards, which bounced far into the sky and became our stars. The eagle chased the raven on the wings of the morning to the uttermost parts of the earth, until the raven flagged, weakened, and let the remaining light drift in a flaming ball to the eastern sky, where it became our sun.

And the raven? Oh, he reinvented himself, as he always does. He's still here.

The real raven, or at least, the one on the beach in this story, made a tart remark and took off, landing on one of the immense sea-washed tree trunks lolling at the top of the sand where the spring gales had thrown them.

Really this is the wrong place, Robert said, for that story. It comes from much further north, and it was one of the first ones to be collected by Europeans so it might not have much at all in common with pre-contact versions. It's probably just a mishmash of mistranslation and exoticism, hopelessly in-authentic. Did you know that there are whole groups of myths about which we know nothing except that they once existed and now don't? Iliads and Odysseys and Aeneids gone into the darkness?

Yes, thought Eli. Yes, he knew that.

She was called Helena and at first he thought she was Jewish. Dark hair in a braid lay heavy between her shoulders and slithered as she moved, dark eyes in a pale face, one of those noses. She was slight, girlish; perhaps with age she would grow into the structure of her bones. He was put off, at first, by her British accent, couldn't but hear superiority or at least snobbery in the way she pronounced 'water' and called the Pacific Ocean 'the sea'. A girl from the Old World, his parents would have said, the world from which their kind had been all but exterminated. Except that here, under these trees and on this shore, in the woods where he still came sometimes on the last traces of First Nations villages, where sometimes a fallen tree turned out to be a fallen totem pole, it was absurd to divide the world like that. Totem poles may have been made only after contact with European sailors, in response perhaps to the figureheads on their ships. All the continents are made of bones and shame, if you see it that way. All of us carry violence and the triumph of the killers. The innocent bystanders died, and their genes and stories with them.

She wore bluejeans and sometimes long skirts with peasant blouses, and early one morning he met her coming up the sandy path from the beach wearing a wet swimsuit and sandals, water still running from the paintbrush tip of her braid down her tanned back and into the meeting of skin and swimsuit above the curve of her behind. She crossed her arms over her chest and he kept his eyes on hers, high, and asked if she swam every morning, if she had swum in England – not, he had imagined, a nation of athletes – if she worried about the sea-lions that they'd seen from time to time down on the rocks. Yes, she said, every morning, and yes, she had been lucky enough to go to a school that had its own pool and yes,

323

a little, but you couldn't swim in the sea at all if you thought about what might be with you and unseen. She didn't ask him any questions back, but it was a start. It would take him weeks to learn that being lucky enough to attend a school with a pool meant that her parents were wealthy enough to pay the fees and progressive enough to educate their daughter as well as their sons, and also that she'd been sent to boarding school at the age of ten and didn't now believe that her parents much cared where she was or what she was doing. It did not take him very long at all to see that she was brave and pragmatic, not just about invisible sea-lions but also about bee-stings on her face and a badly planned roof-repair that went on long into a rainy night. He already knew that she was beautiful to him, and so when summer ended, when the rains came and Bill and Judy moved back to the town for the winter because the track was too muddy for Annie to get to work and the huts too cold and damp for the baby, Helena said come with me, come back to England with me, we can get you away from this stupid war before it's too late, we can start again, a new community, everything you've learnt put to a new purpose, come with me to the Old World and make it new, he said yes. Yes.

It was getting light.

Emma rolled off me and propped herself up on her elbow, which called into being a cleavage she doesn't usually have.

'You do want to go,' she said. 'You want to go to America. Land of your fathers.'

My arm tingled as the blood returned. I thought about it, about our summer lying sunlit and empty a few weeks in the future. We have been to New York, eaten bagels in Central Park and Hershey bars on the Staten Island ferry, taken the girls to MOMA and up the Empire State Building, and also out to Brooklyn to walk down the street where my father grew up, my pilgrimage the negative of those of Americans who appear in the poorer and more picturesque bits of Britain looking for what their ancestors fled. We are all in flight, all trying to raise our forefathers' ghosts. If I want to go to America, it's to the coastline I had just conjured in our dim and landlocked bedroom. I have never seen the Pacific Ocean.

'I don't think so. It's just a story, my dad's America. And we can't afford it. I think I want to go to Austria. Land of my fathers.'

They are all stories. My fathers whose hearts beat true and required intervention, the intervention of the camp guards, to stop. My fathers who needed a reason to die, whose blood knew to keep moving, but who also carried their own destruction – the story of their own destruction – in their Jewish blood.

She frowned. 'When we went to Vienna you said you could hear the echo of jackboots goose-stepping up the streets when you went to sleep.'

I rolled my shoulders. 'I was younger and sillier then. I can hear the echo of Roman legions on the A429 and Tudor monks singing plainchant in the Coventry bus station. Lucky me. Let's go to the Alps. We can show Rose *The Sound of Music* first, she'll love it.'

Emma picked up her phone to check the time. 'I should be getting up. OK. I'll check where there are good hospitals in Alpine towns. Is Switzerland in the EU?'

She stood up, naked and beautiful, her hair wild where she'd rolled her head against the headboard as I held her down.

'No,' I said. 'But they might have reciprocal healthcare arrangements. I'll check.'

She looked at herself in the mirror, gathered up her hair and frowned at herself. 'Another thing, Adam, I've been thinking, when we get back we probably should get a cat. One of those posh breeds that doesn't go out so it can't get run over.'

I knew who would be cleaning its litter tray and taking it to the vet. 'What about that illness?' I said. 'The cat poo one? What about worms and fleas? Doesn't cat hair cause asthma?'

'Toxoplasmosis isn't usually bad unless you're pregnant. They tested Mim, remember, and she doesn't react to cats. It won't get parasites if it doesn't have them on arrival and doesn't go outside.'

'It can still get ill and die,' I said. 'The girls would still have to deal with that sooner or later.'

She met my eyes in the mirror and shrugged. 'We all do. You can't go round not loving things because they'll die. I mean, I can come up with some more reasons if you want them, I know you like reasons, but really I just want to make Rose happy. And I think Mim will probably like it when it gets here even if she says it's a sign of false consciousness to buy cat food while there are people starving under austerity.'

'OK,' I said. 'I'm not going to argue against happiness. I'll look up posh cat breeders. There's probably a new whole world of fun and games out there.'

the next valley and the next, see Europe beginning to fold towards the Mediterranean. There is a little snow in north-facing hollows on the tops, even now, enough for Rose to stop to make a snowball and demand a photo. Today, I hope, if the weather holds and everyone's feeling strong, we will climb the tall mountain on whose summit the sun now rests, join the retired locals and the serious young backpackers on the tram out to the village where we'll buy bread and salami to eat on the summit, and then we'll walk up the forestry track, keeping an eye out for black squirrels in the trees and blueberries underfoot, and then on up the narrower mountain path to a rocky scramble to the top.

And now I am here, and Emma is here, and Miriam is here, and Rose is here. Now I am about to stop writing, to leave my laptop on the wobbly formica kitchen table, return the blanket to the cupboard for the next visitor to keep a dawn watch over the city. I will pull on yesterday's clothes, not waking Emma, try to be quiet as I open and close the heavy front door with its overstated locks. I'll join the old ladies with their high heels, stately hair and shopping trolleys making for the market to get the best produce while the young people and tourists are still in their beds. I'll buy an excess of plums and greengages, *Pflaumen* and I think *Renekloden*, picked yesterday from the orchard surrounding a farm on an Alpine plateau, a farm sheltered by rustling pine trees from the storms of autumn and spring and warmed in winter by a blue-and-white tiled stove the size of a small room. I'll stop at a bakery on the way back for one of the many kinds of bread you can't buy in England and probably a couple of pastries for the girls as well, because the pastries are good and no-one's going to start diabetes in a fortnight's holiday. I will come back, up the stairs with my arms full of paper bags because I'll have forgotten to take a cotton one, and make coffee with the exotic coffee machine before I wake Emma so I can leave a cup at her bedside, its scent adrift, its steam rising in the sunlight that will spill across the bed when I open the shutters. I'll take a shower in the pink bathroom and then rouse the girls, good morning, time to wake up, and I'll set out the bread with salty farm butter and blueberry jam on the iron table on the balcony, where we'll still want to warm our hands on our mugs as we open negotiations about the day's activities, tell Rose to come and sit down, tell Mim that one cup of coffee is more than either of us was allowed at her age.

Stories have endings; that's why we tell them, for reassurance that there is meaning in our lives. But like a diagnosis, a story can become a prison, a straight road mapped out by the people who went before. Stories are not the truth.

Begin with brokenness. Begin again. We are not all, not only, the characters written by our ancestors. I have told my stories now, and we are still here, and the day is hardly begun.

Acknowledgements

The story of the eagle and the raven has been stolen and broken up for parts many times over many years. I took it from Bill Reid and Robert Bringhurst, art historians and anthropologists, in *The Raven Steals the Light* (Vancouver: Douglas and McIntyre, 1988).

The book Adam reads on the train is Jonathan Raban's *Passage to Juneau* (London: Picador, 1999).

I thank Sharon Dixon and Sinead Mooney for reading full drafts and making important suggestions. Max Porter for intelligence, sensitivity and being right, everyone at Granta for their patience and care. Anna Webber at United Agents for kindness and support far beyond the call of duty.

At Warwick: Ian Sansom, Maureen Freely, Tina Lupton, AL Kennedy, David Morley, Will Eaves, Tess Grant, Chantal Wright. The students of the Warwick Writing Programme, who ask the right questions.

Dr Lawrence Youlten kindly shared his expertise in anaphylaxis. All errors of fact or probability remain, as ever, my own.

Also by Sarah Moss and available from Granta Books
www.granta.com

NIGHT WAKING

'Moss writes marvellously (and often hilariously) about the
clash between career and motherhood' *The Times*

'Highly enjoyable' *Daily Telegraph*

Anna Bennett hasn't slept in months.
Overwhelmed by the needs of her two young boys
and opposed on principle to domesticity, Anna is a historian
struggling to write without a room of her own. Stranded on a
Hebridean island where her husband is researching the puffins,
Anna's work changes when her son finds a baby's skeleton
buried in the garden. As an investigation begins, Anna
must confront the island's past while finding a way to
live with the competing demands of the present.

'Tartly humorous, sad and clever' *Sunday Times*

'A brilliantly observed comedy of twenty-first century
manners ... a tightly plotted mystery that keeps the reader
wondering, and hoping, until the final page' *Financial Times*

'The trials of family life are comically and stylishly
depicted ... [an] original and accomplished novel' *Daily Mail*

'I read *Night Waking* with avid enjoyment and no small
amount of recognition' Maggie O'Farrell, *Scotsman*